Gerald Maclean Edwards

Sidney Sussex College

Gerald Maclean Edwards

Sidney Sussex College

ISBN/EAN: 9783742810922

Manufactured in Europe, USA, Canada, Australia, Japa

Cover: Foto ©Andreas Hilbeck / pixelio.de

Manufactured and distributed by brebook publishing software
(www.brebook.com)

Gerald Maclean Edwards

Sidney Sussex College

University of Cambridge

COLLEGE HISTORIES

SIDNEY SUSSEX COLLEGE

BY

G. M. EDWARDS, M.A.

FELLOW AND TUTOR OF THE COLLEGE

LONDON

F. E. ROBINSON AND CO.

20 GREAT RUSSELL STREET, BLOOMSBURY

1899

Printed by BALLANTYNE, HANSON & Co.
At the Ballantyne Press

PREFACE

THIS book owes much to the works of the historians of Cambridge, from Fuller to Willis and Clark; but it also contains a great deal of information never before published, which has been derived from our very complete series of College records. The Master of Sidney has given me much assistance by showing me my way about our Registers, Order Books, and other documents. Many biographical details have been gathered from articles in the *Encyclopaedia Britannica* and the *Dictionary of National Biography ;* from separately published lives of members of the College; and from other works, such as Mr. Kingston's *East Anglia and the Great Civil War*, and Mr. Morris Fuller's *Life of Bishop Davenant.* In writing chapters vii., viii., and ix., I have found Cooper's *Annals* particularly useful. I am indebted to the Master of Trinity for the use of some interesting extracts from the unpublished correspondence of Dr. George Butler; to Mr. John Murray for permission to print some passages from the *Recreations and Studies of a Country Clergyman in the Eighteenth Century;* to the proprietors of the *Cambridge Review* for extracts from that journal; and to Mrs. Yorke of Erddig for the illustration of the Tomb of the Foundress, owing to its position a very difficult subject for a photographer.

CONTENTS

ILLUSTRATIONS

CHAPTER I

THE HOUSE OF THE GREY FRIARS

THE " College of the Lady Frances Sidney, Countess of Sussex," occupies the site of the House of the Franciscans or Friars Minors (*Fratres Minores*), commonly called the Grey Friars. During the thirteenth century it became the custom of the religious orders both in England and abroad to have houses in the Universities to which some of the younger monks were sent for purposes of study. In the next century it was provided by the Constitutions of Pope Benedict XII. that all Benedictine monasteries should send to the *generalia studia* at least one-twentieth of their total numbers.

" These friars," says Fuller, " living in these convents were capable of degrees and kept their acts as other University men. Yet were they gremials and not-gremials, who sometimes would so stand on the tiptoes of their privileges that they endeavoured to be higher than other students ; so that often they and the scholars could not set their horses in one stable, or rather their books on one shelf. However, generally the Chancellors ordered them into tolerable obedience."

The Fransciscans settled in Cambridge early in the thirteenth century. The townsmen gave them as a

A

dwelling-place the "Old Synagogue" said to have been part of the house of Benjamin the Jew, of which the burgesses obtained a grant from the Crown in or before 1224. The Friars found the neighbouring Tolbooth, a portion of which was used as a prison, very objectionable. Accordingly, in a few years, probably about 1240, they migrated to the site now occupied by Lady Sidney's College, where they remained for, as nearly as possible, three centuries. At an inquisition taken in the seventh year of Edward I., *i.e.*, about forty years later, it was found that the Friars Minors in Cambridge had a certain place, where they dwelt and where their church was founded, containing six acres of land and more; but of whom they had the place and whether they had confirmation of the King's ancestors, the jurors did not know. The same King granted twenty-five marks per annum to these Friars; and the grant was renewed by his successors. In 1328 Edward III. granted letters patent to the Warden and Friars for the enlargement of their area by the enclosure of a lane. In 1353 the Warden and Friars gave the King six shillings and eightpence for a licence to acquire two messuages for the enlargement of their mansion.

Fuller states that they had a fair Church, which might be called "the *St. Mary's before St. Mary's*; the Commencement, Acts, and Exercises being kept therein." He is probably right in placing the Church on the bowling-green of his time, which may be seen in Loggan's print to the left (*i.e.*, the north) of the College buildings. Fuller adds that the "depression and subsidency of the bowling-green east and west" mark the dimensions of the Church ; * he says that he had often found " dead men's bones thereabouts." In the excavations for the foundations of our new buildings in 1890 some skeletons were dug up "thereabouts." This seems to show that the graveyard of the Friars lay between their Church and Jesus Lane. Roger Ascham, writing to Thomas Thirleby, Bishop of Winchester, on January 19, 1541 (*i.e.*, after the dissolution of the House), entreats him to help the University in its endeavour to obtain the House of the Franciscans, and adds these words:

Franciscanorum aedes non modo decus atque ornamentum Academiae, sed opportunitates magnas ad comitia et omnia Academiae negotia conficienda habent.

The following Grace of the Senate passed in 1540 refers to these negotiations:

Conceditur ut Vicecancellarius et magister Aynesworthe de collegio Petri possint agere causas et negocia vestra apud Regiam majestatem et dominum Cromwellum Cancellarium nostrum praecipue pro domo et ecclesia Fratrum Minorum hic apud vos, etc.

Before the dissolution the Church had been frequently used for the Commencement Ceremonies. An extract from the University Accounts for 1507–8, quoted by Messrs. Willis and Clark, gives payments to "Robert the carpenter" and others for putting up *fabricam* (*i.e.*,

---

* Willis and Clark (vol. ii. p. 730) think that, if Fuller's view is correct, "we must place the Cloister south of the Church, between it and the Refectory, in order to provide sufficient space for it. It will therefore be represented, at least in part, by the College quadrangle" (*i.e.*, the Hall Court). This coincides with the opinion of Essex given below (pp. 4, 5).

stages) *commensacionis in ecclesia Minorum*, for the
conveyance of the stages from the Schools to the Church
and back again, and for the repair of broken windows
in the Church. In 1523 it was agreed that the Friars
should be paid ten shillings a year for the hire of their
Church at Commencement and for the safe custody of
the *fabrica*, which was apparently now to be kept on
their premises continually.

The Refectory of the Friars stood on the site of the
original, and the present, College Chapel. At least
such was the opinion of James Essex, the architect of
the new Chapel, which was begun in 1776. Fuller had
a different theory :

"Some have falsely reported that the now chapel of the
College was formerly a stable ; whereas it was the Franciscans' ancient dormitory, as appeareth by the con-
cavities still extant in the walls, places for their several
reposure."

To this Essex replies in his notes on the site : *

"This, however, may be doubted, because the cavities
he speaks of were only the doors, windows, and a chimney
of the room. . . . That it was the Refectory appears from
the plan of it, and from the quantity of small bones of
fowls, rabbits, and other animals, with spoons, etc., which
were found among the rubbish when it was pulled down.
. . . On the west side . . . two holes appear in the wall ;
these might receive timber to support the floor of a pulpit
or desk where the Lecturer read the Scriptures to the
Friars while they were at meals. . . . At the south end

* Essex's notes are printed *in extenso* by Willis and Clark, vol. ii.
P. 743, *sqq.*

may be traced the substructure of the foundations to other buildings, which I conceive were the Butteries. . . . The cellars and other offices were ranged on the south next Walls Lane."*

Essex adds that the site of the apartments of the Warden and Friars cannot be traced, but that they were probably between the Church and the Refectory. The Friars had a conduit supplied from a spring in the parish of St. Giles. It is said to have been the cause of frequent disputes between them and the authorities of King's Hall. In the conveyance of the site to Lady Sidney's executors this conduit is specially excepted from the sale. It gave its name to Conduit Street, the old designation of Sidney Street.

The House of the Grey Friars was dissolved in 1538, together with the other religious houses in Cambridge. The surrender to the Crown was signed by William White, the Warden, and twenty-three Friars. It has been mentioned above that the University was very anxious to obtain a grant of the House. A petition on the subject addressed to Henry VIII. is given by Messrs. Willis and Clark. On the petition these words are written in a different hand: "This graunt dyuerse tymes sued for but cold never be opteyned." In December 1546 the buildings and site were conveyed by the King to the Master, Fellows, and Scholars of his Majesty's new College of Trinity. But a valuation made in the previous May by Robert Chester, the King's Surveyor, shows that the buildings had already been destroyed except the " Brewhouse, Malthouse,

* Now King Street.

Millhouse, and Garner," which, together with the site, were stated to have an annual value of £4 6s. 8d. The magnificent Church, which Ascham had called *decus atque ornamentum Academiae*, the Cloister and other buildings were ruthlessly demolished to provide materials for the erection of Trinity College. In the course of the year 1557 no less than 2950 loads of stone were brought there from "the Friars." Messrs. Willis and Clark add this information :

"The charges for the carriage of materials from 'the Friars' set down in the Accounts of Trinity College during the nine years (1548–1557) are incessant; but unfortunately they give but little indication of the nature of the buildings destroyed. The materials were either reduced to lime, or hewn into shapes convenient for use in new buildings, previous to removal. The buildings specified are : the Church; the Belfry containing a peal of bells; the Cloister; the Grave-yard; and the School-house. . . . The Belfry adjoined the Cloister."*

In 1547 Trinity College let a part of the site to William Laing, labourer, of Cambridge. Two years later another portion was leased to Ralph Bicardike, alderman, of Cambridge. In 1562 a third piece, adjoining Jesus Lane, "butting on the east side on a diche commonly called the kynges diche . . . on the west side the kynges highe way called the conduit street," was let to William Hedley, yeoman. The King's Ditch divided the site of the Grey Friars, roughly speaking, into two equal parts, running across

* An entry in the Accounts speaks of " y᷎ corner of y᷎ cloyster next to y᷎ steple."

it from north to south. The ground leased to Hedley was doubtless not let as early as the other portions, because it would not have been clear of building materials, which were not all conveyed to Trinity till 1557 at the earliest. At present we leave Laing, Bicardike, and Hedley in undisturbed possession of their holdings; but we shall return hereafter to the site of the Grey Friars.

CHAPTER II

THE FOUNDRESS

FRANCES SIDNEY was born in 1531. She was the fourth daughter of Sir William Sidney, Chamberlain and Steward of the household to Edward VI. In 1555 she was married to Thomas Radcliffe, Viscount Fitz-walter, whose first wife Elizabeth, daughter of Thomas Earl of Southampton, had died in the same year. Lord Fitzwalter, on the death of his father in 1557, became Earl of Sussex; under this title he is well known to readers of *Kenilworth* as the rival of Robert Dudley, Earl of Leicester.* In the same year he was appointed

---

* "The two nobles, who at present stood as rivals for her (Elizabeth's) favour, possessed very different pretensions to share it; yet it might in general be said that the Earl of Sussex had been most serviceable to the Queen, while Leicester was most dear to the woman. ·· Sussex was, according to the phrase of the times, a *martialist*; had done good service in Ireland and Scotland, and especially in the great Northern rebellion in 1569, which was quelled in a great measure by his military talents. He was therefore naturally surrounded and looked up to by those who wished to make arms their road to distinction. The Earl of Sussex, moreover, was of more ancient and honourable descent, uniting in his person the representation of the Fitzwalters as well as of the Radcliffes. But in person, features, and address, weapons so formidable in the court of a female sovereign, Leicester had advantages more than sufficient to counterbalance the military services, high blood, and frank bearing of the Earl of Sussex."—Scott, *Kenilworth*, ch. xiv.

Lord Deputy of Ireland, whither he was accompanied by his wife and her brother, Sir Henry Sidney (father of the famous Sir Philip Sidney), a member of the Irish Council. Unfortunately Sir Henry, a staunch ally of Leicester, whose sister he had married, proved himself an unsparing critic of Sussex's Irish administration. Again, in 1568, the appointment of his brother-in-law to the office of Lord President of Wales, which was brought about by Leicester, was a bitter mortification to Sussex.

The last years of the Countess were clouded with sorrow, doubtless due in part to the strife between the Leicester and Sussex factions. Her husband died after a lingering illness on June 9, 1583, in his fifty-seventh year. On his deathbed the rivalry of Leicester was still present to his mind; he said to some of his adherents:

" I am now passing into another world, and must leave you to your fortunes and the Queen's graces ; but beware of the ' Gypsy ' (so he called Leicester on account of his swarthy complexion); for he will be too hard for you all. You know not the beast so well as I do."

During the Earl's illness some malicious persons (belonging to the Leicester faction, as we may fairly conjecture) contrived to estrange the Earl's affections from his wife. On this account and also in consequence of some dispute with his executors,* she incurred the displeasure of a Queen ever ready to take offence ; for

* The Earl of Sussex left her all his jewels (valued at £3169), 4000 ounces of gilt plate, coaches, horses, etc. She also had for her life, under his will and certain settlements, some manors in Essex, with estates in Norfolk, and his house at Bermondsey.

"when she smiled," said Sir John Harrington, "it was a pure sunshine that every one did choose to bask in ; but anon came a storm from a sudden gathering of clouds, and the thunder fell in a wondrous manner on all alike."

Lady Sidney attempted to mollify the royal displeasure by a profoundly humble and pathetic letter, quoted by Cooper from Nicholas' *Life of Sir Christopher Hatton*. Unfortunately the spelling has been modernised.

"Most Gracious and most Merciful Queen, I most humbly beseech your Majesty to view these few lines written with many tears and even in the bitterness of my soul, with that pitiful regard wherewith God hath viewed your Majesty at all times and in all cases. And albeit I am now beaten down with many afflictions and calamities hardly to be borne of flesh and blood, yet is there no grief that pierceth me so deeply as that by sinister suggestion I should be defamed to be undutiful to your most excellent Majesty, and injurious to the honour of my dear Lord lately deceased. For the first, I appeal to God himself, the searcher of hearts and revenger of all disloyalties ; for the second, I appeal to none but unto my most gracious Queen, whether I have not from time to time been more careful of his health, honour, and well doing than of mine own soul and safety ; refusing all friends and friendships in this world for so dear a Lord, whom I followed in health and sickness, in wealth and woe, with more care than becomed a true Christian to owe unto any worldly creature. The which, if it be true (as I trust your Majesty in my right and your justice doth acknowledge it is) marvel not, most dread Sovereign, if the vigilant malice of those who have long complotted my ruin, who espied their time, when my Lord through anguish and torments was brought to his utmost weakness, to break the perfect band and love of twenty-eight years continuance, have also by cunning sleights devised and by slanderous speeches instilled into your Majesty's ears the want of that duty, the which I pray God may sooner fail by lack of life than want of loyalty. And thus, most noble Princess, am I trodden down by my inferiors not only in worldly maintenance, which I nothing esteem (having far more by God's goodness than I deserve), but also am touched in the chiefest point of honour and the highest degree of duty, which bringeth on every side such a sea of sorrows as, were it not for the fear of God's revenge, I could with all my heart redeem them with the sacrifice of my life. Wherefore, most gracious Lady, even for the pity which ever hath been engrafted in your Princely heart, I most humbly beseech you, see not your Majesty's poor servant trodden down by the malicious speeches and unconscionable extremities of those who took the advantage of my Lord's painful weakness to work my disgrace, nor increase my just and perpetual grief with your heavy displeasure; praying God that I may rather presently die while I write these lines than that I may live wittingly to deserve your Majesty's just dislike. In the meantime I will not cease to pray to the Almighty for your Majesty's life, health, and prosperity. From the poor careful close of Bermondsey. Your Majesty's poor, but true faithful servant to die at your feet,

"F. Sussex."

This letter was sent on September 18, 1583, through Sir Christopher Hatton. On October 31 the Countess wrote to Lord Burleigh to thank him for pleading her case with the Queen. Apparently her efforts were of no avail, for on April 12, 1585, she wrote from Bermondsey to Sir Christopher Hatton, offering to disprove the malicious speeches of her enemies. Perhaps Elizabeth forgave her during the last years of her life. At all events, after Lady Sidney's death we find the Queen interesting herself in the foundation of her College.

She died at "the poor careful close of Bermondsey" on March 9, 1589, and was buried in Westminster Abbey on April 15. Her tomb fills the place of the altar in the Chapel of St. Paul; on it lies her recumbent effigy in the robes and coronet of a countess; it is surmounted by an arch resting on Corinthian columns. Above are three pyramids and three shields. The whole monument rises to a height of twenty-four feet. There is this inscription, followed by an English version and various texts:

Inclytae Heroinae Franciscae Comitissae Sussex ex nobili & Antiqua Sydneiorum familia ortae, illustrissimo, sapientissimo, & bellicosissimo viro Domino Thomae Radcliffe comiti Sussex nuptae, foeminae multis carissimisque dotibus tum animi, tum corporis ornatae, in sanguine conjunctos, in amicos, in pauperes, in captivos, et praecipue in verbi divini ministros liberalitate & charitate prae caeteris insigni, quae lectionem sacrae Theologiae in Ecclesia Westmonasteriensi Collegiata legendam instituit, & quinque millia librarum per testamentum legavit, quibus vel extrueretur Collegium novum in Academia Cantabrigiensi vel ad augmentum Aulae Clarensis in eadem Academia perquireretur annuus census : de quo perpetuo ali possint magister unus, decem socii, & scholares viginti. Opus certe prae clarum & nunquam satis laudatum. Vixit annos 58. Mort. est 9 Mart. & sepulta fuit die 15 Aprilis, Anno Dom. 1589.

Lady Sidney's will is dated December 6, 1588. After

THE TOMB OF THE FOUNDRESS IN WESTMINSTER ABBEY

giving instructions about her burial and the preaching
of a funeral sermon by Alexander Nowell, Dean of St.
Paul's, she directs her executors to make provision for a
perpetual annuity of £20 for the use of a godly and
learned preacher who is to read two lectures in Westminster Abbey weekly for ever. They are also to
distribute £100 amongst poor and godly ministers in
London and the suburbs. She then proceeds to state
that since the decease of her late lord she had yearly
gathered out of her revenues so much as conveniently
she could, purposing to erect some goodly and godly
monument for the maintenance of good learning. In
performance of the same her charitable pretence, she
directs her executors to employ the sum of £5000
(made up from her ready money yearly reserved, a
certain portion of plate, and other things which she
had purposely left), together with all her unbequeathed
goods, for the erection of a new college in the University of Cambridge to be called the " Lady Frances
Sidney Sussex College," and purchasing some competent
lands for the maintaining of a Master, ten Fellows, and
twenty Scholars, if the said £5000 and unbequeathed
goods would thereunto extend. If in the judgment of
the executors these means appear insufficient for the
erection and founding a new college, she directs that
they be employed for the enlarging of Clare Hall and
for purchasing lands to be annexed to the said College
or Hall, for the maintenance of so many scholars there
according to the rates then used in the University ;
which College should from thenceforth be called " Clare
and Lady Frances Sidney Sussex College."

A few of her other bequests may be mentioned. To

Sir John Harrington and his lady she left much furniture and jewels. Sir John (afterwards first Baron Harrington of Exton) was the eldest son of Sir James Harrington by Lucy, daughter of Sir William Sidney, and therefore a nephew of the Foundress. He has been sometimes confounded with his more celebrated cousin and namesake,* the "saucy godson" of Queen Elizabeth, best known as the translator of *Orlando Furioso*. To her niece, Lady Montagu (Elizabeth, eldest daughter of Sir James Harrington, married to Sir Edward Montagu of Boughton), she bequeathed a trained gown of black velvet embroidered all over with broken trees, a large kirtle, and jewels; to Edward Montagu, a suit of hangings of the story of Holofernes and Judith, with much rich furniture and plate.

She appointed as her executors the above-mentioned Sir John Harrington, her cousin Henry Bosvil, her well-beloved friend Nicholas Bond, D.D. (afterwards President of Magdalen College, Oxford), Robert Forth, D.C.L., "for the like great virtue she had perceived of his fair dealing," her good friend Gabriel Goodman, D.D. (Dean of Westminster), "for his godly and virtuous inclination." Henry Gray, Earl of Kent, she appointed the chief and principal executor of her will, "for the great honour, wisdom, zeal in religion and virtue, which was noted in him," bequeathing to him, as a special legacy, her "fair bason and ewer," and a cup of gold of the value of £100 to be purchased for him. She constituted her good friend, the Lord Archbishop of Canterbury (John Whitgift), as supervisor of her will, and bequeathed to him several pieces of plate.

* A saying of his is quoted on p. 10.

CHAPTER III

THE FOUNDATION

THE Earl of Kent and Sir John Harrington proceeded to the work of founding Lady Sidney's College. Fuller writes:

"These two noble executors in pursuance of the will of this testatrix, according to her desire and direction therein, presented Queen Elizabeth a jewel, being like a star, of rubies and diamonds, with a ruby in the midst thereof, worth an hundred and forty pounds, having on the back side a hand delivering up a heart unto a crown. At the delivery hereof they humbly requested of her Highness a Mortmain to found a College, which she graciously granted unto them.* . . . We usually observe infants born in the seventh month, though poor and pitiful creatures, are vital; and, with great care and good attendance, in time prove proper persons. To such a *partus septimestris* may Sidney College well be resembled, so low, lean, and little at the birth thereof. Alas! what is five thousand pounds to buy the site, build and endow a college therewith? . . . Yet such was the worthy care of her honourable executors, that this Benjamin College—the least, and last in time, and born *after* (as he *at*) the death of its mother—thrived in a short time to a competent strength and stature."

* The licence was not actually granted till 1594.

Some delay ensued ; for it was not till 1593 that, at the motion of the executors, an Act of Parliament was passed enabling Trinity College to sell or let at fee farm the site of the Grey Friars "any locall Statutes of the said Colledge or any statute or lawe of this Realme to the contrarie notwithstandinge." Thereupon Queen Elizabeth wrote to the Master and Seniors of Trinity, *requiring* them to sell or grant the site to the executors at some reasonable price,

"considering that their suite tendeth to a common benefite of our Realme, to the amplifying of our Universitie, and the beautifying of our towne of Cambridge."

She adds that she has no need to use any arguments (since " the same tendeth to the advancement of learning, whereof you are professors ") ; and that the recent Act of Parliament fully dispenses them from the provisions of their Statutes forbidding such alienations. However, for their "better satisfaction and contentment," by her royal prerogative she discharges and dispenses "with you and every of you touching all your said Statutes and ordinances in that behalfe."

On July 25, 1594, the Queen granted her licence by letters patent to the executors of the Countess to found and build a College on the site of the Grey Friars or some other convenient spot ; to appoint a Master, Fellows, and Scholars who are to be a body corporate and politic ; also to make Statutes and appoint a Common Seal. This—the Charter of the College—is a lengthy document. The most interesting and important part of it may be quoted here:

" Nos . . . bonum, laudabile, et pium institutum praefatae Comitissae in praemissis considerantes, et intime
quantum in nobis est ea omnia et singula quae fidem
Christianam orthodoxam quoquo modo concernere poterunt
cupientes promoveri . . . licentiam dedimus . . . praefatis
Comiti et Johanni Harrington * quod ipsi ac haeredes
executores et assignati sui, seu eorum aliqui vel aliquis, ad
Christi unici Mediatoris nostri Evangelium propagandum
ac in laudem et honqrem Dei Omnipotentis, hujusmodi
Collegium perpetuum Sacrae Theologiae, liberalium scientiarum, philosophiae, bonarum artium, et linguarum, de
uno Magistro, decem Sociis, et viginti Scholaribus graduatis
aut non graduatis vel pluribus vel paucioribus ut praedictum
est, juxta ejusdem Collegii ordinationes et statuta per ipsos
Comitem et Johannem Harrington . . . facienda, con-
denda, statuenda, et stabilienda, in villa sive Universitate
Cantabrigiae praedictae, in quodam loco ibidem cognito
vel vocato per nomen nuper scitus domus de *le Graye
Friers* infra vel prope villam Cantabrigiae in dicto comitatu
nostro Cantabrigiae dudum dissolutae vel in aliquo loco
convenienti infra vel prope villam praedictam erigere,
fundare,· et stabilire possint et valeant perpetuis futuris
temporibus duraturum : Et quod iidem Comes et Johannes
. . . idoneam personam theologum in Magistrum, et pro
primo Magistro ipsius Collegii, necnon alias personas quas-
cunque in primos Socios et primos Scholares per ipsos
Comitem et Johannem Harrington . . . eligendas et
assignandas praeficere, creare, et ordinare valeant secundum veram intentionem, propositum, et effectum testa-
menti et ultimae voluntatis praefatae nuper Comitissae,

---

* It is stated earlier in the Charter that Henry, Earl of Kent,
and Sir John Harrington have taken upon themselves the execution of the will of the Countess of Sussex with the full consent of the
rest of the executors.

et secundum ejusdem Collegii ordinationes et statuta . . . :
Et ulterius volumus . . . quod praedictum Collegium
cum sic erectum, factum, fundatum et stabilitum fuerit,
Collegium dominae Franciscae Sidney Sussexiae in perpetuum appelletur et nuncupetur : Et quod Magistri, Socii,
et Scholares Collegii illius sint et erunt unum corpus cor-
poratum et politicum in re, nomine, et facto, habeantque
successionem perpetuam."

No settlement had yet been made with Trinity
College. About a year after the granting of the
Charter, Archbishop Whitgift, who had already exerted
his influence, in the matter of the site, with the College
over which he had previously presided (1566-1577),
received a letter from the Master and Seniors. They
state that, at his Grace's motion and for the foundation
of a College, they have not been unwilling to part with
the site of the Grey Friars to no small damage and
prejudice of their College inheritance ; but, considering
the delays and slender recompense for so large and
beneficial a grant, they venture to make an appeal to
him :

"We are bould eftsonnes to recommend the serious
consideracion thereof to your Graces wisdome and wonted
care of our poore Colledge, well hopinge that as we have
referred our demaunds in this behalf to your Graces deter-
minacion, so your Grace wilbe well pleased to award vs,
above the fee farme of twenty markes, some proporcion of
monie answerable to the buildinges and other comodities
of stone and stuffe, aswell within as above the ground,
which by estimacion of workemen beinge of great valew we
are content to leaue behinde vs."

Then they go on to suggest alternative courses, one of which is to except from the sale such lands and tenements as may be well spared, "leavinge sufficiencie for the scite, buildinges, Courts, backsides, and other offices of the intended foundacion."

The Archbishop's reply, which is curt and slightly sarcastic, is dated "from Croydon the last day of July 1595." With regard to the amount to be paid to the College "for an olde buylding standing within the wall of the Grey-Fryers now used for a malting-howsse; or whether any consideracion should be made therefore or noe," and also with regard to the allowance which "the Master should have for his charges in commyng vp and downe to London the last Trinitie terme for the perfecting of the assurance of the said Grey-Friers,"—the Archbishop is unable to settle these points, "being notwithstandinge of no great importance," without conference with some members of the College, which cannot well be till the next Term. Accordingly, he heartily prays them "for the avoyding of further excuses and delayes in so good a purpose" to complete the business "with as muche expedicion as may bee." After committing them to "the tuicion of Allmightie God," he signs himself "your assured loving friend Jo. Cantuar." This letter had the desired effect. The conveyance of the site is dated September 10, 1595. It is stated therein that the Master, Fellows, and Scholars of Trinity

"for and in consideracion of a certayne somme of monye to them in hand paid before then sealling of these presentes and of the yerelie rent in and by these presentes hereafter reserved. . . . Have bargained and solde . . . vnto Henrie Earle of Kent Sir John Harrington Robert Forthe and Nicholas Bonde . . . All that parcell of land conteyning by estimacion Three Acres be it more or lesse called or knowne by the name of y⁰ late scyte of the howse of y⁰ Graye Fryers . . . nowe enclosed with a stone wall . . . To have and to hold y⁰ said parcell of land . . . for euer . . . yelding and paying therefore yerelie to the said Mʳ Fellowes and Scholers the yerelie rent of Thirtene powndes sixe shillinges eight pennce."

The rent is to be paid half-yearly by equal portions within forty days after Michaelmas and Lady Day under the forfeiture of £5 a month during non-payment. A covenant is added to the effect that, "whereas the said Mʳ Fellowes and Schollers have abated very greatly of the price of the value and worthe of the said grownde," if the College to be erected by the will of the Countess is not built within the seven years next ensuing, then these present Indentures and everything therein contained are to be "vtterlie voyde frustraite and of none effecte."

It is worth noticing that (1) the amount to be paid down is not specified in the conveyance; (2) the site is said to contain three acres, whereas its real extent is about double; (3) it is parted with "*for ever.*" Sometimes it is said that the "lease" of Sidney will "fall in" to Trinity; this idea probably arose from the fact that a rent is paid. The money to be paid down was soon fixed by the Archbishop, who wrote thus to the Master:

" I have signified to Sir John Harrington that for further recompence of the bargayne betwixt you concerning the

Friers hee shall yield vnto you one hundred markes. You may signifie so muche vnto the Companie if you thinck good. It is my order wherevnto all parties haue promised to stand. Vale in Christo. From Croydon the xviith of Septemb. 1595.

" Y^r assured loving frend,

" Jo. CANTUAR."

Sir John Harrington seems to have been greatly astonished at the Archbishop's award. He sent to the Master the hundred marks along with the following letter, from which it will be seen that the executors had now sealed the conveyance:

" Good Mr Doct^r Nevill, I have stayed to send vnto you longer than I purposed for that . . . I have been enforced to send to all the executors generally. . . . But now having procured them all to seale I have sent the assurance vnto you, not doubtinge but as you haue euer delt freindly and lyke a gentleman in this accion, you will now be contented to passe the assurance for the gray friers as it is agreed vnto by your Counsell. . . . I suppose his Lordship hathe awarded you a farr greater somme than you either expected or would your self haue demaunded, and I haue appointe this bearer to deliuer you so much of the same somme a you will take, prayinge you to haue consideracion that how much you shall abate of this somme, so much shall Sydney Colledge be furthered and bettered by your good meanes and fauour. And so I commit you to God. Burley the 3 of October 1595.

" Your very assured Frend,

" JOHN HARYNGTON."

On October 10 the Earl of Kent wrote a similar, but less pointed letter. He entreats the Master's " good

favour and furtherance in passeing thoroughe and finny-
shing the assuraunce of the Graye Friers "; and adds
these words:

"The time hathe bynne longe, the charges and trobles
very greate to the executors to bring this to passe that
hathe bynne done, the money remaininge but very small
to finnyshe that which is begune. Wherein what favour,
with expedition, yourselfe and fellowes will vochsaffe to
shewe us, we will be all righte thankfull vnto you."

The correspondence relating to the conveyance of the
site is given in full by Messrs. Willis and Clark (vol. ii.
pp. 731–6), who point out that no receipt of the hundred
marks, or of any part of that sum, is to be found in the
Bursar's books of Trinity College, the series of which
for this period is quite complete. Hence it seems probable that the College took Sir John Harrington's hint.

It is surprising to find that the building of the
College was begun nearly four months before the
execution of the conveyance. The first Master writes
in his " day-book," which we still possess:

"The first stone of this College was laid by myselfe on
the 20th day of May 1595, in the presence of Dr. Soame
Dep. Vice. Chan., Dr. Barwell, Dr. Cowell, and others."

Other entries in the same book prove conclusively
that the work was begun at this time, not in May
1596, the date given in all the printed statements
on the subject which I have read. The date of the
actual foundation of the College is February 14, 1596.
On that day the Earl of Kent and Sir John (afterwards
Lord) Harrington, by a deed under their hands and
scals, founded the College, consisting of a Master, James

Montagu, M.A., of Christ's College, Dean of the Chapel
Royal, three Fellows and four Scholars (the other
members of the Society to be appointed afterwards).
The first Master was born in 1568. He was the fifth
son of Sir Edward Montagu of Boughton, by Elizabeth,
daughter of Sir James Harrington of Exton, and therefore a grand-nephew of our Foundress (see p. 14). His
eldest brother, Edward, was created first Lord Montagu
of Boughton in 1621 ; and the third brother, Henry,
became first Earl of Manchester in 1626. In the year
of the foundation Lord Harrington granted to the
College an annuity of £30 per annum to be paid out of
the Manor of Bagington in the county of Warwick.
He also assigned to the College a bond for £600.
Further, in 1608, "in full accomplishment of the
will of the Foundress," he conveyed to Dr. Montagu,
the first Master, now Bishop of Bath and Wells, and
others, in trust for the College, the Manor of Saleby in
Lincolnshire. Whereupon the College released Lord
Harrington of "all obligation under their Foundress's
will," since he had, as they affirmed, "bestowed as much,
nay more than was bequeathed to them by the same."
The executors reserved to themselves or the survivor
of them, or to their executors, the power of making a
body of Statutes for the College. They also reserved to
themselves during their life the power of removing the
Master or any of the Fellows or Scholars ; of appointing
to all vacancies ; and of altering any Statutes which
they themselves should make.

So Lady Sidney's "little babe" throve, "(thank God
and good Nurses !) well-batteled."

CHAPTER IV

THE ELIZABETHAN STATUTES

THE original Statutes were framed by the Executors of
the Foundress and given to the College in 1598. They
are to a large extent copied from the Statutes of
Emmanuel College, which was founded in 1584. They
are verbose, cumbrous, and ill-arranged ; they must
be three times as long as the Statutes of 1882 under
which we now live. Their provisions are fortified by
elaborate oaths and cumulative penalties, some of them
gradually mounting up from a farthing fine to expulsion.
A few of the Statutes were, as we shall see in the next
chapter, afterwards amended by the Earl of Kent, the
surviving executor. We may feel sure that some
others very soon became obsolete. But it is clear from
our College Order Books and other records that the
Statutes as a whole were loyally carried out for more
than 260 years ; in 1860 they were superseded by a new
body of Statutes. A sketch of the more interesting
portions of the old Statutes is given here to enable the
reader to form some idea of the College life and discipline of three hundred years ago.

The Preface to the Statutes, which has been re-
suscitated and now appears at the head of the Statutes
of 1882, is a very florid document ; but it is interesting

in that it asserts the object of the foundation with great clearness. Two important passages may be quoted here :

"Finis ille unicus nobis propositus est Gloria Dei et Aedificatio Ecclesiae in optime instituenda juventate ; ut fiat Collegium, respectu Ecclesiae, seminarium quoddam in quo non nisi optima quaeque germina plantari, ea plantata largifluis scientiarum imbribus irrigari volumus, usque dum ad tantam maturitatem excreverint, ut inde transferantur in Ecclesiam, quae eorum fructu opipare pasta crescat in plenitudinem Christi."

"Nec modo seminarium augustum et conclusum nimis, verum in se amplissimum campum Collegium esse cupimus ; ubi juvenes apum more de omnigenis flosculis pro libita libent, modo mel legant, quo et eorum procudantur linguae et pectora, tamquam crura, thymo compleantur ; ita ut tandem ex Collegio, quasi ex alveari evolantes, novas in quibus se exonerent sedes appetant. Haec mens nostra, hic finis ; quem qui non respicit, ad quem qui non collineaverit, hunc morsibus et aculeis, modis denique omnibus vexent, donec pro fuco ex alveari pepulerunt."

The functions of the MASTER are almost entirely disciplinary and bursarial. To James Montagu and his successors the executors give *authoritatem in Socios et Scholares omnes ejusdem Collegii, eosdem gubernandi, regendi, puniendi, admonendi, et rem domesticam totius Collegii administrandi.* But they do not allow the said James or his successors to do anything *sub nomine Collegii, nisi ex majoris partis Magistri ipsius et Sociorum assensu.* To prevent excessive severity on the part of the Head towards the Members, the Master is to impose all penalties in the presence of the Dean and

the Senior Fellow, in order that they may be witnesses
in case of an appeal to the Vice-Chancellor, which the
Statutes allow.   It is directed that, if any Fellow
or Scholar not content with the decision of the
orum domesticum fail in his appeal, he is to be
expelled.   But the Master is not only to restrain the
bad ; he must provoke to greater goodness, by rewards
and kind treatment, *quos viderit religioni, doctrinae et
probitati diligentius insudare.*   The rewards suggested
are preferences in appointments to College offices and
benefices, and in the assignment of chambers in College.
No one except a Fellow is to have a chamber to himself.
To the Master the executors assign the chambers which
they have directed should be built for his use.   *Et ne
forte tot labores incassum a Magistro ipso absque
emolumento subeantur*, it is ordained that he receive as
his annual stipend £20 in two half-yearly payments,
besides 2*s.* a week for Commons and 26*s.* 8*d.* a year
for the wages of his *Famulus.*   He is also to have for
his own use the garden, one pigeon-house (*Colum-
barium*), and the produce of all the College grounds
except the Fellows' orchard (*Pomarium*).

Then follow elaborate directions for the election of a
new Master.   He is to be an Englishman, a Master of
Arts at least, and in Holy Orders, the possessor of
many good qualities here enumerated, and one who
*Papismum, Haereses, superstitiones et errores omnes ex
animo abhorret et detestatur.*   This last clause, as we
shall see afterwards, became historical (see p. 151).   If
any Fellow can be found answering to this description,
he is to be elected ; if not, recourse must be had to a
former Fellow ; if no former Fellow is suitable, it shall

be lawful to elect *ex Collegio Trinitatis et eo deficiente ex tota Cantabrigiae Universitate.* This provision led to trouble on an important occasion (see p. 210). Next the executors, having reserved to themselves (or the survivor of them) the right of nomination and admission to the Mastership, Fellowships, or Scholarships, give at great length rules to be observed at the election of a Master. Only the more interesting provisions need be mentioned here. Seven days after the publication of the vacancy all the Fellows, Scholars, and Pensioners are to assemble in the Chapel at 5 A.M. After Morning Prayer a sermon is to be preached by the Senior Fellow or his deputy, exhorting the Fellows to choose a Master according to the Statutes and the wants of the College.

Postea Eucharistia, id est Coena Domini, celebrabitur cujus omnes Socios, Scholares, Pensionarios, caeterosque inhabitantes participes esse volumus. Finitis autem his omnibus pietatis ac religionis exercitiis quibus Electores ad debitum officium alacrius et religiosius praestandum excitentur—

the Senior Fellow, having directed all except the Fellows to withdraw, is to associate with himself as scrutineers the two Fellows next Senior. After an oath of fidelity to the Statutes, to be taken on the Holy Gospels, these three are to receive the votes which are to be given in writing as follows: *Ego N.T. eligo in Magistrum hujus Collegii N.N.* If the major part of the Fellows cannot agree on one person at the first or second scrutiny, then the election is to be delegated to the five Senior Fellows, who must complete the election there and then under pain of the loss of their Fellowships *ipso facto*

—certainly a drastic method of ensuring an election. The Senior Fellow or, if he himself be elected, then the next Senior, is bound to declare the election and to admit the person elected *sub poena manifesti perjurii et perpetuae expulsionis a Collegio*. The new Master is then to take an oath of great length, the most important part of which is directed against Popery in the following words:

Ego N.T. Deum testor me veram Christi Religionem Papismo et caeteris haeresibus contrariam ex animo complexurum; Scripturae authoritatem vel optimorum hominum judiciis praepositurum, caetera quae ex verbo Dei nulla ratione probari possunt pro humanis habiturum; authoritatem Regiam in hominibus ejus dominationis summam et externorum episcoporum et principum et potestatum quarumcumque jurisdictioni minime subjectam aestimaturum, etc. etc.

To assist the Master in his disciplinary work, a DEAN or CATECHIST is to be appointed. He is to be elected annually by the Master and the major part of the Fellows. His duties are: (1) Every year within three days after the Great Audit (*Magnus Computus*) to read aloud the Statutes in the presence of all the Fellows and Scholars. (2) Every Friday during Term to preside at a Theological Disputation in Chapel of two hours duration, from 4 to 6 P.M. (3) *Eundem etiam volumus Sociorum suorum in Divinis Officiis celebrandis negligentias annotare.* He is to approve legitimate excuses for absence or unpunctuality (*tarditas*) and to punish delinquents. Note that the "delinquents" here mentioned are Fellows. (4) He is to appoint from among the students two "Monitors," who are to note on mark-sheets instances of unpunctuality, absence, or neglect on the part of their fellow students, both at College Chapel and at Exercises in the Schools. These sheets are to be posted on the screens every Friday. (5) On Sunday at 3 P.M. for the space of one hour he is to expound some Article of the Christian Faith, and he is to examine according to his judgment all the Scholars, Pensioners, and servants dwelling in College, so as the better to note the progress of each one of them. If necessary, the other Fellows are to assist the Dean in this examination. The annual stipend of the Dean is to be 43s. 4d.

Precise details are then given as to the penalties to be imposed by the Dean. A Fellow is to be fined for each "tardiness" at Chapel one halfpenny; for each absence one penny; for each neglect of his course (*cursus et ordinis*) in reading prayers twelve pence. At Disputations in College "tardiness" on the part of a Fellow involves a fine of one penny, absence fourpence, and neglect of his course 6s. 8d. The students are to be fined for "tardiness" at Chapel one halfpenny; for absence one penny; for neglecting a course in the Schools twelve pence if they are grown up (*si adultus fuerit*); if not, they are to be punished with the rod (*virga corrigatur*).* "Tardiness" is thus defined: (1) at Disputations, *post Respondentis expositam sententiam;*

* " The prolongation of the whipping age to the verge of manhood is perhaps peculiar to the English Universities. . . . The Statutes of Brasenose—founded in 1509—are the first which exhibit the undergraduate completely stripped of his medieval dignity, tamed and reduced to the schoolboy level, from which he did not begin to emerge till towards the close of the seventeenth century. Here he is subjected to the birch at the discretion of the College Lecturer

(2) at Chapel, *post primum Psalmum.* The proceeds of all fines are to go to the Fellows' Table.

The Chapel Services were under the control of the Master, not the Dean as at the present time. Every day, especially on Sunday, all the Fellows, Scholars, Pensioners, and other dwellers in the College are to be present at Public Prayers, in which the Master is to take part. At the beginning of each Term *at least* he must preach a, sermon to the Fellows and Scholars. Next the object of the foundation of the College is emphasised once more; it is to provide suitable persons for the ministry of the Word and Sacraments. The College is to be a nursery (*Seminarium*) from which the English Church may summon pastors and teachers. A solemn warning is addressed to Fellows and Scholars :

Sciant itaque Socii et Scholares, qui alio consilio se Collegio obtrudent quam ut Sacrae Theologiae se addicant tandemque in Verbo praedicando laborent, spem nostram frustrari locumque Socii aut Scholaris praeter institutum nostrum occupare ; quam rem serio eos admonemus uti diligentur curent scituros se aliquando fraudis per eos admissae reddituros Domino rationem.

The very solemnity of this declaration seems to betray a lurking fear that the object aimed at was not likely to be completely attained. At all events, the stern logic of facts soon proved that the ideal of Lady Sidney's executors could not be realised ; for their College even in its early years produced, as we shall see, not clerics only, but also soldiers, poets, lawyers, doctors, and even a newspaper-editor. Nor were the clerics all

for unprepared lessons, playing, laughing, or talking in lecture, making ' odious comparisons,' etc."—Rashdall, *Universities*, vol. ii. p. 622.

Anglicans by any means; some were Presbyterians, and one at least was a Romanist.

The STEWARD (*Seneschallus*) is to receive in advance from the Master, Fellows, Scholars, and Pensioners the monthly payments for Commons; the amount of these payments is to be fixed by the Master. With the money thus received the Steward is to provide for the purchase of victuals. Every Saturday after dinner a weekly account is to be rendered by the Steward or the Manciple to the Master and Fellows. No Fellow is to be absent from this weekly audit without the Master's permission under pain of a fine of two pence.

There is to be a KEEPER OF THE COMMON CHEST (*Custos cistae communis*). This Chest, in which all the College money is to be placed, must be kept in the Treasury along with other chests containing the College muniments. Every chest is to have three keys of different make; of these the Master is to have one, the Senior Fellow another, and the *Custos* another. The College Seal is to be kept in a little chest, the key of which is given to the Master. There is to be an audit twice a year, one within a month after Easter, the other within a month after Michaelmas; at which the Master is directed to render to the Fellows a true and faithful account of receipts and expenses, and to exhibit to them all the College treasure and muniments.

Every Scholar and Pensioner must have a TUTOR who is to render an account of the conduct and diligence of his pupils and to instruct them when necessary, especially *in Religione sincera et vera Dei cognitione*. No one may act as Tutor except the Master or one of the

Fellows. The number of pupils to be taken by each Tutor is to be carefully limited by the Master. Every Tutor must have two or more of his pupils sleeping in his own chamber. We may picture the Tutor enthroned on his high bed with, perhaps, four pupils on their little truckle-beds in each corner of the room. The students are not allowed to go out into the town without permission from their Tutors, except to attend lectures in the Public Schools or other exercises, sermons or other academic functions. The possibilities of this early tutorial system are beautifully exemplified in the account given of Joseph Mede of Christ's, the friend of our own Richard Howlett, who was Cromwell's Tutor. The first question which Mede used to address to each of his pupils in the evening was this: *Quid dubitas?* (What doubt have you got in your reading to-day?)

" For he supposed," it is added, " that to doubt nothing was to understand nothing. When he learned their doubts, then he resolved their *Quaeres,* and so set them on clear ground to proceed more distinctly. Then, having by prayer commended them and their studies to God's protection and blessing, he dismissed them to their lodgings."

The Master and Fellows are to choose one of their number to be LECTOR. The title given to this official in the Trinity Statutes is a clearer one, *Lector Primarius—i.e.,* Head Lecturer, *qui caeteris praesit.* Immediately after morning chapel the bell is rung and Lectures begin in Hall. The Head Lecturer is to listen to the other lecturers for an hour; he will examine the students when necessary, or cause them to be examined by *Sub-Lectores*. The Master is to determine the subjects to be studied in each class and the method to be pursued. The Head Lecturer should himself lecture occasionally on Plato, Aristotle, or Cicero; and he is to superintend all disputations and exercises throughout. *Sub-Lectores* are to be chosen from among the Fellows, if possible; if not, they may be Masters of Arts or Bachelors who are not Fellows. The Head Lecturer is to give punishments for "tardiness" at Lectures, Disputations, and Examinations: to "grown up" students fines of a farthing, a halfpenny after half-time (*ultra medietatem*), and a penny for absence; if not grown up, *virga corrigantur*. Any student who after frequent punishment refuses to reform is to be brought by the *Lector* before the Master and Fellows; if after this he persists *in notabili negligentia sua*, he must be expelled. The stipend of the *Lector* is to be 13*s.* 4*d.* a quarter.

The FELLOWS are to be Englishmen, Masters of Arts, or Bachelors at least; they are to be chosen from among the Scholars, the poorer students being preferred. A preference is also to be given to natives of the county of Kent and to pupils of Oakham and Uppingham schools. If no Scholars are found suitable, then other students are eligible—*semper tamen ex egentioribus probioribus et doctioribus.* If the Master or any Fellow proposes an affluent person, the penalty is loss of half a year's dividend. *Hos vero pauperes sive ex Collegio sive ex Academia eligi volumus.* They are to be well versed in Hebrew, Greek and Latin. They must also understand the principles of Rhetoric, Dialectic, and

c

Physics, and be able to make practical use thereof. Above all things they must be professors of pure Religion without taint of Popery or other heresies, conforming their lives and characters thereunto. They must also have studied for six full years in the University of Cambridge. When a Fellowship is vacant, the Master is to appoint two Examiners from among the Fellows. The Examination is to last three days, 8–10 A.M., or longer, on each day. Greek and Hebrew are taken on the first day, Rhetoric and Logic on the second, Physics on the third. There is also a Theological examination by the Dean on the third day. The Master and any of the Fellows are at liberty to take part in the examination, provided that everything is done decently and in order. The formalities of the Fellowship election are then explained; the oaths and other proceedings being somewhat similar to those used at the election of a Master. The studies of the Fellows are next referred to. Besides studying Philosophy and other University exercises, they are to take part in the weekly College Disputation in Theology; each Fellow is to take his turn as respondent, and there are to be two opponents. All Fellows are to be admitted to Holy Orders within three years after their election under pain of losing their Fellowships.

Amongst practices forbidden to Fellows may be mentioned the frequenting of taverns and bearing of arms. No Fellow may presume to be out of College after 9 P.M. from Michaelmas to Easter, or after 10 P.M. from Easter to Michaelmas, except for some grave cause to be approved by the Master. No Fellow may keep dogs or hawks (*rapaces aves*), or play at dice, hazard, or cards (*tesseris, alea, aut chartis ludat*)—*ne remittendi quidem animi gratia*. It appears that some Colleges did allow cards in Hall at Christmas. A Fellow must not scorn his senior; he must give way to him in College and out, in Chapel and Hall, in the schools and in the street. *Et quoniam boni bene merentur et digni sunt praemio*, each Fellow is to receive from the Master an annual stipend of twenty shillings. Further, two shillings are to be paid weekly to the Steward for the Commons of each Fellow ; and for clothes every Fellow is to have an annual allowance of twenty shillings. But any Fellow not in Holy Orders must be content with his Commons and dress allowance, receiving no stipend till he is ordained. If a Fellow obtains a property, pension, or benefice without charge, the annual value of which exceeds £20, he vacates his Fellowship *ipso facto ;* this also occurs in the case of institution to a benefice of any value whatsoever to which the cure of souls is attached. All Fellows must proceed to the degree of Bachelor of Divinity in due course ; they are to vacate their Fellowships seven years after they are of standing for the D.D. degree, not reckoning the time of holding certain specified offices. A Fellow may have thirty " play-days " (*dies lusorios*) in each year, during which he may absent himself from College, provided that he ask permission from the Master with all due respect. For an urgent cause to be approved by the Master he may be absent for a second period of thirty days. For another urgent cause, or for the same cause now rendered more urgent, to be approved by the Master and the major part of the Fellows, he may be absent for a third period of thirty days.

The SCHOLARS are to be elected from among those students who are *pauperiores, probiores, aptiores*, not yet Bachelors of Arts, nor admitted to the Sacred Ministry. They must have proposed to themselves to study Theology, and to take Orders; *sintque saltem mediocriter instructi et periti in Graecis, Rhetorica, et Logica*. Preference is to be given *ceteris paribus* to those in need and to natives of the counties of Kent and Rutland. The method of examination and election is left to the Master and Fellows. Newly elected Scholars are required to take an oath of obedience to the Statutes and the College authorities. It is directed that the Scholars, in batches of six or thereabouts week by week, wait at the Fellows' table, carrying in and out such things as are necessary, *in prandiis, coenis, et biberiis*. For the explanation of the meals called *biberiae* we must go to the Statutes of other Colleges— *e.g.*, at Jesus,

omnes Socios, Scholares, et Commensales, cum ad biberiam campana sonuerit, statim aulam ingredi volumus, et convenienter silentio observato, postquam biberint, sine diuturna mora inde recedant.

The *biberiae* consisted of a pewter of beer and a piece of bread. One of these meals was breakfast; this was after morning Chapel, which was at five o'clock. The dinner hour in the early days of the College was ten; supper was at five. To return to the Scholars: they are also to take their turn at reading the Scriptures (*Biblia*) during meals in Hall; and all present are to listen attentively till the Master directs the Scholar to cease reading. The Scholars are to have an allowance of twelve pence a week for Commons. If they exceed this allowance, they must pay the difference to the Steward ; but when their weekly Commons come to less, they are to receive the balance.   Four Scholars and no more are to sleep in one chamber.   An allowance for dress is made to each Scholar, amounting to 14*s*. 8*d*. per annum ; the clothes are to be of a colour to be determined by the Master.   No Scholar may be absent for more than forty days in one year except for some reasonable cause.

The greatest care is to be taken to prevent the admission of FELLOW-COMMONERS and PENSIONERS from corrupting the members of the Foundation.   Any students admitted as such must be of unblemished character ; they must promise to adapt themselves in all respects to the life of the Fellows or Scholars, as the case may be, and to obey the Statutes of the College. No one may be admitted *ad mensam et convictum Sociorum* unless he be either a Master of Arts at least, or the son of a knight or one of higher rank, except for some cause to be approved by the Master and the major part of the Fellows.   Fellow-Commoners are to pay 2*s*. a quarter *in usus necessarios*.   Ordinary Pensioners (*qui in Scholarium convictum admittentur*) are to be charged 12*d*. a quarter.

The Students must attend Public Prayers in the College Chapel *absque ulla exceptione*, and often go to University Sermons ; they are also directed

contentionibus et rixis abstinere ; modestiam omnem vultu, gestu corporis, et vestitus genere et forma praeferre ; literis sic diligenter incumbere ut fructu ipso diligentiam suam contestetur.

If they do not meet with the approval of the Master in

these matters, he is to admonish them in the presence of
the Dean; recalcitrants are to be " put out of Commons "
till they reform themselves. The stoppage of Commons
to students who had no pocket-money would mean
starvation. If a student after a second and third
admonition still fails to give satisfaction to the Master,
he is to be summoned to plead his cause before the
College, and if the Master and the major part of the
Fellows so decide, he is to be expelled. To prevent
waste of time, foolish talking and trifling, it is ordained
that no students, except they be Masters of Arts, may
presume to assemble in their chambers *aut ludendi aut
epulandi aut confabulandi gratia aut quocumque alio
nomine.* An offender if " grown up " is to be fined by
the Master twelve pence for each offence; *sin puerilem
actatem non excesserit, verberibus per Decanum castigetur.*
The students' chambers are to be visited twice at least
in each week by the Fellows singly or in pairs; they
must take careful note of what is being done there,
commending the industrious and upbraiding the slack.
On the next day they are to report any offenders against
this Statute, so that they may be punished as is above
directed. The students would doubtless be expected to
be reading in the little studies (*studiola* or *musaca*),
generally five or six feet square, partitioned off from
the chambers.* To warm themselves on cold evenings
they had to repair to the common fire in the Hall;
for at this time there were no fires in the College

---

* " In English College rooms the usual arrangement was that
each scholar had a study of his own adjoining the windows. Thus
at New College: *in inferioribus cameris quatuor fenestras et quatuor
studiorum loca habentibus sint semper quatuor scholares vel socii collocati*

rooms. The Fellows had their own " Parlour Fire "
(see p. 91). The obligation to converse only in Latin
within the precincts of the College, which is found in
the Statutes of most of the older Colleges, is not
mentioned in the Sidney Statutes. Probably the
requirement was now becoming obsolete.

This chapter may appropriately end with our own
Fuller's benediction on the College, his *Child's Prayer
for his Mother*, as he calls it :

" Now though it be only the place of the parent and
proper to him as the greater to bless his child, yet it is the
duty of the child to pray for his parents ; in which relation
my best desires are due to this Foundation, my mother
for my last eight years in this University. May her lamp
never lack light for the oil, or oil for the light thereof!
Zoar, is it not a little one ? Yet who shall despise the day
of small things ? May the foot of sacrilege, if once offering
to enter the gates thereof, stumble and rise no more!
The Lord bless the labours of all the students therein,
that they may tend and end at His glory, their own
salvation, the profit and honour of the Church and
Commonwealth."

In the words of Coleridge, Sidney men may well
respond :

" God bless thee, dear old man ! "

(Statutes, p. 88). These studies were apparently movable structures,
being sometimes treated as part of the furniture. . . . Students
slept in the part of the room left unoccupied by the separate
studies."—Rashdall, *Universities,* vol. ii., p. 669.

CHAPTER V

JAMES MONTAGU, FIRST MASTER

On February 20, 1596, the executors by their attorney
gave possession of the site of the Grey Friars to James
Montagu, M.A., Master, and to William Wood, M.A.,
and John Maynard, B.A., in the name of the Fellows
and Scholars. As has been already stated, the College
buildings had been begun in the previous year. The
architect was Ralph Simons, who had built Emmanuel
and "thoroughly reformed a great part of Trinity
College." Afterwards, in 1598, with Gilbert Wigge as
his partner, he "undertook" to build the Second Court
of St. John's, in which work "the undertakers were
undone," and Simons lost the use of one of his hands.
Wigge was his partner in the Sidney work also.
From the beginning the Master wrote day by day in
his account book, still preserved in the College, the
various items of receipt and expenditure, from which
may be gathered many interesting particulars with
regard to the rate of wages and cost of materials
at the end of the sixteenth century. Apparently
Ralph Simons could not write; for in the Master's
day-book he always signed his name in large capitals
like a child. His printed signature may be seen under
his design of part of the Second Court of St. John's

(reproduced by Willis and Clark). It is interesting to note that more than half of the sum received from Lady Sidney's estate to found and endow the College was expended in the erection of the Hall, the Master's Lodge, and the Hall (*i.e.*, the northern) Court. These buildings formed the whole of the College when it was opened in 1598. The style of architecture may be seen in Loggan's print (made about 1688), a reproduction of which forms the frontispiece of this book. The Hall Court is the left-hand Court in Loggan's print. Harraden, writing in 1814—*i.e.*, before the buildings were covered with cement—says that

"the whole College is built of dark-coloured brick, partially intermixed with stone ; the effect of the whole is so gloomy that no correctness of form or distribution of parts can counteract its impression."

At first, however, the brick-work was "rose-red." So says Giles Fletcher in his Latin poem on the Colleges published in 1633.

> Haec inter media aspicies mox surgere tecta
> Culminibus niveis roseisque nitentia muris :
> Nobilis haec doctis sacrabit femina musis,
> Conjugio felix, magno felicior ortu,
> Insita Sussexo proles Sidneia trunco.

The arrangement of the Hall, Kitchen, Buttery, and Master's Lodge was much the same as at present, with a few exceptions. The Hall had an open timber roof (now covered by a flat ceiling) and no music-gallery. The structure which now projects in front of the Hall blocked up two windows on the east side.

"There was originally," say Messrs. Willis and Clark, "a square turret in each angle of the court as at Emmanuel College. The one to the right served as a porch to the Lodge ; the one to the left served the same office for the College Parlour. A similar turret projected from the middle of the façade and furnished a porch for the Hall of a more ornamental character than the others."

The original Parlour (or Combination Room) is now the reading-room of the Taylor Library. The present buttresses of the garden front of the Hall and Lodge are a later addition. The north and south sides of the Court consisted of ranges of chambers in three floors, with garrets in the roof lighted by small windows, as may be seen in Loggan's print. The position of the College Gate, opposite the entrance to the Hall, is also shown by Loggan.

Fuller says that the College "continued without a Chapel some years after the first founding thereof until at last some good men's charity supplied this defect." In the *Adversaria* of John Sherman, Fellow of Jesus, quoted by Baker, it is stated that the Chapel was added two years after the other buildings were completed, *i.e.*, only four or five years after the "first founding" of the College. The Chapel and the Library over it were formed out of the ruins of the refectory of the Grey Friars, the walls of which had been left standing.* It seems probable that the Chapel was only roughly fitted up at first, and that it was afterwards much improved, partly at the expense of Dr. Montagu (when he had become Bishop of Bath and

* It had recently been used as a malthouse ; see p. 19.

THE HALL AND MASTER'S LODGE: GARDEN FRONT

Wells) during Dr. Ward's Mastership. Cole, the antiquary, writing in 1748, says that Montagu

" wainscoted the altar end of the Chapel in a very handsome manner : but this was done, as I should guess, when he was Bishop of Bath and Wells; for over the altar is carved the arms of that See impaling his own."

The original Chapel stood almost exactly on the same site as the present one. It was never consecrated. Fuller writes sensibly on the subject :

" Others have complained that it was never ceremoniously consecrated, which they conceive essential thereunto, whilst there want not their equals in learning and religion who dare defend that the continued series of divine duties (praying, preaching, administering the sacrament) publicly practised for more than thirty years, without the least check or control of those in authority, in a place set apart to that purpose, doth sufficiently consecrate the same."

On August 28, 1598, the Earl of Kent sent the first copy of the Statutes to the Master ; another copy, with several alterations, was forwarded in the same year, or that following. Up till January 5, 1611, the Executors exercised their right of appointing to the Mastership, Fellowships, and Scholarships. In September 1598 the College was open for the reception of students. By August in the following year ten Fellows had been nominated by the executors. The Senior Fellow or President was Samuel Wright, who entered Corpus in 1577 and afterwards migrated to Magdalene. He took the B.A. degree in 1580. A friend of his published in 1612 *Divers godly and learned Sermons of a reverend and faithfull servant of God, Mr. Samuel Wright,*

*Bachelor of Divinitie, late President of Sidney Colledge
in Cambridge, deceased.*

The most distinguished member of the infant society
was Thomas Gataker, formerly Scholar of St. John's,
who was now twenty-two. After his appointment in
1596, he was tutor and chaplain in the house of William
Ayloffe at Braxted, while the Sidney buildings were in
progress. In 1598 he came into residence, before they
were quite completed. He shared his chamber with
another very able Fellow, William Bradshaw, whose
acquaintance James Montagu had made in Guernsey.
Bradshaw had a tutorship there, having failed in 1595
to obtain a fellowship at Emmanuel, his own College.
When riding up to Cambridge to enter on his new
duties, Bradshaw had a narrow escape from drowning at
Harston Mills, four miles from his destination. He
took Orders and used to preach in the villages around
Cambridge. Unfortunately he soon got into trouble
for espousing the cause of John Darrel, the " Exorcist,"
whose impostures were exposed by Samuel Harsnet,
Master of Pembroke. Bradshaw felt compelled to leave
College. Gataker, who had in a short time gained a
high reputation as a successful tutor, followed his
friend ; he moved to London at the end of 1600.
Shortly afterwards Montagu visited him with the view
of inducing him to return to Cambridge as Hebrew
Professor. Gataker declined ; whereupon the Master
helped him to obtain the Preachership at Lincoln's Inn.
In 1611 he became Rector of Rotherhithe, and in 1643
one of the Westminster Assembly of Divines. He was
not an extreme Puritan, being in favour of a "well-
regulated prelacy." As a classical and biblical scholar

he was very famous. He wrote a treatise on the *Nature and Use of Lots*, and he was chiefly responsible for the annotations on the Bible issued by the Assembly of Divines. He also wrote some of the lives in Fuller's *Abel Redivivus*. A splendid edition of his classical works, including a commentary on Marcus Aurelius, was published, after his death, at Utrecht in 1698. Bradshaw was a more zealous champion of Puritanism than Gataker. He wrote an enormous number of tracts in its support, the most celebrated of which was *English Puritanisme*.

Another well-known name in the first list of Fellows is that of Samuel Ward, who came from St. John's. He was afterwards a celebrated preacher at Ipswich. He must not be confounded with his more famous namesake, the third Master of the College. Francis Aldrich, of Clare, afterwards second Master of Sidney, was also one of the first Fellows.

The Master must have been very active in securing students for his College. From September 1, 1598, to Michaelmas 1599—*i.e.*, in the first year of the College—there were no less than forty admissions. John Brereton, one of the first batch of Scholars, was afterwards, as we shall see, a notable benefactor. William Wilmer, afterwards a knight, was the first Pensioner; he gave books to the Library. Jeremy Dike was afterwards a Fellow and subsequently Vicar of Epping. He was a celebrated preacher, and the author of tracts on the Eucharist and other subjects. John Pocklington, Scholar, was afterwards a Fellow, Prebendary of Lincoln and Canon of Windsor, and author of *Sunday no Sabbath* and *Altare Christianum*, which, by order of the

House of Lords, were publicly burnt by the common hangman in London and the two Universities. One of these forty freshmen afterwards made a name for himself in English history—viz., Edward Noel, afterwards well known as the second Viscount Campden. He was the son of Sir Andrew Noel and was born in 1582. His mother was Mabel, daughter of Sir James Harrington; this explains why he came to Sidney. Early in life he served in the wars in Ireland, where, in the words of his epitaph, " he was a knight baneret." In 1617 he was created Baron Noel of Ridlington; and in 1629 he succeeded his father-in-law as Viscount Campden, having previously obtained a grant of the reversion of this title. Like many Sidney men who came after, he was an enthusiastic royalist. In 1631 he paid £2500 into the Exchequer as a loan for the public service; and he assisted in the levying of ship-money in his county. In 1640 we find him a member of the Council of Peers at York. When war broke out, he received a commission from the King to raise 500 horse, and afterwards three regiments of horse and three of foot. But before he could complete his task he died, in March 1643, in the royal quarters at Oxford.

Some of the earliest students of the College had migrated from other houses; for in our Degree Register we find presentations for degrees from Sidney as early as Lent 1599, when Pocklington and one of the Harrington family took the B.A. At the summer *Comitia* Richard Cleburne, one of the Fellows, took his M.A. along with Daniel Dike, afterwards the first Fellow on Sir John Hart's foundation. Daniel was the brother of Jeremy Dike mentioned above. He was a

notable Puritan. Fuller describes him as " that faithful
servant in discovering the deceitfulness of man's heart."
His book on this subject was translated into Latin by
the Librarian of the Bodleian. The first recorded list
of annual College officers is that of October 1604:
Decanus, Mr. Cleburne; *Lector*, Mr. Stafford; *Seneschallus*, Mr. Ward; *Hebræus Lector*, Mr. Pocklington.

In the second year of the College (Michaelmas 1599
to Michaelmas 1600) the number of admissions was 27.
In the eight succeeding years down to the end of
Montagu's Mastership the numbers were 19, 24, 16, 17,
12, 23, 22, 14. In October 1600 a very remarkable
man was admitted, George Goring, afterwards Earl of
Norwich, who was born in 1583. In early life he served
in Flanders, and was made a knight in 1608. Having
a rare gift for wit and drollery, he became a favourite
courtier of James I:; he is described as " Master of the
games for fooleries." Charles I. too was very fond of
Goring, who by the royal favour established himself as
a great monopolist. We are told that " Sir George
Goring leads up the march and dance with the
monopoly of tobacco and licensing of taverns." In
1641 his income was £26,000. He spent his money
freely in the King's service. " I had all from his
Majesty," he said, " and he hath all again." In
1644 he was created Earl of Norwich, as a reward for
his services as ambassador to France, on account of
which Parliament impeached him for high treason.
The unsuccessful part which Goring played as general
in the second civil war is well known. He was brought
to trial by Parliament and condemned to death; but
was afterwards respited, thanks to the casting vote of

the Speaker. He was soon set at liberty, and joined Charles II. on the Continent. At the Restoration he was appointed Captain of the King's Guard. He died in 1663, and was buried in Westminster Abbey.

In 1606 Richard Dugard was admitted as a Sizar; he afterwards became the leading Tutor of the College in its most flourishing period. Fuller says that he had the honour of his intimate acquaintance.

" He had a moiety of the most considerable pupils, whom he bred in learning and piety in the golden mean between superstition and faction. He held a gentle strict hand over them, so that none presumed on his lenity to offend, or were discouraged by his severity to amend. He was an excellent Grecian and general scholar; old when young, such his gravity in behaviour; and young when old, such the quickness of his endowments."

Dugard was an intimate friend of Milton. He died at Fulletby, Lincolnshire, of which he was Rector, in 1653.

"1606. *Mr. Joan: Young Scotus admissus est in Coll: qui gradum magistri in Artibus in Scotia sumpserat.*" Young was elected a Fellow in the same year that he took his *ad eundem* degree, and was Dean of the College in 1612. He afterwards became Dean of Winchester. He was the son of Sir Peter Young, diplomatist and tutor to James I. He is described as " the first Scottish man who ever took degree in the University." Mr. Mullinger remarks that

" the statement, though not to be accepted without quali- fication, brings home to us very forcibly the small amount.

of polite and lettered intercourse that existed between England and Scotland prior to the union of the crowns."

Scotchmen went to Paris, Padua, and Geneva, but very rarely to Oxford or Cambridge.

Meanwhile another building began to rise, the College endowments mounting up with great rapidity during the next fifty years. The number of benefactions received during that time, most of them from former students of the College, is quite extraordinary. In fact during our first half-century we obtained almost all the property which we now possess. An account will now be given of those endowments which came in during Dr. Montagu's Mastership.

In 1599 Edward Montagu of Hemington (afterwards first Baron Montagu of Boughton), brother of the Master, granted to the College by lease for 1000 years forty-five acres at Burwash in Sussex (then leased out for three lives with a reserved rent of £3 per annum) on condition that, till the lives were out, the yearly rent should be laid out in books of Divinity for the Library; and that afterwards, when in all likelihood the estate would bring in £10 per annum, it should be employed towards the maintenance of three Scholars. Two of them are to be Northamptonshire men born, and of Oundle School, and the third a Sussex man born, if any such shall be found fit Scholars. They are to have all the privileges of the Scholars of the Foundation.

In 1601 Leonard Smith, citizen and fishmonger of London, bequeathed £120 with all his goods, for founding a Fellowship (to be called "Mr. Smith's Fellowship") on condition that the person nominated by the Company of Fishmongers be upon every vacancy

admitted to it, if qualified by the Statutes of the College.
The College agreed to found this Fellowship for £120,
it being provided that the Fellow be in Priest's Orders
within three years after his admission, under pain of
expulsion, and that his tenure be limited to six years.
He is to have the same allowance as the Fellows of the
Foundation, an equal share in the dividend, and all
other privileges. Moreover, in 1604 the College for
£60 covenanted to found a Scholarship of equal value
with those of their Foundress and with the same
privileges. It was agreed that a Scholar nominated
by the Company of Fishmongers within three months
after notice from the College be admitted if he be
found fit ; or else that the College fill the Scholarship.
Scholars of Holt School in Norfolk are to have the preference.

The celebrated benefaction of Peter Blundell belongs
to the same time. He was born at Tiverton in 1520.
From a most humble beginning he rose to a great
position in the kersey trade and accumulated a vast
fortune. He died in 1601, bequeathing (after ample
legacies to his nephews) £40,000 in various benefactions, the most important of which was the endowment
of Blundell's School at Tiverton, which was founded in
1604. He directed that £2000 should be set apart for
founding six Scholarships (for members of his school) in
Oxford or Cambridge, or in both Universities. The
carrying out of this bequest was left to the discretion
of Sir John Popham, Chief Justice of the Common
Pleas, who ordained that two of the Scholarships
be founded at Balliol, two at Emmanuel, and two
at Sidney. In 1603 " Emmanuel College refusing Mr.

Blundell's Scholars," he assigned four Scholarships to
Sidney, ordering that "such one of the two antientist
Scholars or Fellows as the Master shall think most fit
for it, shall read yearly a Greek or Hebrew Lecture and
have for it out of Mr. Blundell's Estate £5 per annum;
and that the Master out of the same shall have £4 per
annum and the College £2 per annum." But it was
not till 1616 that the matter was finally settled. In
that year the College agreed with the Feoffees of
Tiverton School

"for £1400 for purchasing the Manor of Itterby (lying in
or near the Parish of Clee in the County of Lincoln) to
maintain for the future Mr. Peter Blundell's 2 Fellows
and 2 Scholars heretofore maintained by the Feoffees,
and that their Foundation in the College be confirmed
and that they be called the Fellows and Scholars of Mr.
Peter Blundell."

In all their public sermons and commemorations they
are to mention Mr. Blundell as their Founder and a
special benefactor to the College. The Scholarships
are to be filled, from Tiverton School only, by a majority
of the Feoffees with the advice of the Master of the
school. Both Fellows and Scholars are to be " as of the
Foundation and Body of the College " and to have all
the privileges thereof. Upon a Blundell Fellowship
becoming vacant, the Senior Blundell Scholar is to be
elected to it, if he be of six years standing and a B.A.;
if not, he is to continue as he is, till he be of such standing. In the meantime another Scholar is to be sent
for from the School. If the Scholar sent "shall be
insufficient and not prove towardly for learning, after 3

years trial he may be removed and expelled." The
Fellows are to have, over and above the allowance of
those of the foundation a stipend of £5 16s. per annum,
and the Scholars £6 8s. in addition. Mr. Blundell's
Fellows are to be tutors to his Scholars gratis. If any
of these Scholars reach M.A. standing before a Fellowship is vacant, he retains his Scholarship till a vacancy
occurs and may take pupils "in the name of Mr.
Blundell's Senior Fellow." At seven years standing
both Fellows and Scholars must apply themselves to
the study of Divinity and go into Orders as soon as
"by law they may;" their places being made void by
the acceptance of any benefice with cure of souls, or
charge of school, or after ten years from M.A. standing.
One of Mr. Blundell's Fellows, if either of them be
willing, or else some other Fellow

"shall yearly read a Greek or Hebrew Lecture every week
in Term time in such manner and form as the Master shall
judge meet, receiving yearly of the College for the same £5."

There is to be a sermon in Chapel on St. Peter's Day, in
commemoration of Mr. Blundell, by one of his Fellows or
Scholars, if any be willing; or else by any other Fellow
(appointed by the Master) who shall have 10s. for the
same. On the same day 40s. is to be allowed by the
College for "exceeding through the Hall."

In 1603 Sir John Hart, Alderman of London,
bequeathed to the College £30 for the use of their new
Library and £600 to purchase an estate of £42 per
annum which should be conveyed to the College, the
annual income to be thus distributed: £2 to the
Master, £4 to a Greek Lecturer to be chosen by the

Master and Fellows, £10 each to two Masters of Arts to be Fellows, £4 each to four poor Scholars, Scholars of Coxwold School to have the preference both for Fellowships and Scholarships. Later on—in 1618—the College for £200 covenanted to allow Sir John Hart's Fellows an equal share in the common dividend and all other privileges of the Fellows of the Foundation.

Shortly afterwards John Freestone, of Altofts in the county of York, bequeathed £500 for the purchase of an estate of £25 per annum to be assured to Emmanuel College for ever, the income to be thus distributed: £10 for the maintenance of a Fellow, £5 apiece for two Scholars, £5 for the "reparations and benefit of the said College," on condition that the Fellow and Scholars have "like preferment every way" with those of the foundation. In 1607 Emmanuel College "gave leave to settle the Fellowship and two Scholarships of John Freestone Esqre in Sydney College." About eighty acres of land near Stamford and several houses there, of the annual value of £25, were conveyed to the College, on condition that none but a Yorkshire man born and one of Mr. Freestone's Scholars, if any of them be qualified, be eligible for the Fellowship.

Our first Master was not only a wise and beneficent Head of his own House; he also conferred a great benefit on the town of Cambridge.

"Nor did he while private Master of this College confine his Munificence within the Walls thereof; for the King's Ditch in Cambridge being at that Time very offensive to the Inhabitants, he at ye Expence of an Hundred Pounds brought a clear running Water into it, to the no small

Conveniency and Pleasure both of the Town and University." (Cole.)

But Sidney and Cambridge were not to retain his services for long. Signs of his coming preferment were manifested on a notable occasion.

In 1602, "upon the setting of that bright Occidental Star, Queen Elizabeth," James VI. of Scotland succeeded to the English crown. "By many small journeys and great feastings" he travelled from Scotland to London. Fuller waxes eloquent on the subject :

"Always the last place he lodged in seemed so complete for entertainment that nothing could be added thereunto; and yet commonly the next stage exceeded it in some stately accession ; until at last, April 27th, his Majesty came to Hinchinbrook, nigh Huntingdon, the house of Master Oliver Cromwell,* where such his reception, that, in a manner, it made all former entertainments forgotten, and all future to despair to do the like. All the pipes about the house expressed themselves in no other language than the several sorts of the choicest wines. . . . Hither

---

* "When Sir Henry Cromwell of Hinchinbrook passed away in 1603, his son Oliver (not *the* Oliver, but his uncle), entertained King James at Hinchinbrook. . . . This Oliver Cromwell was then knighted ; but in 1627 there was a change at Hinchinbrook, which Sir Oliver sold to the Montagues (in later times the Earls of Sandwich). . . . Robert Cromwell, brother of this Sir Oliver, had married Elizabeth, the young widow of William Lynne of Bassingbourn. Her maiden name was Steward, and she was a daughter of William Steward, farmer of the tithes at Ely. About the year 1591 Robert Cromwell and his wife settled down in the town of Huntingdon to farm his portion of the family estate left to him, and in a substantial house. . . . . In this house Oliver Cromwell was born on April 25, 1599, the fifth child of a family of ten."—A. Kingston, *East Anglia and the Great Civil War*, p. 5.

came the Heads of the University of Cambridge in their scarlet gowns and corner caps, when Mr. Robert Naunton, the Orator, made a learned Latin oration, wherewith his Majesty was highly affected. The very variety of Latin was welcome to his ears, formerly almost surfeited with so many long English speeches, made to him as he passed every corporation. The Heads in general requested a confirmation of their privileges (otherwise uncourtlike at this present to petition for particulars) which his Highness most willingly granted."

James must have thoroughly enjoyed the gathering; for he delighted in the society of scholars and theologians, being really something more than the pragmatical pedant he is commonly represented to have been. He singled out the Master of Sidney for special honour.

"Here one might see the King (passing over all other Doctors for his seniors) apply himself much in his discourse to Dr. Montagu, Master of Sidney College. This was much observed by the courtiers (who can see the beams of royal favour shining in at a small cranny) interpreting it a token of his great and speedy preferment, as indeed it came to pass."

In 1603 Montagu was appointed to the deanery of Lichfield, and was transferred to that of Worcester in the following year. These preferments did not in those days necessitate the resignation of the headship of a College. In 1608 he was made Bishop of Bath and Wells;- he was consecrated on April 17, when he resigned his Mastership. He was most active in promoting the restoration of Bath Abbey, which was in a ruinous state, contributing £1000 from his own purse.

When Prince Charles and his brother-in-law visited Cambridge in March 1613, they were accompanied from Newmarket by Bishop Montagu and other noblemen. The Earl of Northampton, Chancellor of the University, was also expected ; but, says Hacket, " the frugal old man appeared not."

In 1616 Montagu was translated to Winchester. In the same year the King employed his services in an important matter. James took a great interest in the Universities, being very anxious that they should follow a *via media* between Popery on the one hand and Puritanism on the other. With this end in view, he imposed subscription to what he called his " three darling Articles" as a necessary preliminary to the taking of any Cambridge degree. These Articles contained an assent to the doctrine and discipline of the Church of England. The King's orders on this subject are dated December 3, 1616; he delivered them in his own person to the Vice-Chancellor and some of the Masters of Colleges at Newmarket. A few days later Bishop Montagu wrote this letter to the Vice-Chancellor :

" I have sent you his Majesty's hand to his own directions. I think you have no precedent that ever a King, first with his own mouth, then with his own hand, gave such directions ; and therefore you shall do very well to keep the writing curiously and their directions religiously, and to give his Majesty a good account of 'em carefully ; which I pray God you may. And so, with my love to yourself and the rest of the Heads, I commit you to God. From the Court, the 12th of Dec. 1616.

" Your loving Friend,

" JAMES WINTON."

To Bishop Montagu was also entrusted the duty· of
editing King James's *Works*, and translating them into
Latin. The English edition was published in 1616;
the Latin version in 1619. The King presented to
the University Library copies bound in velvet and
gold.

His tenure of the bishopric of Winchester was very
short ; he died at Greenwich on July 20, 1618, aged
fifty, and was buried in Bath Abbey. Our College
Register says : *Ad episcopatum Winton. translatus,
eundem, cum in eo administrando biennium vix exegisset,
cum sede Beatorum commutavit.* He was succeeded by
the famous Lancelot Andrewes. In his will he was not
unmindful of Sidney, bequeathing to the College a
perpetual annuity of £20 per annum to be paid out of
the Manor of Copingford, in the county of Huntingdon,
by the Montagu family. Of this sum twenty marks
were intended to be for the discharge of the rent of the
site payable to Trinity College ; and twenty nobles were
to be disposed of as the Master and Fellows should
think most for the good of the College.

Bishop Montagu's connexion with the College brought
to Sidney in its early days many members of a famous
family. Six nephews of his and three grand-nephews
joined the College. The first Master's brother, Henry
Montagu, first Earl of Manchester, had three sons there,
*Edward and *Walter (admitted together in 1618) and
James, afterwards known as James Montagu of Lackham
(admitted 1624). His brother Edward (1562–1644) first
Baron Montagu of Boughton, already mentioned as a
benefactor of the College, also sent three sons to Sidney,
*Edward, *William, and Christopher, admitted in three

successive years, 1631-2-3. The three grand-nephews of
the first Master who joined the College were *Edward,
eldest son of the second Baron Montagu (admitted
1651), James, son of James Montagu of Lackham
(admitted 1653), and another James, sixth and youngest
son of Edward Montagu, Earl of Sandwich, the famous
Admiral (admitted 1681). Of these, the five whose
names are marked with an asterisk were distinguished
men, and deserve some notice here.

Edward Montagu, afterwards famous as the second
Earl of Manchester, was elected M.P. for Huntingdon
in 1623 and 1625. At Charles I.'s coronation he was
made a Knight of the Bath. In 1626 he was raised to
the Upper House with the title of Baron Montagu of
Kimbolton, and in the same year he obtained the
courtesy title of Viscount Mandeville, when his father
was created Earl of Manchester. Being allowed only
a small income, he did not go to Court, and inclined
towards the popular party. In the Long Parliament
he became the acknowledged leader of that party in the
House of Lords.

"Kimbolton Castle had, in these stormy times, meant
for the Huntingdonshire people an embodiment of the Star
Chamber, Ship-money, and the 'Bishops' War,' which the
Earl of Manchester had supported with his influence and
his money. But there was a strange pathos in the fact
that the old Earl had, so to speak, one foot in the grave,
and that his son, Edward Montagu, the young Viscount
Mandeville and the future Earl, was by the irony of events
to be the leader of the Puritan party in the House of
Lords, and destined to reverse all the late traditions of his
house in a few short months." (Kingston.)

Later on we shall have more to say of the Earl of
Manchester.

Walter Montagu took his M.A. degree in 1627. He
was a most valuable member of the Royalist party,
especially as a diplomatist. In France he was employed
in several important negotiations, principally with
regard to the marriage of Princess Henrietta Maria,
with whom he formed a life-long friendship. He was
arrested by order of Richelieu and imprisoned in the
Bastille, but he soon regained his liberty. In 1628 we
find him negotiating with the Cardinal for an exchange
of prisoners. Subsequently he was an attaché at the
Embassy at Paris. In 1635 he joined the Roman
Church. In 1643 he was imprisoned in the Tower by
order of Parliament ; a compromising letter in cypher
from the King to Montagu had been intercepted. He
remained a prisoner till 1647, when he was allowed out
on bail to take the waters at Tunbridge Wells. Two
years later, being ordered to leave the country, he went
to France once more, and soon became Abbot of
Nanteuil, near Metz. Afterwards he held the Abbey of
St. Martin near Pontoise till 1669 ; his income then
was about £5000 a year. He spent most of his money
in befriending the English Royalists who had escaped
to France. The last years of his life were spent in
Paris, where he died in 1677. His literary works
gained some celebrity, notably the *Miscellanea Spiritu-
alia.*

Edward Montagu (1616–1684), afterwards second
Baron Montagu of Boughton, was Member for Huntingdon in the Long Parliament. He espoused the
popular cause. He succeeded to the peerage in 1644.

In 1646 he treated for the surrender of Newark, and was one of those who received the King's person from the Scots, attending him till his escape in 1647. Afterwards he eagerly welcomed the Restoration.

William Montagu was called to the bar in 1641. He was M.P. for Huntingdon in the Short Parliament, and for Cambridge University in 1660. In 1676 he was made Lord Chief Baron of the Exchequer. Ten years later James II. removed him from the Bench, because he failed to give an unqualified approval to the prerogative of dispensation. Montagu quietly returned to his practice at the Bar. In January 1689 he was nominated assessor to the Convention. He died in 1706.

Edward Montagu (1635-1665), son of the second Lord Montagu, was educated at Westminster. He acted as negotiator between Charles II. and his cousin Admiral Montagu (afterwards Earl of Sandwich). Subsequently he was Master of the Horse to Queen Catharine. In 1665 he was killed at Bergen in an attack on the Dutch fleet.

CHAPTER VI

A SHORT REIGN

In April 1608 the Earl of Kent appointed Francis Aldrich, one of the Fellows, to the Mastership in the place of James Montagu, now Bishop of Bath and Wells. Aldrich was born in Kent in 1577. He was admitted at Clare Hall in June 1589, being then only twelve years of age. He took the B.A. degree in 1593 and the M.A. in 1596; and in 1598 became, as we have seen, one of the first Fellows of Sidney. He took his B.D. in 1603. His career, which we may feel sure was regarded as one of great promise, was cut short by death on December 27, 1609, at the age of thirty-two. He was buried in the Church of St. Margaret at Canterbury. A tablet erected by his brother Simon bears this inscription:

"Francisco Aldrich Sanctae Theologiae Doctori et Collegii Sidnesussexiensis in Academia Cantabridgiensi quondam Praefecto praematura morte absumpto et in communi cum patre sepulchro condito Simon Aldrich Monimentum pietatis ergo posuit."

Then follow these quite respectable elegiacs:

Septima saevit hyems ex quo mandavimus urnae
    Ter charum juncta cum pietate patrem;

Et jam te socii solamen dulce doloris
    Horridior reliquis septima tollit hyems.
Te, Frater, cui Vitam anni, spondebat Honores
    Virtuti faciles Praesulis almus amor.
Dum nova Sidnaei Dominum Musaea salutant,
    Alterum et a primo te decus esse putant,
Spem magnam specimenque domus primordia fausta
    Quam cite festina morte perisse vident!
Sed periisse vetat mortis mors altera Christus
    Et tua supremo spes rediviva rogo.

By his will dated November 1, 1609, Aldrich bequeathed to the Sidney Library twelve folio volumes to
be selected by his brother. To Humphrey Moorer, one
of the Fellows, he left the "joint ring which he was
wont to wear, and two new leather chairs," also
Zanchius, *de Redemptione*, Zanchius, *de Natura Dei*,
and Thomas Aquinas, *Summa*. After these and other
legacies he gave the rest of his goods to his "tender
and careful mother," of whom in a manner he had
received them all.

Our Degree Register shows that Aldrich took his D.D.
at the summer *Comitia* of 1609. In October 1608
these College appointments were made: Mr. Pocklington, *Lector* and Hebrew Lecturer; Mr. Kay, Greek
Lecturer; no Dean is mentioned. In the following
October we find: Mr. Pell, Dean; Mr. Eston, *Lector*;
Mr. Pocklington, Hebrew Lecturer; Mr. Kay, Greek
Lecturer. From October 1607 to October 1608 there
were only fourteen admissions. In the next year the
number rose to eighteen; among these are two notable
names: John Bramhall, prelate, statesman, and stalwart
champion of Anglican orthodoxy; and Thomas May,

scholar, poet, and historian, most brilliant and versatile, but, in the not unfair judgment of Marvell, " most servile wit and mercenary pen."

This is Bramhall's admission register under the year 1609 : *Joannes Bramhall admissus in Convictum Scholarium Februar. 21ᵐᵒ*. The following note is added : *Evasit Episcopus Derensis in Hibernia ; et hoc quoque anno* (viz., 1661) *Archiepiscopus de Armagh et Hiberniae Primas.*

John Bramhall was the son of Peter Bramhall of Casleton, near Pontefract; he was born in 1594. He was at school at Pontefract ; and was admitted at Sidney on February 21, 1609, and took his B.A. in 1612. The dates of his other degrees are M.A. 1616, B.D. 1623, D.D. 1630. His D.D. thesis is described as strongly anti-papal. He was ordained in or about 1616 ; he held a living in York, and also the rectory of Elvington, Yorkshire. Subsequently he became Archdeacon of Meath. As a Royal Commissioner he did wonders for the Irish Church ; in four years he recovered £30,000. In 1634 he was made Bishop of Derry. He exercised great influence both in the Irish Convocation and in Irish politics. In 1641, owing to accusations brought against him, especially a baseless charge of complicity with the Irish Insurrection, he was obliged to leave Ireland. He lived in Yorkshire till 1644 ; he sent his plate to the King and supported the Royalist cause by his writings. In 1644 he went abroad for some years, staying for a considerable time at Brussels. In 1660 it was thought he would have been made Archbishop of York. However, in the following year he became Archbishop of Armagh and Primate of Ireland.

Shortly afterwards he was made Speaker of the Irish House of Lords. He died in 1663. His voluminous works testify to the strength of his Anglican and Royalist opinions; he also wrote against Hobbes, whom he met during his travels on the Continent. Cromwell looked upon him as Laud's *alter ego* on account of his poor presence and rigid Anglicanism; he used to call him " Irish Canterbury." The Presbyterians had a great dislike to " Bishop Bramble."

Thomas May was born in 1595, and joined the College as a Fellow-Commoner on September 7, 1609. He took his degree in 1612. Clarendon says that

" since his fortune could not raise his mind, he brought his mind down to his fortune by a great modesty and humility in his nature, which was not affected, but very well became an imperfection in his speech, which was a great mortification to him."

His early literary efforts were chiefly dramatic. He wrote two comedies, *The Heir* and *The Old Couple*. The latter was acted in 1620. His three tragedies were on classical subjects, *Antigone*, *Agrippina*, and *Cleopatra*. Next he devoted himself to translations from the classics. His *Lucan's Pharsalia* (1627) was much admired. In 1630 he published an English continuation of Lucan in seven short books, in which he brought down the history to the death of Cæsar. His Latin version of this, *Supplementum Lucani* (1640), is printed at the end of the Variorum Edition of Lucan (London, 1818). It is a spirited performance, and shows that May was a really good Latin scholar. Wood says that it is written "in so lofty and happy Latin

Hexameters that he hath obtained much more reputation abroad than he hath lost at home." By command of the King, May wrote two narrative poems, *The Reign of Henry II.* (1633) and *The Victorious Reign of Edward III.* (1635). On the death of Ben Jonson in 1637 he hoped to obtain the Laureateship. Disgusted at the appointment of D'Avenant, "he fell from his duty," as Clarendon says, and joined the popular party. In 1646 he became one of the "Secretaries for the Parliament"; in the following year he published his *History of the Long Parliament.* A very good judge, Mrs. Hutchinson, in her *Memoirs of Colonel Hutchinson,* pays the book a high compliment; she says that "Mr. May's history is impartially true, save some little mistakes in his own judgment and misinformations which some vain people gave him of the state." Subsequently he published in Latin a *Breviarium* on the same subject. He was very energetic in the service of the Parliament up to the time of his death, which was said to have been caused by "tying his nightcap too close under his fat chin and cheeks." He was buried in Westminster Abbey; but in 1660 his body was dug up and thrown into a pit in St. Margaret's Churchyard, and his monument was demolished.

The following College account belonging to Aldrich's time is interesting:

Master's and Fellows' Allowances for the Half Year between the Annunciation and the Feast of St. Michael the Archangel 1608:

	£	s.	d.
Imp: to the M^r of the Coll: Allowance	10	0	0
It: from Sir John Hart	1	0	0

It : Fellows of the Foundation   24   0   0
It : Sir John Hart's Fellows   10   0   0

                                            45   0   0

Scholars Allowances.
Scholars of the Foundation   14   6   0
Sir John Harts 4 Scholars   8   0   0

                                            22   6   0
Other Expences   42   8   8

Summa Expens :   109 14   8
Summa Receptuum for the same ½ year   125   8   3

Remains   (*sic*)   13 17   7

Whereof 13*l*. 10*s*. was divided, 2 Parts to the Master and to each Fellow one.* 7*s*. 7*d*. to be accounted at the next Accounts.

* The history of the Fellows' dividend is interesting. No provision is made for it in the Statutes. The first dividend was at Lady Day 1604, when £17 8*s*. was divided (£7 8*s*. having been carried from the last account). Other early dividends are as follows :

	£	*s.*	*d.*		£	*s.*	*d.*
Mich. 1604	21	0	0	Mich. 1607	0	0	0
L. D. 1605	11	14	2	L. D. 1608	0	0	0
Mich. 1605	37	5	0	Mich. 1608	13	10	0
L. D. 1606	23	16	5	L. D. 1609	0	0	0
Mich. 1606	11	18	0	Mich. 1609	8	2	0
L. D. 1607	0	0	0	L. D. 1610	19	7	5

For another set of accounts, see Appendix.

CHAPTER VII

MAGISTER EXIMIUS

AFTER the death of Dr. Aldrich, the Executors appointed to the Mastership Samuel Ward, B.D., formerly Scholar of Christ's, where he was admitted in 1589, and Fellow of Emmanuel. He held, along with the Mastership, the Rectory of Great Munden in Hertfordshire and the Archdeaconry of Taunton; and afterwards, as we shall see, the Lady Margaret Professorship. His Diary, now in the Sidney Library, deals chiefly with his earlier Cambridge life. It is to a great extent simply a catalogue of his own shortcomings recorded from day to day. Most of the reflections contained in it are of no great interest, except that they give evidence of a wonderfully simple and blameless nature. For instance, he accuses himself of "my negligence in serious meditating of my catechising," "my negligence in hearing and calling to mynd the *common-place*," "my thought of pride att reading of Greek, commencing of teaching my auditors the Greek accents," "my over great dinner," "my intemperance in eating plums," "my little pity of the boy which was whipt in the Hall," "surmisings of M. N. that day when he were speaking of them that saught prayse, as we were coming downe Gogmagog." Fuller, who knew Ward well, bears testimony to the gentleness of his nature and the acuteness of his intellect in a striking passage which is quoted at the end of this chapter. The lengthy correspondence between Ward and Usher, contained in Richard Parr's life of the Archbishop, abounds in evidences of his profound erudition and his constant readiness to place it at the disposal of other scholars. He was one of the translators of the Bible, whose work was completed in 1611, " having cost the workmen as light as it seemeth twice seventy times seventy-two days and more." Ward was on the Committee which was entrusted with the Apocrypha; he had among his colleagues on this Committee the Master of Caius, the Master of Jesus, and the Greek Professor.

With regard to ecclesiastical matters, Ward was singularly pessimistic and "puritanical," as we should now say, though we shall find that he was not accounted a Puritan by those who knew him best (see p. 80). When at Emmanuel, he could write thus :

" Aug. 12, 1604. Observe two plots laid to bring our College to the wearing of the surplice. 1. Dr Googe hath prescribed it to be worn in Magd. College; 2d. Dr Mountagu hath also appointed it to be worn in Sidn. College. Now what remaineth but that we (unless we will be singular) should take it up ? There is no way of escape for any thing I can possibly discern. Our trust is in the name of the Lord."

Five months later he says :

" Remember on Wednesday Jan. 18th was the day when the surplice was first urged by the Archbp. to be brought into Eman. College. God grant that other worse things do not follow the so strict urging of this indifferent ceremony. Alass! we little expected that King James would have been the first permitter of it, to be brought into our College, to make us a derision to so many that bear us no good Will."

Dr. Ward was admitted Master on January 9, 1610, and took his D.D. degree in the same year. Early in his reign there were many changes in the body of Fellows. Four new Fellows were appointed in 1610; among these Richard Howlett and Robert Daggett proved most useful members of the Society, which in the two following years was further strengthened by the accession of Paul Micklethwait (who had migrated from Caius, and was afterwards Master of the Temple), Richard Garbutt, and Richard Dugard. In these five the Master had excellent lieutenants as College officers and "pupil-mongers." At the very beginning of his Mastership the number of admissions showed a tendency to increase. In 1610–11 there were fifteen Freshmen, In the five following years the numbers were 20, 25, 26, 32, 28.

On January 5, 1611, the Executors of the Foundress took an important step. By the right reserved to them they had hitherto chosen Masters, Fellows, and Scholars. They now gave the College leave to elect to all future vacancies according to the Statutes. In the following year they directed that, whereas much more than Lady Sidney's legacy had been expended in building and endowing the College, and yet the estate was not sufficient for the maintenance of a Master and ten Fellows, there should in future be seven Fellows only, unless the revenues of the College should hereafter be sufficiently increased. They also directed that, whereas the Master was allowed by the Statutes only £20 per annum and two shillings a week for Commons, and each Fellow only forty shillings per annum and two shillings a week for Commons, in future the former should have an additional stipend of £5 12s. and each of the latter an addition of £2 16s.

Very soon after this Harrington died. His last years had been clouded with misfortune arising from the royal favour. In April 1603 he had entertained James I. at Burley on the Hill during his progress from Scotland. At the Coronation in July he had been created Baron Harrington of Exton. In the same year he was appointed guardian of the Princess Elizabeth. Owing to her extravagance the office was by no means a pleasant one. The annual allowance of £1500 granted to Lord Harrington for the purpose proved to be wholly inadequate, and he became involved in debt. The Princess was a constant trouble to him. Quite worn out with anxiety, he died at Worms in August 1612. His daughter Lucy, " the favourite of the Muses," who married the third Earl of Bedford, was a benefactor to our Library. His son John, who succeeded to the title, was a student at Sidney. Thomas Gataker described him as " a mirror of nobility." He was an excellent scholar and linguist, and the bosom friend of Henry, Prince of Wales, by whose death in 1613 he was much overcome. His own end came in the following year. His funeral sermon was preached by " T. P. of Sidney Sussex College."

In 1614 the Earl of Kent, as surviving executor, made certain " recognitions " of the Statutes, amending some

regulations which had been found to be unsatisfactory.
He now ordained (1) that the Fellowships should be
open to Scotchmen and Irishmen as well as Englishmen ;
(2) that the four Senior Fellows might, under certain
conditions, be absent from College for six months in
every year; (3) that the Statute terminating the tenure
of Fellowships at seven years from D.D. standing be
repealed, and that they be tenable for life, provided
that no other Statutes are infringed; (4) that the
College have power to appoint a Fellow other than the
Dean *ad Catechizandi munus;* (5) that the method of
examining and electing Scholars be the same as that
appointed by the Statutes in regard to Fellows.

The first notable admission under Ward's Mastership
was that of the celebrated Hollander, John Reede, who
entered as a Fellow-Commoner in 1613. He was made
Canon of Utrecht in 1620, and was afterwards known as
the Lord of Ronsvorde. In 1644 he came to England
as ambassador from the Low Countries with the object
of reconciling King and Parliament. He visited
Charles I. at Oxford, who created him Baron Reede.
In 1652 he became President of the States General.
This office he held for many years. He lived till
1683.

The year 1616 was an *annus mirabilis* in the history
of the College. For it was then that our "Chief of
men," Oliver Cromwell, was admitted. In his year were
three other well-known Puritans, Richard Minshull,
afterwards Master of the College, Jeremiah Whitaker,
who became a member of the Assembly of Divines,
and James Garbutt, afterwards a Fellow and a well-
known preacher. Cromwell entered as a Fellow-Com-

moner; in the same year there were three other Fellow-
Commoners, John and Henry Savill, Yorkshiremen, and
Christian Hulsbos, from the Low Countries. Another
Huntingdon man, John Cooper, entered as a Pensioner.
In all there were twenty-eight entries in that year.
The annual College officers elected in 1616 were:
Decanus, Mr. Howlett; *Lector*, Mr. Smith; *Seneschallus*,
Mr. Mascall; *Sublectores*, Mr. Haine, Mr. Denne, Ds.
Bell.

The College must now have been full to overflowing.
From John Scot's Manuscript in the British Museum,
which gives an account of the University in 1617, we
learn that Sidney had then 117 residents, the total
number being 2270. Before the erection of the Clerke
building, which was probably begun in 1628, there
cannot have been more than thirty-five chambers in
College; and residence in lodgings was not allowed.
Even the Combination Room was used as a sleeping-
place; in one of our account-books there is this
note:

"In the fellowes parlour for want of chambers there
kept Mr. Edmund Eston; after him Mr. Thomas Kaye.
Then Mr. Robert Daggett; Mr. Richard Dugard; Mr.
Edmund Bell; Mr. Thomas Wood; Mr. John Land."

But we must return to our Oliver. Of his parentage
something has been said already (p. 54). Nothing is
known about his early years except that he was educated
at Huntingdon Grammar School under Dr. Thomas
Beard. He entered the College on April 23, 1616,
two days before his seventeenth birthday. Here is the
register of his admission:

THE CROMWELL PORTRAIT

Oliverus Cromwell Huntingdoniensis admissus ad commeatum sociorum Aprilis vicesimo tertio tutore Magistro Richardo Howlet.

" While Oliver Cromwell," says Carlyle, "was entering himself of Sidney Sussex College, William Shakespeare was taking his farewell of this world.   Oliver's father had most likely come with him ; it is but some fifteen miles from Huntingdon; you can go and come in a day.   Oliver's father saw Oliver write in the Album at Cambridge ; at Stratford Shakespeare's Ann Hathaway was weeping over his bed. The first world-great thing that remains of English History, the Literature of Shakespeare, was ending ; the second world-great thing that remains of English History, the armed appeal of Puritanism to the Invisible God of Heaven against very many visible devils on Earth and elsewhere was, so to speak, beginning.   They have their exits and their entrances.   And one People in its time plays many parts."

Between the entry of Cromwell's admission and the next entry a zealous royalist of the Restoration time has inserted this little philippic :

Hic fuit grandis ille impostor, carnifex perditissimus, qui, pientissimo rege Carolo primo nefaria caede sublato, ipsum usurpavit thronum, et tria regna per quinque ferme annorum spatium sub protectoris nomine indomita tyrannide vexavit.

There is a tradition that Cromwell was lodged in the chamber which has a projecting window looking into Sidney Street at the north-west corner of the College. Being a Fellow-Commoner, he would probably have had only one " chamber-fellow."   Unfortunately nothing is known for certain of the College career of Sidney's greatest son. ' Owing to the death of his father in June 1617 he was obliged to leave College after a year's residence.

Heath writes that Cromwell

" was more famous for his exercises in the fields than in the Schools, being one of the chief matchmakers and players at football, cudgels, or any other boisterous sport or game."

Statements about Cromwell in Heath's *Flagellum* must be accepted with caution. There is no doubt, however, that football of a kind was played in his time   Mr. Rashdall says :

" I have come across no allusion to football before 1574, when it is forbidden at Cambridge, but in 1580 allowed only within the College precincts, *non adulti* offenders to be flogged."

D'Ewes speaks of a football match between Trinity and St. John's in 1620, *i.e.*, four years after Cromwell's entry. The tradition that Oliver led a riotous life at Cambridge appears to be due to two sources, (1) the royalist ribaldry of a later day, such as this statement quoted by Bates : *Saxeae frontis histrio flagris ignominiose caesus Cantabrigia cessit, et ab eo tempore schismaticis navavit opem ;* (2) the self-condemnation frequent in men of his religious persuasion. Thus, referring to his early life, he writes to his cousin Mrs. St. John : " Oh, I lived in and loved darkness and hated light ; I was a chief, a chief of sinners." Such words must not, of course, be taken too literally. A descendant, who bore his name, published in 1820 the *Memoirs of the Protector*, with the object of setting his reputation in the true light; for he used to say,

"the Cavaliers made him a devil, and the Roundheads a saint; whereas the truth is he was neither the one nor the other, but he was a man with a character of his own."

After leaving Sidney, Cromwell went to London to study law. It is said that he joined one of the Inns of Court; but no record of his admission can be discovered. After his marriage on August 22, 1620, at St. Giles', Cripplegate, to Elizabeth, daughter of Sir John Bourchier of Felsted, he returned to his native town.

" In the quiet routine of a farmer's life he fulfilled for nearly ten years, without any incident chronicled in history, the ordinary duties of a country gentleman. We are left to imagine, so far as we can, the silent and unnoticed growth of a great soul, limited as yet in its outgoings to the cares of a farm,—the thoughts that struggled and sank to rest in the stillness of home, the powerful religious convictions, the 'splenetic fancies,' the deep fits of melancholy, that ultimately resulted in an open profession of Christianity, and a steady adherence thenceforward to that strict and earnest form of it which had received from its enemies the derisive name of Puritanism. The house of Oliver Cromwell became from this time a resort of 'godly men'; and in their prayers and preachings, their interests and their grievances, he took a zealous and active part." (A. Nicolson.)

In 1618 the Master of Sidney was chosen by James I. as one of the divines to attend the Synod of Dort. He was reputed to be the author of the *Judicium de Quinque Articulis Remonstrantium* found among the Acts of the

Synod. This assembly met in November; it was a Synod of the Netherland Church, the foreign deputies being asked to attend merely to give the benefit of their advice. The "Five Articles" had been addressed by the Arminians (or Remonstrants) to the States General in 1610; they henceforth became known as the five points of Arminianism.

The three other divines selected to represent the English Church were George Carleton, Bishop of Llandaff, Joseph Hall, Dean of Worcester, and John Davenant, President of Queens' College, Cambridge. Before leaving England they repaired to Newmarket to receive instructions from the King. Ward and Davenant had a second interview with his Majesty at Royston; he talked familiarly with them for two hours, and prayed that God would bless their endeavours. Unfortunately they missed the Dutch man-of-war which had been sent to fetch them; so they crossed in a small vessel.

The sentence against the Remonstrants was published at the 144th sitting of the Synod. In a letter to Archbishop Usher, Ward writes:

"On April 23rd the Canons were signed by all the members of the Synod. Arminians were pronounced heretics, schismatics, teachers of false doctrine. They were declared incapable of filling any clerical or academical post."

In a later letter written from Sidney on May 26, 1619, he says:

"We had a solemn parting in the Synod, and all was concluded with a solemn Feast. This was upon Thursday

April 29. The Saturday we went to the *Hague* to take our leaves of the States General, where we resolved, while our Ship was made ready, to see *Leyden, Amsterdam,* and *Harlem,* which we did the week following. Upon the Monday we, purposing to go to *Leyden,* early in the morning were informed that *Bernevelt* was to lose his head that morning, which was executed. Upon the tenth of *May* we loosed from the *Bril,* and arrived at *Gravesend* the thirteenth of *May:* And visited his Majesty at *Greenwich* as we came by, who graciously did receive us. And thus, I thank God, we are safely returned to our homes."

Ward brought from Amsterdam an enormous chest, which he presented to the College Treasury. We still have it. In his will he bequeathed to the College the gold medal which he received in memory of his presence at the Synod. This has disappeared.

In 1619 Paul Micklethwait, who was then the College *Lector,* began the practice of keeping an elaborate register of admissions with careful biographies of those admitted. The earlier entries, which are very brief, were copied afterwards from a book now no longer extant into the blank pages which he left at the beginning of his register. There were thirty entries in the year 1619–20. It is interesting to note the schools at which these youths were educated. Twenty came from these " public schools " as they are here described: Eton (2), Westminster, Tiverton, Durham, Alford, Luton, Milton Abbott, Grimsby, Lewes, Louth, Newcastle (2), Oakham (2), Wakefield, Northwich, Sutton, Rochester, Coxwold. One had migrated from Trinity, Cambridge ; another from Trinity, Oxford. The remaining eight were educated either at private schools or *in paternis aedibus*. The Fellows in this year were Richard Danford, B.D., Richard Howlett, B.D., Robert Daggett, B.D., William Smith, B.D., Richard Garbutt, M.A., Paul Micklethwait, M.A., Richard Dugard, M.A., John Mayne, M.A., John Denne, M.A., Edmund Bell, M.A. In the next year the number of entries rose to forty; but it fell again to twenty-nine and twenty-six in the two following years. In 1622 Richard Dugard's nephew, William Dugard, entered as a sizar. He was afterwards Headmaster of Merchant Taylors' School, and a noted classical scholar. He wrote a Greek grammar and a *Rhetorices Compendium*, and edited some of Lucian's dialogues. In the following year Montagu Bertie entered as a Pensioner in his fifteenth year, along with his little brother Roger who was only twelve. Entrance at the age of twelve was not an extraordinary occurrence at this time, as may be seen from this charming passage, which Mr. Mullinger quotes from Peacham's *Compleat Gentleman*:.

" These young things of twelve, thirteene, or fourteene, that have no more care than to expect the next carrier, and where to sup on Fridayes and fasting nights; no further thought of studie than to trim up their studies with pictures and place the fairest bookes in openest view, which, poore lads, they scarce ever opened, or understand not ; that, when they come to logicke and the crabbed grounds of art, there is such a disproportion between Aristotle's *Categories* and their childish capacities, that what together with the sweetnesse of libertie, variety of companie, and so many kinds of recreation in towne and fields abroad (being like young lapwings apt to bee snatched up by every buzzard) they prove with Homer's willow ὠλεσίκαρποι, and as good goe gather cockles with Caligula's people on the sand, as to attempt the difficulties of so rough and terrible a passage."

Montagu Bertie, afterwards second Earl of Lindsey, was the eldest son of the first Earl by Elizabeth, only daughter of Edward, first Lord Montagu. At Edgehill, where he was in command of a regiment, he made a desperate attempt to rescue his father, and finally surrendered, so that he might share his captivity, for he was wounded. He remained for some time in Warwick Castle. At Naseby we find him in command of part of the reserve. Subsequently he was in attendance on the King as Gentleman of the Bedchamber. After the execution he was one of those who accompanied the King's body to Windsor. At the Restoration he was made a Knight of the Garter, and was appointed one of the judges for the trial of the Regicides. He died in 1666

In 1620-1 the Master of Sidney served the office of Vice-Chancellor. In February 1623 he was elected to the Lady Margaret Readership in Divinity, much to the joy of his predecessor, John Davenant, who now felt sure that the same kind of teaching would be continued from the Lady Margaret Chair. In that age of learned theologians this appointment was a great distinction. Some of Ward's lectures were published after his death, viz., *Determinationes Theologicae, Tractatus de Justificatione, Praelectiones de Peccato Originali.* " His Theses," says Russell in his *Memorials of Fuller*, "attest his readiness in the scholastic Theology of

those times, now peradventure too lightly esteemed."
Ward's friends used to urge him to publish some of his
writings; but he was very loath to prepare anything
for the press. In 1630 he wrote to Usher that he
hoped to " revive " his Lectures on *Grace* and *Free-will*,
and " to do the like" with his " Readings upon the
Eucharist." Later on we find Usher pressing him to
put his writings in good order, " that in them you may
live and speak unto the Church when you are dead."
Fuller, writing in his *Worthies* of Ward's later days,
says that

" he was counted a Puritan before these times, and Popish
in these times, and yet being always the same was a true
Protestant at all times."

The important series of letters from Bishop Davenant
to Dr. Ward, preserved in the Bodleian, bear interesting testimony to the latter's theological position.
These letters, which are spread over a period of
twenty years (1621–1640), show that he was thoroughly like minded with the Bishop, a sober English
Churchman. A perusal of Ward's correspondence
with Archbishop Usher will lead the reader to the
same conclusion.

The College was now increasing in numbers; so was
the University as a whole. In 1623 the total was
2998. The residents at Sidney numbered about 130.
In 1623-4 the number of entries was 27. Among
them was George Ent, son of Josiah Ent, merchant,
described in the Register as *Anglobelga*. He had been
educated for four years in Wallachia and for three
years at Rotterdam. He afterwards attained great

celebrity as a physician and was one of the founders of
the Royal Society. Apparently the first Sidney man
who took the degree of M.D. was a contemporary of
Ent's, named Samuel Remington, who, after leaving
Cambridge, went the round of the Continental medical
schools after the manner of that time, studying at
Leyden, Padua, Paris, and Montpellier. On returning he maintained these two theses for his M.D.:
(1) Ἰχθυοφαγία *quadragesimalis est fames sana*, "Fish-
eating in Lent is a healthy form of fasting"; (2) *Dysen-
teria postulat venae sectionem*, "Dysentery requires
bleeding." His "Opponent" was Alexander Fraser,
described as a *Scotobritannus*, who had been his companion abroad.

In 1624 there was what Fuller calls a "tough
canvass for Trinity Lecture," *i.e.*, the Lectureship at
Holy Trinity Church. A Fellow of Sidney, Paul
Micklethwait, "an eminent preacher," was one of the
candidates; he was supported by the Bishop of Ely and
all the Heads of Houses. But Dr. John Preston,
Preacher at Lincoln's Inn and afterwards Master of
Emmanuel, was favoured by the townsmen who contributed to the Lectureship.

"The contest," says Fuller, "grew high and hard, inso-
much as the Court was engaged therein. Many admired
that Dr Preston should stickle so much for so small a
matter as an annual stipend of eighty pounds, issuing out
of more than thrice eighty purses."

Thanks to the Duke of Buckingham's intervention
Preston "carried it clear." Two years later another
Sidney man engaged in an unsuccessful contest. James

F

White stood for the Greek Professorship vacant by the death of Andrew Downes, " one composed of Greek and industry." White had four rivals.

" How much was there now of Athens in Cambridge, when, besides many modestly concealing themselves, five able competitors appeared for the place ! All these read solemn lectures in the Schools on a subject appointed them by the electors, namely the first verses of the three-and-twentieth book of Homer's Iliads, chiefly insisting on χαῖρέ μοι ὦ Πάτροκλε καὶ εἰν 'Αΐδαο δόμοισι, &c. But the place was conferred on Mr. Robert Creighton, who, during Mr. Downes's aged infirmities, had, as Hercules relieved Atlas, supplied the same, possessed by the former full forty years."

On March 30, 1625, Charles I. was proclaimed King at Cambridge. The Master of Sidney was a contributor to the volume of poems with which the University celebrated the occasion. In the summer the plague prevailed to an alarming extent in London and other parts of the country. On August 1 a Grace passed the Senate for the discontinuance of Sermons at St. Mary's and Exercises in the Schools. But Cambridge was as yet free from infection. Writing on August 3 to Archbishop Usher, Ward says :

" This week I had purposed to have brought my whole family to *Munden*, but this day I received a letter, that one of my Workmen at my Parsonage had a Sister who was suspected the last *Saturday* to die of the Plague at *Standon*. I thank God we are yet well at *Cambridg*."

Ward's mastership, professorship, country parish, and archidiaconal functions in the West must have kept him fully occupied. Besides there are occasional visits to London on legal business. Writing from London on February 13, 1626, the Master says:

" I have been here above a fortnight, for to get a Licence of Mortmain for the holding of 240 Acres of Capite Land, which a Gentleman would give to our College ; but I find great difficulty in effecting it, so as I fear me I must return *re infecta.*"

The discovery of the "Fish-Book" in 1626 caused a tremendous sensation in Cambridge. It was looked upon as an omen of coming calamities. Dr. Ward writes thus to Archbishop Usher on June 27 :

" There was last week a Cod-fish brought from *Colchester* to our Market to be sold; in the cutting up which there was found in the Maw of the Fish a thing which was hard ; which proved to be a Book of a large 16°, which had been bound in Parchment ; the Leaves were glewed together with a Gelly. And being taken out, did smell much at the first. . . . The Book was intituled *A Preparation to the Cross.* It may be a special admonition to us at *Cambridg.* . . . I think the Book was made in King *Henry* the Eighth's time, when the Six Articles were a-foot. The Book will be printed here shortly."

The Archbishop replies thus:

" The Accident is not lightly to be passed over, which (I fear me) bringeth with it too true a Prophesy of the State to come ; and to you of *Cambridg* (as you write) it may be a Special Admonition, which should not be neglected. It behoveth you who are Heads of Colledges and 'Ομόφρονες to stick close to one another."

The " Fish Book " was afterwards published under the title of *Vox Piscis*.

Here may be mentioned an interesting little episode. The Master received a letter from Dr. William Harvey, whose epoch-making discovery had been made known to the world shortly before. The great physician requested that a curious skull, still preserved in the College Library, should be sent up for the inspection of the King. It is encrusted with carbonate of lime, which resembles a petrifaction of the flesh. Captain William Stevens, one of the elder brethren of the Trinity House, brought it in 1627 from Crete, where it was found about thirty feet below ground, in digging a well near the town of Candia. Here is Dr. Ward's reply :

> " Sir,
>
> " I receyved your letter by which I understand his Majesty's pleasure that I should send up the petrifyed Scull which wee have in our Colledg library, which accordingly I have done, with thee case wherein we keep it. And I send in this Letter both thee key of the case and a note which we have recorded of the Donour and whence he had it. And so with my affectionate prayers and best devotions for the long life of his sacred Majesty and my service to your self I rest
>
> " At your command
>
> " SAMUEL WARD."

Sidney Coll. Junii x
   Die Solstitiati.
To his much honoured frend
Doctor Harvey one of his
Majestys Physitians att his
house in the Blackfryars be
this delivered.

Harvey's reply, miserably written, is on the back of Ward's letter. It is still preserved in the Library ; a facsimile was printed in 1849 by Dr. G. E. (afterwards Sir George) Paget.

"Mʳ Doctor Ward I have showed to his Majesty this scull incrustated with stone, which I receyved from you, & his Majesty wondered att it & look'd content to see soe rare a thinge. I doe now with thanks retorne to you & your Colledg the same with the key of the case & the memoriall you sent me inclosed heare in thinking it a kinde of sacriledg not to have retorned it to that place where it may for the instruction of men heare after be conserved."

A Sidney man already mentioned, Sir George Ent, afterwards President of the College of Physicians, was a devoted friend and disciple of Harvey, and had the distinction of giving to the world his master's book *Exercitationes de Generatione Animalium.* Ent's account of the circumstances which led to the publication is very interesting. He visited Harvey in 1650 at his brother Daniel's house at Combe.

" I found him," he says, " with a cheerful and sprightly countenance investigating, like Democritus, the nature of things. Asking if all were well with him—' How can that be,' he replied, ' when the state is so agitated with storms and I myself am yet in the open sea ? And indeed, were not my mind solaced by my studies and the recollection of the observations I have formerly made, there is nothing which should make me desirous of a longer continuance.' "

Harvey had been with the King at Oxford, and there he had devoted much time to the subject of generation ;

he had collected a large number of observations, which he was in no hurry to publish. Ent prevailed on Harvey to give him his manuscripts with authority to print them if he thought well.

"I went from him," he says, "like another Jason in possession of the Golden Fleece, and when I came home and perused the pieces singly, I was amazed that so vast a treasure should have been so long hidden."

In the years 1624–9 the number of entries remained very stationary. The numbers are 27, 26, 26, 26, 23. In 1629–30 there is a drop, there being only ten admissions. This, as is explained in the Register, is *propter pestem in oppido Cantabrigiensi graviter saevi-entem*. The plague broke out in the spring of 1630. The University was for a time dissolved and the students dispersed into the country. Dr. Ward writes on the subject to Archbishop Usher on May 25:

" There hath hapned the most doleful dissolving of our University and the most suddain dispersion of our Students that ever I knew, occasioned by the Infection brought hither by a Souldier or two, dismissed long since from the King of Sweden's Army, in February last. So as, whereas this time was our chief time of the Year for Acts and Dis-putations, now our School-gates are shut up, and our Colledges left desolate and empty almost. . . . I pray God we may be sensible of our Sins and his heavy Hand, and may by serious Repentance meet him, that so he may forgive our Sins, and heal our Town and Land."

The Vice-Chancellor, Dr. Henry Butts, remained at his post, and with the help of the town authorities did

wonders in calming the panic-stricken townsfolk and
instituting sanitary precautions. Writing to Lord
Coventry he said : " Myself am alone, a destitute and
forsaken man, not a Scholler with me in College, not a
Scholler seen by me without." There were 347 deaths
from the plague in the town. In the next year Cambridge was itself again. The students returned and
great preparations were made for the reception of the
King and Queen, who came in March ; " they were
entertained at Trinity College with Comedies and expressed candid acceptance thereof."

Just before the appearance of the plague there
migrated to Sidney (November 5, 1629), one whom
Coleridge has called " incomparably the most sensible,
the least prejudiced, great man of an age that boasted a
galaxy of great men,"—Thomas Fuller. He was the
eldest son of Thomas Fuller, B.D., *Lector Primarius*
of Trinity and afterwards a Northamptonshire Rector.
Young Fuller was born in 1608 and was soon recognised
as " a boy of pregnant wit." He entered Queens', of
which his uncle John Davenant was President, and took
his B.A. in 1625. Fuller, having been " overlooked " in
a Fellowship election at Queens', was removed by
Davenant, now Bishop of Salisbury, to Sidney, of which
he became a devoted member. Some months previously
the Bishop had written thus to his " very loving friend
Dr. Ward " :

" I am informed they have made a late election at
Queens' Colledg, and utterly passed by my nephew. . . .
I am loat Mʳ ffuller should be snatched away from the
University before hee bee growen somewhat riper. His
ffather is p'swaded to continew him there, untill I can

provide him some other means ; but hee think it will bee
some disparagement and discouragement to his sonne to
continew in that Colledg, where he shall see many of his
punies stept before him in preferment.   In which respect
hee is very desirous that hee should remoov unto your
Colledg, there to live in fellowes commons till hee shall
bee otherwise disposed of.   Wee nether intend to make
him fellow in yours or any other Colledg, but only that
hee may bee conveniently placed for the continuance of
his studyes.   1 pray doe him what kindenes conveniently
you may in helping him to a chamber and study, and in
admittance into fellowes commons with as little chardg
as the orders of your howse will give leave."

Fuller's " chamber-fellow " during part of his residence
at Sidney was another Fellow-Commoner, young Roland
Lytton, only son of Sir William Lytton of Knebworth,
ancestor of the present Lord Lytton.   Roland joined
the College in January 1632.   Fuller writes thus to him
(dedication to § iv. of *History of Cambridge*):

" I ought to consider College life truly golden; for I
recall with delight our life at the time when we formerly
devoted ourselves to letters at Sidney College, I under
the chief direction of Dr. Ward, you under the tutorship
of Master Dugard, who have now both joined the ranks of
the blessed.   But besides this happiness which was common
to me with others, it was my especial honour to be
associated with you in the same chamber."

Fuller was soon appointed Minister of St. Benet's by
Corpus Christi College, " freely without my thoughts
thereof."   He held this cure for three years.   Hobson,
the famous Cambridge carrier, was one of his parish-

ioners. At St. Benet's Fuller's quaint and eloquent sermons attracted great attention. He was also esteemed as a poet; his poem called *David's Hainous Sinne* was written at this time. It was dedicated to three Sidney men, the sons of the first Lord Montagu. In 1631 Bishop Davenant gave him a prebendal stall in Salisbury Cathedral. In 1634 he became Rector of Broadwindsor in Dorsetshire. Here he remained for six years, and wrote the *Holy War* and *Sacred and Prophane Studies*. The first volume of his sermons was published in 1640 under the title of *Joseph's Particoloured Coat*. His eldest son John, born at Broadwindsor in 1641, entered Sidney in 1657, and edited his father's *Worthies of England* in 1662. We shall return to Thomas Fuller later on.

Two noteworthy benefactions next claim our attention. In 1627 Sir Francis Clerke of Houghton Conquest in Bedfordshire came forward as a benefactor, or more than a benefactor, in the judgment of Fuller:

" As for the bounty of Sir Francis Clerke, it exceeded the bounds of benefaction and justly entitled him to be a by-founder. The giver doubled the gift, if we consider, First : his estate was not a great one for one of his condition. Secondly : he had a daughter ; and generally it is observed that parents are most barren and the childless most fruitful in great expressions of charity. Thirdly : he was altogether unknown to the College and the College to him ; surprising it on a sudden with his bounty, so much the more welcome because not expected. Yet such his liberality that he not only built a fair and firm range of twenty chambers (from the addition whereof a second court resulteth to the College), but also augmented the

Scholarships of the Foundation, and founded four Fellowships and eight Scholarships more. Herein his favour
justly reflected on his countrymen of Bedfordshire,
preferring them before others to places of his own
foundation."

The King granted to Sir Francis Clerke a licence of
Alienation in Mortmain of his manors of Pilling
Shingay and Pilling Rowsbury to the College. In the
following year, 1628, he alienated the same and also
conveyed to the College his other property at Wootton
for founding four Fellowships and eight Scholarships
and for increasing the Scholarships of the first Foundation. In the deed of Foundation it is ordained
that none are to be eligible for these Scholarships
except persons born and educated in the County of
Bedford, and at the schools of Eaton-Socon and
Houghton Conquest especially; and that none be
eligible for the Fellowships but one of the Scholars.
The four Junior Scholars are each to have an allowance
of £5 per annum and the four Senior twenty nobles
per annum till they are of standing for M.A., and

" each two of them to have Chamber up 2 Pair of Stairs in
Sir Francis Clerke's Building and one of his Fellows for
their Tutor gratis."

Each of the Clerke Fellows is to receive twenty marks
per annum, their Fellowships to cease as soon as they
are of standing for D.D.; they are each to have a
middle chamber in Sir Francis Clerke's building,
choosing according to seniority. They are also to
partake in all College offices, in the privilege of taking

pupils, and in the use of the Garden, Library, and
Parlour (*i.e.*, Combination Room) fire. If through an
increase in the rents of the estate or a charitable
addition to it Sir F. Clerke's Fellowships become equal
in value to those of the Foundation, then his Fellows
shall partake in the common dividend and enjoy all
other privileges of Fellows of the Foundation. It was
also agreed that £30 per annum out of the rents of the
Clerke estate be divided equally among the Scholars of
the first Foundation, and that the College pay yearly
out of the estate to the Churchwardens and Overseers of
Houghton Conquest £10 for their poor.

The date of the erection of Sir Francis Clerke's " fair
and firm range of twenty chambers " is not recorded ;
but we may suppose that the building was begun soon
after the execution of the deed of foundation. Its
original architecture may be clearly seen from Loggan's
print ; the new block is on the south side of the College
just overlapping the south end of the Chapel ; so that
the College had now three parallel ranges of chambers.
The twenty chambers of the Clerke Building, five on
each floor, can easily be traced in the block as it now
stands. The Clerke Fellows would occupy four out of the
five chambers on the first floor, and, as each of them
was to " have a Chamber over their heads which shall
be for two Scholars," four more chambers would be thus
accounted for. This would leave no less than twelve
chambers at the disposal of the College, a considerable
item in a magnificent benefaction. The present par-
titioning of the second floor rooms in the Clerke
building may represent the original arrangement, the
bed-room and " gyp-room " of to-day being the

"studies" of the two Scholars who slept in the present "keeping-room" (see p. 38).

To this time belongs another splendid benefaction, that of Sir John Brereton, whose name appears on the first page of our Register of Admissions as one of the first batch of Scholars. Fuller's remarks on his wise generosity are most sensible :

"He was, as I may term him, one of the aborigines of the College, one of the first Scholars of the House ; and afterwards became his Majesty's Sergeant for the Kingdom of Ireland. At his death he was not unmindful of this his mother, to whom he bequeathed a large legacy, about two thousand pounds. Now, whereas some *bene*factors in repute are *male*factors in effect (giving to colleges δῶρα ἄδωρα), namely such as burden and clog their donations to maintain more than they are able, whereby their gifts become suckers impairing the root of the foundation, Sir John's gift was so left at large for the disposal thereof, that it became a gift indeed and really advanced the good of the College."

Sir John died in 1626, having left to the College one half of his ready money, goods, chattels, and credits, which should remain unbequeathed at his death, for such uses as the Regius and Margaret Professors of Divinity should think most expedient for the good of the College. In 1634 the College purchased of the Earl of Monmouth

"Cridling Park, being part of the Manor of Cridling in the County of York, and the Pasturage and Feeding for 200 Sheep in the Town-fields and territories of Darrington and Knottingley in the said County, with all their appurtenances, for £2670, being the legacy of Sir John Brereton; on this condition, that they pay yearly to the King £4 10s. out of the same."

In the same year Dr. Ward, the Master, as Margaret Professor, and Dr. Samuel Collins, Regius Professor of Divinity, by the authority committed to them under Sir John's will, assigned the annual rent of Cridling Park, being £140, and of the Sheep-walk, being £3, to the following uses (all the payments to be yearly):

£12 12s. for the increase of the Master's stipend.

£6 14s. to each of the 7 Fellows of Lady Sidney's Foundation for the increase of their stipend.

£6 14s. to Mr. Leonard Smith's present Fellow, during his being Fellow; and afterwards £4 of that sum to go the College Treasury, and only £2 14s. to the said Fellow for ever.

£4 14s. to each of Sir John Hart's Fellows.

40s. to Mr. Freestone's Fellow.

£3 14s. to each of Mr. Peter Blundell's Fellows.

20s. to each of the 20 Scholars of the first Foundation.

£6 13s. 4d. for a Mathematick Lecture in the College.

£5 for a Lecture in Ecclesiastical History.

£5 to him that is both Library Keeper and Chapel Clerk.

30s. for addition to expense of the Feast of the Foundress.

£3 10s. for the expense of a yearly commemoration of Sir John Brereton, £3 for the Feast and 10s. for the Preacher.

40s. to the Master for wages to a man.

40s. for 2 liveries for 2 servants of the Master.

£3 for the stipend of the "Register" of the College.

£6 6s. 8d. for the increase of the College Treasury.

£3 for the further increase of the same, after the determination of a suit depending on the rent of the Sheep-walk above mentioned. In 1638 it was decided by the Lord Chancellor that the College should have quiet possession of the Sheep-walk which was part of the purchase by Sir John's Legacy.

The distribution of an income of £143 a year among so many objects may appear at first sight to have been an unwise frittering away of the Brereton bequest. But, in comparison with the original stipends allotted by the Statutes, the additions granted were by no means insignificant, especially when we remember that money in those days went much further than it does now. We may feel sure that the arrangements made by Dr. Ward and Dr. Collins brought to the Society a great increase of personal comfort and educational efficiency. Free and unfettered legacies to universities and colleges have been amazingly rare. The trustful bounty of Sir John Brereton was most thoughtfully handled; but no Sidney benefactor has ever come forward to follow his wise example, at least to any considerable extent.

In the years 1630–1636 the College reached the zenith of its prosperity, if numbers may be taken as a criterion. The admissions in these years numbered 38, 34, 46, 35, 34, 41. The total number of residents at this time must have been about 150. The entry of 46 in 1632–33 is the largest in the whole history of the College. It included four freshmen from Eton and three from Westminster. As an interesting illustration of the tutorial system of those days, it may be noted that these 46 students were distributed among 13 tutors. Flathers had 9 of them as his pupils, Dugard

and Daggett 7 each, Pendreth and Butler 5 each,
Minshull 4, Bretton and Garbutt 2 each, and 5 others
one each. In this list of freshmen there is one name
which afterwards became famous, that of Seth Ward,
who was admitted in December 1632. He was born in
1618, the son of John Ward, Attorney of Buntingford
in Hertfordshire, " of good Reputation for his fair
Practice, but not rich." John Ward probably died in
Seth's childhood ; his mother, we are told,

" he commended extraordinarily for her Vertue, Piety and
Wisdom, to whose good Instructions and Counsels, he used
to say, he ow'd whatever was good in him."

He was taught " his first rudiments of Latin " in the
Grammar School at Buntingford, though he had not
" the benefit of an happy Institution, his Master being
a weak Man." Yet, thanks to his mother's encourage-
ment and his own talents and industry, he was thought
fit for the University at the age of fifteen. Alexander
Strange, Vicar of Buntingford, recommended Seth to
Dr. Samuel Ward, to whom he was in no way related.
He was admitted as " Master's Sizar " ; the College
Register states :

16 *ferme aetatis annum agens admissus est sizator sub
Reverendo Collegii Praefecto Doctore Ward Decemb. 1 et
postea traditus in tutelam Magistro Carolo Pendreth.*

The Master, as Walter Pope tells us in his biography of
Seth,

" took young *Seth* under his more especial care, lodging
him in his own Apartment, and allowing him the use of
the Library ; in a word, treating him as if he had been his
own and onely son. When he first went to the University,

he was low of stature, and as he walked about the Streets, the Doctors and other grave Men would frequently lay their Hands upon his white Head, for he had very fair Hair, and ask him of what College he was, and of what standing, and such like questions, which was so great a vexation to him that he was asham'd to go into the Town, and, as it were, forc'd to stay in the College and study. I said before that he had the benefit of the College Library, and our young Student shew'd this Favour was not ill bestow'd upon him, by making good use of it, and so happily improving that advantage, that in a short time he was taken notice of, not only in that College, but also in the University."

Of the intimate relations existing between the Master and himself Seth wrote this beautiful account many years afterwards, when he was Bishop of Salisbury, in the stylish Latin he had learnt from the study of his favourite Cicero:

" Ille me puerum quindecennem a schola privata (ubi me tunc aegre habui) ad Academiam florentissimam vocavit, ille me infirmum atque valetudinarium existentem recreare solitus est & omni modo refocillare, ille mihi animum ad studia . . . accendere solebat, ille mihi librorum usum suppeditavit, ille me in Collegii florentissimi societatem (quam primum licebat) cooptavit, ille mihi magister unicus erat & patronus, & spes & ratio studiorum. Ego interim (ut fieri decuit) ipsi vicissim soli addictus eram. . . . Continuo ipsi ad manum adfui ejusque ad nutum me composui . . . Aderam ipsi quotidie in Musaeo studiorum ejus conscius, nunc oculis atque ore, nunc manu, ipsi inserviens, nunc chartulas jussu illius ordinans, nunc calamo transcribens, nunc authores si quid erat opus conferens & notans ; non deeram ipsi in domesticis, si qua foret usus."

For his Tutor, Charles Pendreth, he had not so much reverence. Pope says that Seth's growth in knowledge was not due to any instruction he received from him ; for Pendreth,

"tho' he was a very honest Man, yet was no Conjurer, nor of any fame for Learning. I have often heard the Bishop repeat some part of his Tutor's Speeches, which never fail'd to make the Auditory laugh."

The dearth of mathematical teaching in those days is well illustrated by Seth's experience :

" In the College Library he found by chance some books that treated of the Mathematics, and they being wholly new to him, he inquired all the College over for a Guide to instruct him that way, but all his search was in vain ; these Books were *Greek*, I mean unintelligible, to all the Fellows of the College.* Nevertheless he took courage and attempted them himself *proprio Marte*, without any Confederates or Assistance, or Intelligence in that Countrey, and that with so good Success, that in a short time he not only discovered those *Indies*, but conquer'd several Kingdoms therein, and brought thence a great part of their Treasure, which he showed publicly to the whole University not

---

* " The explanation of the remarkable indifference evinced for the studies then known as ' mathematical ' is not solely to be found in a spirit of conservatism. A statement made by Wallis, the eminent mathematician, who entered at Emmanuel in 1632, throws additional light upon the subject. Even at that time, he tells us, mathematics were more studied in London than at either of the Universities, owing to the fact that the subjects included under that designation were looked upon as appertaining to practical life rather than to the curriculum of a University, ' as mechanical and the business of traders, merchants, seamen, carpenters, or the like, and perhaps some almanack makers in London.' "—Mullinger, *University of Cambridge*, p. 403.

G

long after. When he was Sofister he disputed in those Sciences, more like a Master than Learner, which Disputation Dr. *Bambridge* heard, greatly esteemed, and commended. This was the same Dr *Bambridge* who was afterwards *Savilian* Professor of Astronomy at *Oxford*."

Two years after Seth Ward's admission, *i.e.*, in 1634, another famous name was added to our Register, that of Roger L'Estrange, second son of Sir Hamon L'Estrange, born at Hunstanton in 1616, and educated for one year at Westminster and two years at Eton. Clarendon describes him as " a man of good wit, and a fancy very luxuriant and of an enterprising nature." In early life he was quite the Don Quixote of the Royalist party. His attempt to recover Lynn for the King in 1644 is one of the funniest episodes in English history. In this wild enterprise he was taken prisoner by the Parliament and condemned to death. Afterwards he was reprieved and kept in Newgate till 1648. He now gave up soldiering, and took to literature ; he was a most zealous and successful pamphleteer in favour of Monarchy and the Church. In 1663 he was appointed Licenser of the Press ; in the same year he started a weekly journal called the *Intelligencer*, a single quarto sheet sold for a halfpenny.

At the time of the Commencement in the summer of 1634 the Master of Sidney wrote a very melancholy letter to Archbishop Usher. Here are some extracts from it :

" Though sundry Doctors did favour him (Mr. Tourney)* and would have had him to be the Man that should answer

---

* He had been accused of inclining to Popish doctrine.

Die Comitiorum, yet he is put by, and one Mr. Flathers of our Colledg chosen to answer, whose first question is *Sola fides justificat ;* the 2nd *Realis praesentia Christi in Eucharistia non ponit Transubstantiationem.* The truth is, there are some Heads among us that are great Abettors of Mr. Tourney, who no doubt are backed by others. I pray God we may persist in the Doctrine of our Church, contained in our Articles and Homilies. Innovators are too much favoured now-a-days. . . . It may be you are willing to hear of our University affairs. I may truly say, I never knew them in a worse condition since I was a member thereof, which is almost 46 years. Not but that I hope the greater part is Orthodox ; but that new Heads are brought in, and they are backed in maintaining Novelties, and them which broach new Opinions (as I doubt not you hear) ; others are disgraced and checked when they come above, as my self was by my Lord of York the last Lent, for favouring Puritans in Consistory."

Three weeks later he writes in a much happier frame of mind :

" Our Commencement is now over, where Dr. Baden did well perform his part, who answered the Act *Vesperiis Comitiorum.* And so did the Batchelor of Divinity *Die Comitiorum*, being one of the Fellows of our Colledg. The Vice-Chancellor, Dr. Love, did well perform his part, especially in encountring with one Franciscus de S. Clara [but his true name is Davenport], who in a book set forth at Douay would reconcile, *si diis placet*, our Articles of Religion with the Definitions of the Council of Trent. But we have dismissed the Auditors this Year with much more content than they were the Year before. Our Stirs we had a little before the Commencement are prettily well over."

At Commencement in the next year Fuller came up to Cambridge to take his B.D. After the ceremony he gave the regulation "treat" which cost him "seven score pounds"! These feasts must have been on an extravagant scale. They were abolished some years afterwards under the Puritan *régime*. In the following summer (1636) Seth Ward took his B.A., and, our Register adds, "about this time was made Chappell clerke."

"At his Act for Batchelour of Arts, his Questions were concerning the *Julian* and *Gregorian* Account of the Year, which gave occasion to Mr. *Thorndike*, then Proctor, to take especial notice of him, and intitled him to the Acquaintance and Friendship of most of his ingenious Contemporaries, amongst whom some prov'd afterwards very eminent, as Dr. *Pearson*, the learned Bishop of *Chester*, Sir *Charles Scarborough*, Mr. *Rook*, &c." (W. Pope.)

In a document sent to Archbishop Laud in September 1636 are many complaints about the behaviour of Cambridge students and the state of the chapels. This report is said to have been drawn up either by Dr. Cosin or Dr. Sterne, in preparation for the Archbishop's projected Visitation. The management of most of the College Chapels is severely criticised.

"In Sidney Coll. they have no Consecrated Chappell; they read the Lessons after an order of their owne and not as they are appointed in the Kalendar. Are much like Emmanuel for the rest."

Elsewhere in the report it is stated that in Sidney and four other Chapels "the Table (notwithstandinge the King's pleasure declared for all Colledges when himself ordered it to be sett up at King's) stands still below as it did and poorly furnished."

This complaint is also interesting :

"Upon Frydays and all Fasting days . . . in Schollers' Chambers are generally the best Suppers of the whole week, and for the most part of flesh meate all. We know not what fasting is; this we know, that then the custom is for pupils to goe to their Tutors for supper money to spend in the Towne, and that their Tutors do commonly allow them twice as much for a fasting night as the College Commons doe any night of the week besides."

In the Archbishop's report of his Province for the year ending Christmas 1639 occurs this statement :

"I likewise find by my Lord the Bishop's account that there are divers particulars of moment and very fit for redress . . . most of them in the University and Town of Cambridge. As namely, that Emmanuel, Sidney, and Corpus Christi Colleges have certain Rooms built within the Memory of Man, which they use for Chappels to all Holy Uses; yet were never Consecrated."

The Master had himself already incurred the Archbishop's displeasure as a pluralist. In 1634 he writes on the subject to Usher with delightful naïveté.

"I intreated my Lord of *Canterbury* to speak to the Dean of *Wells* that now is, who had sundry times excepted against me for not residing three months *per Annum*, as I should by Charter, which I nothing doubt but it was by his instigation. He promised me then he would ; but not having done it yet, I repaired again to my Lord's Grace

about it in *November*. . . . I told him my Case was not
every Man's Case ; and that I had a Benefice at which I
desired to be in the Vacation-time ; but nothing would
prevail.   And yet, as I told him, I am every Year at *Wells*,
sometimes a month or six weeks.   I think they would have
me out of my Professor's place, and I could wish the same,
if I could have one to succeed according to my mind, for
then I should have leasure to transcribe things. . . . We
have a Vice-Chancellor that favoureth Novelties both in
Rites and Doctrines.   I could write more, *sed manum de
tabula.*"

In October 1639 Bishop Davenant writes to the
Master about John Fuller (the brother of Thomas),
who entered Sidney in 1632 and had just taken his
M.A.   He says that John

"has resolved to betake himself to the studie of the Civil
Law. . . . I conceav it will be most fitting for him to converse with men of the same profession ; and therefore I
have advised him to remove unto Trinity Hall."

In the same year we find Seth Ward *Sublector* in his
College ; in 1640 he took his M.A. ; in 1642 he was
elected to the College Praelectorship in Mathematics,
an office not often occupied in the seventeenth century.
He suffered a brief suspension from his M.A. just after
he had obtained it.   His biographer tells us that the
Vice-Chancellor

"pitcht upon Mr. Ward to be *Praevaricator*, which in Oxford
we call *Terrae filius ;* and in that place he behaved himself
to the general satisfaction of the Auditory."

The *Praevaricator* played the part of Devil's Advocate
in a Disputation.   A man with a reputation for ready

wit would be selected for the office. Doubtless Seth Ward took full advantage of his opportunity; for the Vice-Chancellor took offence and suspended him from his Degree.

"Dr. *Cosin* was not an Enemy to Wit, but perhaps he thought not fit to allow it to be so freely spoken in so sacred a Place [Great St. Mary's]. . . . However the next day before the end of the *Commencement* he revers'd his Censure. The Reader may imagine his Fault was not great, when so severe a Judge as Dr. *Cosin* should impose no greater Punishment upon him, and take it off in so short a time."

In the Chapel and in College Disputations Seth Ward's brilliant literary gifts must have been most valuable.

"His sermons were strong, methodical, and clear, and, when Occasion required, pathetical and eloquent; for, besides his Skill in the Mathematics, he was a great lover of *Tully* and understood him very well. In his Disputations his Arguments were always to the purpose, and managed with great Art, his Answers clear and full." (W. Pope.)

These two lists belonging to the year 1639–1640 are interesting:

Fellows 1639–40.		*Officiar : Electio Oct.* 1, 1639.
Robert Daggett		*Decanus.*
Richard Dugard		Mr. Hayne
James Garbutt		*Lector.*
Richard Minshull		Mr. Daggett, Jun.
Clement Breton	S.T.B.	
John Butler		*Seneschallus.*
Charles Pendreth		Mr. Wallace
Joseph Hayne		*Catechista.*
William Wallace		Mr. Pendreth

William Daggett ⎫
Theophilus Dillingham ⎪
John Lawson ⎪ M.
John Dillingham ⎬ in
Seth Ward ⎪ Art.
William Hodges ⎭

Lector Hebraeus.
Mr. Butler
   Lector Graecus.
Mr. Theoph. Dillingham
   Sublectores.
Mr. Lawson
Mr. Joan. Dillingham
Seth Ward *Art. Baccal.*

Theophilus Dillingham, who came from Emmanuel in 1638, was appointed Master of Clare in 1654.

In 1640–1 the number of admissions, which had been declining in the last four years (26, 18, 16, 16), rose to 32. In the next year there were 20 entries; in the next only two. In November 1642 the Praelector, John Dillingham, admitted two students, one of whom was Thomas Richardson, afterwards Lord Cramond. Then follows this memorandum: *Grassante bello civili cesserunt armis togae, nec plures hoc anno admissi sunt.*

We now come to the last Act in Dr. Ward's Mastership. In this an old pupil was "protagonist"; for Cromwell now became a commanding figure in Cambridge. His political connexion with the Borough seems to have arisen from the leading part which he took in the drainage of the fens, and especially from his successful opposition to the Royal Commissioners. Hence he is said to have earned his title of "Lord of the Fens"; but this is doubtful. This is the account which Heath gives of Cromwell's first public introduction to Cambridge Town. His friends had strongly recommended him to the Mayor, who, though a royalist, exercised his right of conferring the freedom of the borough on Cromwell. On January 7, 1640, he appeared in the Town House "arrayed in a scarlet coat with a broad gold lace, and was sworn and saluted by the Mayor." Cromwell had, according to custom,

"caused a good quantity of wine to be brought into the Town House, with some confectionery stuffe, which was liberally filled out, and as liberally taken off, to the warming of most of their noddles."

His friends are said to have taken advantage of this occasion to suggest that " Mr. Cromwell would make a brave burgess" for Cambridge Town. He was soon elected. It is stated that about this time he lived at Cambridge in a small house in the White Bull Yard near St. Clement's Church. The new Parliament was dissolved in three weeks. In the next—*i.e.*, the Long Parliament—Cromwell again sat for Cambridge, and he soon made his mark. After his speech at the beginning of the Long Parliament Lord Digby said to Hampden : " Pray, Mr. Hampden, who is the sloven who spoke to-day ? " The answer was,

"That sloven you see before you hath no ornament in his speech ; but if we should ever come to a breach with the King—which God forbid !—that sloven will be the greatest man in England."

An interesting conflict soon occurred between Cromwell and another Sidney man, Edward Montagu, now Lord Mandeville, and afterwards Earl of Manchester. Cromwell was a member of a Committee of the House which had to discuss the question of some waste land enclosed and sold to the Earl of Manchester. Cromwell took the side of the Fenmen "with great passion," as Clarendon tells us. Lord Mandeville claimed to be heard on his father's behalf and "with great modesty

related what had been done." Cromwell replied with
extreme rudeness ; and Clarendon remarks that

" every man would have thought that, as their natures and
their manners were as opposite as possible, so their interest
could never have been the same."

Clarendon himself was Chairman of this Committee.

On the King's return from Scotland in November
1641 the University of Cambridge published a volume
of congratulatory verses. The Master of Sidney was
among the contributors. On June 29, 1642, the King
wrote to the University, asserting his " perpetual care
and protection for such nurseries of learning," and
assured the colleges that whatever was paid to John
Poley, Fellow of Pembroke and one of the Proctors,
would be received "as a very acceptable service." He
offered eight per cent. interest on all loans. Three
weeks later Mr. Secretary Nicholas wrote that Oxford
had sent in £10,000 to the King, and Cambridge " a
fair proportion also." We have this historic entry on
the subject in our *Acta Collegii :*

"July the 2, 1642. It were ordered by the M^r, Mr.
Garbut, Pendreth, Haine, Ward, being the major part then
present, that £100 should be taken out of the Treasury for
the K's use, and so much plate as hath been given to the
M^r and ffel. for admissions of ffellow-commoners should be
set apart in lieu of it, till it bee repaid."

The hundred pounds were paid the same day to Mr.
Poley. St. John's paid £150 at the same time.

On July 24 the King wrote to the Vice-Chancellor,
desiring that the plate of the different colleges should
be deposited in his hands " for the better security and

safety thereof"! Most of the colleges obeyed the royal wish. But we have no record of the despatch of any plate from Sidney; probably the College had very little to send.* Its money contribution alone was a most handsome present from a poor treasury. The greater part of the surrendered plate was conveyed to Nottingham in August. Its value is said to have been about £10,000. A small portion was intercepted by Cromwell, who "lay in wait for the rich booty at a place called Lowler Hedges betwixt Cambridge and Huntingdon." On August 15 Parliament received this intelligence:

"Mr. Cromwell in Cambridgeshire has seized the magazine in the Castle at Cambridge, and hath hindered the carrying of the plate from that University; which, as some report, was to the value of £20,000 or thereabouts."

This account must be, to say the least, a gross exaggeration.† The royalist view is given in the not very trustworthy *Querela Cantabrigiensis.*

* The only valuable pieces of plate now belonging to the College are the Communion Plate and the Loving Cup, all given by the Earl of Kent, and the Ewer and Basin given by the second Lord Harrington. All these are remarkable for their beauty.

† There seems no reason to doubt the account which Clarendon gives of the matter: "The whole affair was transacted with so great secrecy and discretion that the messengers returned from the two Universities in as short a time as such a journey could well be made; and brought with them all, or very nearly all, their plate, and a considerable sum of money, which was sent as a present to his Majesty from several of the Heads of Colleges out of their own particular stores; some Scholars coming with it and helping to procure horses and carts for the service; all which came safe to Nottingham, at the time when there appeared no more expectation of a treaty, and contributed much to raising the dejected spirits of the place. The plate was presently weighed out and delivered to the several officers, who were entrusted to make levies of horse and foot, and who

"One Master *Cromwell*, Burgesse for the Towne of *Cambridge*, and then newly turn'd a man of Warre, was sent downe by his Masters above, at the invitation of the Master below (as himselfe confessed) to gather what strength he could to stop all passages that no Plate might be sent: But his designes being frustrated, and his opinion as of an active subtile man thereby somewhat shaken and endangered, he hath ever since bent himselfe to worke what revenge and mischiefe he could against us."

Three Heads of Colleges, who had been specially ·forward in the matter of the plate, were sent up to London as prisoners. On August 17 Parliament gave instructions to Cromwell and the Mayor and three aldermen of Cambridge

"to exercise and train all the Train Bands and Voluntiers in the Town of Cambridge . . . to defend it from all hostile attempts, . . . to disarm all Popish Recusants and all other ill-affected persons."

The *Querela Cantabrigiensis* states that at this time "a Scholar could have small security from being stoned or affronted as he walked the streets." Many soldiers were quartered in the colleges. On March 4, 1643, the House of Lords ordered that the University "shall have a Protection of this House"; this, it is stated in the ordinance, is to prevent any disturbance happening to the "quiet and studies of the Scholars" on account of the "great multitude of soldiers resorting from several places to the Town of Cambridge." On March 20

received it as money ; the rest was carefully preserved to be carried with the King when he should remove from thence."—*History of the Rebellion*, vol. ii. pp. 49, 50.

"upon the bruit of Prince Rupert's coming into Buckinghamshire several thousands of men were sent to defend Cambridge by the five associated Counties."* On July 12 the Governor of Cambridge Castle reported to Parliament: "Our Town and Castle are now very strongly fortified, being encompassed with breastworks and bulwarks."

The Vice-Chancellor and Heads of Houses, "solemnly assembled in the Consistory" on March 30, 1643, were requested to make contributions to the Parliamentary cause, "so to redeem their forwardness in supplying the King. Which performed by them would, notwithstanding their former crooked carriage in the cause, bolster them upright in the Parliament's esteem." But they replied that "such contributing was against true religion and a good conscience." The Master of Sidney was

"in the Convocation House, when all the members of the University there assembled (many of them 60 years old and upwards) were kept prisoners in the Public Schools on an exceedingly cold night till near one in the morning, without any accommodation for food, firing or lodging; and, to complete this outrage, it was done on Good Friday,

* The "Eastern Association," of which Cambridge was the head-quarters, had been formed in the previous winter. Two Sidney men, Cromwell and the Earl of Manchester, were the leading figures in it. Cromwell, now a colonel, during the spring of 1643 was successful in quelling all royalist attempts in East Anglia, striking the final blow in the capture of Lowestoft. He then turned his attention to Lincolnshire. In August Manchester took the command of the Eastern Association, with Cromwell serving under him. In October they joined Fairfax at Boston, and defeated the royal forces at Winceby. During the remainder of the year Cromwell was attending to the affairs of the Association, spending some time Ely, of which he had been appointed governor a few months before.

whence it maybe supposed they went with empty stomachs, and all this for no other reason but because they could not in conscience comply to contribute anything to that detestable war against His Majesty."

The *Mercurius Aulicus* (a Royalist newspaper) for April 22, 1642, states that

"the Lord Grey of Wark and Master Cromwell did the last week deal very earnestly with the Heads of Colleges to lend £6000 for the public use."

It is added that Cromwell, having met with a refusal and having kept most of the Heads in custody till midnight, afterwards remarked that he and his friends

"would have been content with £1000 or less for the present turn ; not that so little money could have done them good, but that the people might have thought that one of the two Universities had been on their side."

The story may be continued in the interesting record of Seth Ward's biographer :

"St. John's College was made a Gaol by the Parliamentary Forces, commanded by the Earl of *Manchester ;* and amongst the rest Dr. *Samuel Ward,* Master of *Sidney* College was imprisoned, whither Mr. *Ward* accompanied him voluntarily, and submitted to that confinement, that he might assist so good a Man and so great a Friend in that Extremity. I have heard him say that Imprisonment seem'd at first to him very uneasie, but after he had been a little time used to it, he liked it well enouf, and could have been contented not to have stir'd out all the days of his Life. The great Inconvenience of so close a Confinement, in the heighth of a hot Summer, caused some of

Doctor *Ward's* Friends to mediate for his Removal, at least for some weeks, which was granted, and in the beginning of *August* the Doctor was permitted to go to his own House, to which also Mr. *Ward* accompanied him and carefully ministered unto him. Within a Months time after his Inlargement, the good Old Man fell into a dangerous Distemper, caused by his Imprisonment, whereof he died the seventh of September following in the year of our Lord 1643."

We have Seth Ward's own account of Dr. Ward's last days in his beautiful preface to a volume of the Master's theological lectures published in 1658:

" Cum paulo ante obitum, saeviente bello civili, libertate per aliquot hebdomadas privatus est, me aerumnarum participem habuit & curarum, me mensae socium & cubilis, & cum paulo post, ingenti bonorum omnium luctu atque gemitu, mea vero animi consternatione & stupore, Deo unde profectus fuerat reddenda esset anima ejus sanctissima, ego ab ipsius latere nunquam discessi ; quin etiam . . . morientis oculos clausi, corpusque tandem exanime meis aliorumque humeris impositum ad tumulum detuli."

Seth Ward told Walter Pope that the Master's last words were " God bless the King and my Lord Hopton." He was the first person buried in the Chapel of the College which he had ruled wisely and well for thirty-three years. Fuller has a quaint and pathetic passage about his old Master's end :

" Among these was Dr. Samuel Ward, Master of Sidney College and Divinity Professor, Lady Margaret's (or 'the King's' shall I say ?) in the University. For, though the former by his foundation, he may seem the latter by his resolution. Yet was he a Moses, not only for slowness of speech, but, otherwise, meekness of nature. Indeed, when in my private thoughts I have beheld him and Dr. Collins (disputable whether more different or more eminent in their endowments), I could not but remember the running of Peter and John to the place where Christ was buried. In which race John came first as the youngest and swiftest; but Peter first entered into the grave. Dr. Collins had much the speed of him in quickness of parts; but let me say (nor doth the relation of a pupil misguide me), the other pierced the deeper into underground and profound points of divinity. Now, as high winds bring some men the sooner into sleep, so I conceive the storms and tempests of these distracted times invited this good old man the sooner to his long rest, where we may fairly leave him and quietly draw the curtains about him."

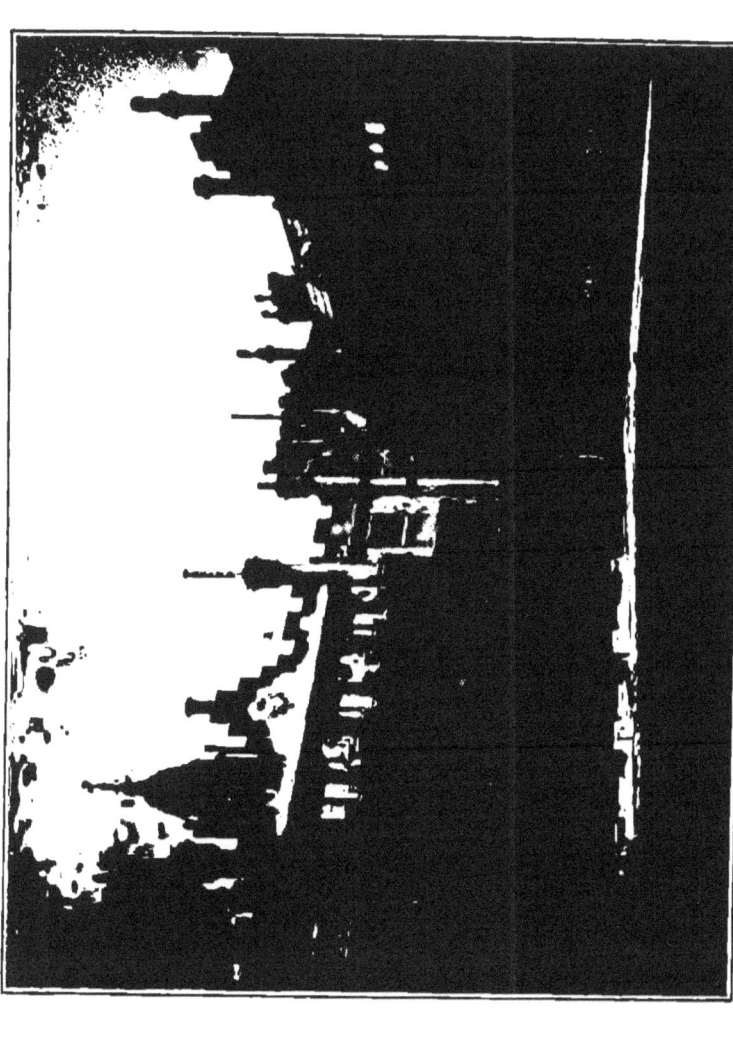

From a photograph by]   THE HALL COURT   [J. Palmer Clarke, Cambridge

CHAPTER VIII

THE PURITAN MASTER

" Now," says Fuller, " approached the general doom of
' malignant members ' (so termed) in the University."
The chief instrument employed by Parliament in these
proceedings was a member of Fuller's College. On
December 5, 1643, the following letter from the Earl of
Manchester was read in the House of Peers :

" By virtue of the Ordinance of Sequestration, the
Sequestrators of the Town of Cambridge have sequestered
all the Lands and Profits belonging to those Colleges
which did convey their Plate to the King : This is likely
to breed a great Distraction in the University, by reason
that the Fellows and Scholars of those Colleges must be
driven to very great Extremities, having no other Livelihood or Subsistence. . . . I have made Stay of any further
Proceeding, until I receive Direction from your Lordships
and the House of Commons, which I shall be ready to
obey in this and in all Things else."

The Lords referred the matter to the Commons, who
on December 12 referred it to a Committee. On
January 6 Parliament passed an ordinance staying the
proceedings of the Sequestrators, and restoring to the
Colleges control over their revenues, on one condition,
viz. :

H

"that their Receivers or Treasurers shall be approved by Edward Earle of Manchester, Serjeant Major Generall of the Parliament's Forces in the County of Cambridge and the other associated Counties."

The next parliamentary ordinance was less merciful to the University. On January 22, 1644, power was given to the Earl of Manchester to eject such Masters, Fellows, and Students as

"he shall judge unfit for their Places and to place other fitting persons in their Roome, such as shall be approved of by the Assembly of Divines sitting at Westminster."

This commission arose out of the proceedings of the Assembly of Divines, whose first act was to petition Parliament to abolish "all monuments of idolatry and superstition" and "more especially the whole body and practice of Popery." In February, Manchester, accompanied by his chaplains, Mr. Ash and Mr. Good, repaired to Cambridge to undertake his "reformation of the University"; he was also charged to deal with "scandalous Ministers" in the five Associated Counties. The Committee constituted by the Earl to reform the University consisted of about forty members; but the average attendance was only five or six. First of all they held their sittings at the Bear Inn in the corner of Market Passage; afterwards they met in Trinity College, and the "Scandalous Ministers Committee" sat at the Bear.

The harshness of the Commissioners' proceedings was chiefly due to the two chaplains, to whom the Earl, "most mild in himself," as Fuller allows, handed over most of the business. Even Clarendon says that he was

" a man of gentle and generous nature," and " never guilty of any rudeness towards those he was obliged to oppress." In the *Querela Cantabrigiensis* it is alleged that an oath of discovery was tendered to many members of the University, who universally refused it,

" as against all law and conscience, as being thereby made to accuse their nearest and dearest friends, benefactors, Tutors, and Masters, and betray the members and acts of their Societies contrary to their peaceable Statutes."

On Februry 24 Manchester served a warrant on the College requiring that the Statutes should be sent to him, together with the names of all the members of the Society and also a certificate stating who were present and who absent, and a " Notice of the expresse time of their Discontinuance who are now absent." Immediately afterwards the Earl sent the following warrant:

" These are to will and require you upon Sight hereof, to give speedy Advertisement, Viis, Mediis & Modis, to the Fellowes, Schollars, and Officers of your Colledge, to be resident at your said Colledge the tenth day of March next ensuing, to give an account wherein they shall be required to answer such things as may bee demanded by mee, or such Commissioners as I shall appoint."

This was followed by yet another document requiring the Master to give in the names of all members out of residence, and the records of all College Acts passed during the last twelve years. Fuller comments on the shortness of the notice given to non-residents:

" Whereas many Scholars, being absent more scores of miles than they had days allowed them (besides the danger of armies interposed) could not, if receiving warning, repair at the time appointed. But because many of them were suspected to be in the King's army, twelve days were conceived for them as much as twelve months no time being short for those who were willing, and none long enough for such who were unwilling, to take the Covenant. The Covenant, being offered, was generally refused ; whereupon the recusants were ordered, without any delay, to pack out of the University three days after their ejection."

As a matter of fact, Manchester, on being informed that the time was too short, extended it to April 3. Five days later sixty-three Fellows of Colleges and many scholars also were ejected for non-appearance in answer to Manchester's summons. Among them was one Fellow of Sidney. The College was directed to sequestrate the profits belonging to his Fellowship, to be disposed of to such person as the Earl should appoint in his room, and to "cut his name out of the Butteries." Soon afterwards many other Fellows, including four from Sidney, were ejected for refusing to take the Covenant and opposing the proceedings of Parliament. Eleven Heads of Houses were put out of their Lodges. The "malignant" Master of Sidney, as we have seen, had anticipated ejection by his death. The Masters of Corpus, Trinity Hall, Christ's, and Magdalene, "by the especial favours of their friends and their own wary compliance continued in their places."

A new Master of Sidney, favourable to the Parliament, had been appointed some months previously after an election dominated by intrigue and armed force. On September 13, 1643, the Fellows assembled to elect a successor to Dr. Ward. They were divided between Robert Thorndike, of Trinity, a royalist, and Richard Minshull, B.D., a Fellow of the College, who, as has been said, was a student with Cromwell, and now espoused his cause. They met at 5 A.M. in the Chapel; during the service which in obedience to the Statutes preceded the election some of the Parliament's soldiers broke in and carried off John Pawson, one of the royalist Fellows. The account of the matter given in our *Acta Collegii* is very interesting:

"Impr: before the election of Mr Minshull to be Maister of the College, Mr Seth Ward in presence of Mr Garbut, Minshull, Pendreth, Lawson, Hodges, Seyliard, Gibson, Matthewes, Bertie, made a protestation against the election (which was by statute to bee perfected before 12 of the clock at noone that day) because Mr Pawson was taken away by souldiers sent from the Committee, so that he could not give his voice with others. Notwithstanding the rest of the ffellowes proceeded on and Mr Minshull was elected and admitted before 12 of the clock that day.

"2. There were present at the election, Mr Garbut, Minshull, Lawson, Hodges, Seyliard, Bertie, the other withdrawing themselves and refusing to repaire into the Chapell againe, when they were sent for to give their suffrages.

"3. Five of the forementioned ffellowes, viz., Mr Garbut, &c., consented in Mr Minshull, and Mr Hodges only suspended his vote, giving for no body."

The *Querela Cantabrigiensis* says that John Pawson

"was violently pluck't from the Communion as he was

ready to receive that holy Sacrament before the solemn Election of a Master of that College, and thrown into Gaol to the great disturbance of the Election."

It is added that " since he hath proved himself an arrant honest man and is rewarded for it with a Fellowship in S. John's," *i.e.*, he took the Covenant. This was doubtless the reason for the following College Order :

"Jan. 13, 1644. The M^r and all the ffellowes ordered that Mr John Pawson should have his whole allowance paid him from the time he left his fellowship to the time of his admission into St. John's, which was Nov. 18th 1644."

Walter Pope thus completes the story :

" Mr *Mynshull* was admitted Master, the other eight * only protesting against it, being ill advised, for they should have adher'd to their Votes. Two of them whereof Mr *Ward* was one, went to *Oxford*, and brought thence a *Mandamus* from the King, commanding Mr *Mynshull* and the Fellows of *Sidney* College to repair thither and give an account of their Proceedings as to that Election. This Mandamus or peremtory Summons was fix'd upon the Chapel door by Mr *Linnet*, who was afterwards a Fellow of *Trinity* College, but at that time attended on Mr *Thorndike*. On the other side, one Mr *Bertie*, a Kinsman of the Earl of *Lindsey*, being one of those who voted for Mr *Mynshull*, was also sent to Oxford in his behalf; this Gentleman, by the Assistance and Mediation of my Lord of *Lindsey*, procur'd an Order from the King to confirm Mr *Mynshulls* Election, but he, not thinking this Title

* Pope is mistaken about the numbers here and earlier in his narrative.

sufficient, did corroborate it with the Broad Seal, to which
Mr *Thorndike* consented, Mr *Mynshull* paying him and the
rest of the Fellows the Charges they had been at, in the
Management of that Affair, amounting to about a hundred
pound."

The Fellows of Sidney ejected by Manchester were
Seth Ward, Edward Gibson, Robert Bertie, John
Lawson, and John Pawson. Pope tells us how in the
spring of 1644 Seth Ward and Edward Gibson

"were summoned to appear before the Committee of
Visitors, then sitting at *Trinity* College, and tender'd the
Covenant and other Oaths, which they refused, declaring
themselves unsatisfied as to the Lawfulness of them. Then
they desired to know if the Committee had any Crime to
object against them. They answered they had not : they
declared the reason why they ask'd was that they understood some were ejected for not taking the Covenant and
others for Immoralities ; to which they received this
Answer, that those were words of course put into all their
Orders of Ejection. Such was the Carriage of those Commissioners, not only to take away the Livelihood of those
they expell'd, but also their good Name and Reputation,
and so render them unpitied and not worthy to be relieved.
In the month of *August* following, Mr *Ward*, who was
absent, received the news that his Ejection was voted and
put into Execution."

Fuller wonders how many of the Fellows turned out
of the different Colleges were able to gain a livelihood,
and he is reminded of the Greek proverb, ἢ τέθνηκεν ἢ δι-
δάσκει γράμματα, " He is either dead or teacheth school,"
adding that we must conceive that the same was " the

hard hap of such Fellows that survived the grief of their ejection," many of whom "betook themselves to the painful profession of schoolmaster; no calling which is honest being disgraceful, especially to such who, for their conscience' sake, have deserted a better condition." No such "hard hap" befell Seth Ward. His ejection from Sidney proved a great stepping-stone in his career. For a time he "diverted himself with Dr. Ward's Relations in and about London." He saw much of the celebrated William Oughtred, author of the *Clavis Mathematica*.

"He was invited by the E. of *Carlile* and several other Persons of high Quality with profers of large and honourable Pensions to come and reside in their Families. Nay, I have heard him say that even then when he was in those straits and might have truly said, 'Silver or Gold or Preferment I have none,' he was proferr'd several rich Matches, but he had no inclination to Matrimony, whilst he labour'd under those Circumstances." (W. Pope.)

At last he accepted the invitation of "his friend and countryman" Ralph Freeman of Aspenden in Hertfordshire, "in the Parish wherein he had sucked his first milk." There he stayed off and on till 1649. In that year he lived for a short time with Lord Wenham of Thame Park, Oxfordshire,

"rather as Companion than Chaplain, it being more safe for him to be near Oxford than Cambridge, and, as it proved in the event, much more advantageous."

In 1649 Dr. Scarborough recommended him to John Greaves, Savilian Professor of Astronomy at Oxford,

as a suitable successor. The Professor wished to resign his chair instead of waiting to be ejected; for
the Visitation of the University of Oxford had now
begun. Ward was at first loath to entertain Greaves's
proposal.

"After many thanks for so great and unexpected a
Favour, he objected the difficulty of effecting it, saying he
could not with any reason expect to enjoy quietly a public
Professors place in *Oxford*, wher 'twas notoriously known
that he was turn'd out of *Cambridge* for refusing the
Covenant. Mr Greaves reply'd that he and his friends
had consider'd that Obstacle and found out a way to
remove it; and it was effectually removed a little while
after by the means of Sir *John Trevor*, who . . . had great
Interest in the Committee which dispos'd of the places of
those who were ejected, and by that brought Mr *Ward*
into the Professors Chair, and preserv'd him in it without
taking the Covenant or Engagement."

Dr. Wilkins, Warden of Wadham, who had already
gathered in his College several scientific celebrities,
induced him to join that house. For ten years he lived
there in "the chamber over the gateway"; he was
Christopher Wren's predecessor not only in his College
rooms, but also in his University Professorship.[*] He
took part in the weekly meetings of an "experimental
philosophical club," which first met at Oxford in 1648,
and which Aubrey says "was the *incunabula* of the
Royal Society." According to the official *Record of the
Royal Society* (p. 2), this Oxford society was an offshoot
of an older society which used to meet at Gresham

* Wells, *History of Wadham College*, p. 75.

House and other places in London. This private
society, meeting partly in London, partly at Oxford,
afterwards became the nucleus of the Royal Society,
which obtained its charter in 1662, Wilkins and Seth
Ward being amongst its first members. As Professor,
Ward won golden opinions, " never failing of a good
auditory," and giving private teaching gratuitously ;
he was also renowned as a preacher. Pope says :

" I have heard him say, and he was no Lyar, that, in all
the time he enjoy'd the Astronomy Professors Place, he
never miss'd one reading Day."

An amusing story told by the same writer gives us
some idea of the Oxford view of Seth Ward's opinions
and prospects :

" Tho' he was so complyant and useful in his Station at
Oxford, yet he could never wear off, neither indeed did he
desire it, the imputation of being a Cavalier and Episcopaly
inclin'd, this was often hit in his teeth as the unpardonable
Sin and the Leaven of the Farisees, but it did him no
hurt. Amongst the rest a Person of Honour, afterwards
married to a Peer of this Realm, who then lived about
twenty miles distant from *Oxford* in a Family well known
to Dʳ *Wilkins* and Dʳ *Ward*, and often visited by them.
This Lady drolling with him used these words : *Doctor*
Ward, *I am confident you believe the King will come in, and
that you shall be a Bishop.* Madam, replyed he, *I think
neither the one or the other impossible.* But I esteem it so
improbable, said she, *that if it happens in my life-time I
promise, before these witnesses, to present you with a pair of
Lawn Sleeves of mine own handiwork, which would be no small
Mortification to one of our persuasion*, said she laughing, for
she was a Presbyterian. . . . Dʳ *Ward* return'd her his

humble thanks, adding, *If there should be an occasion, he would give her Ladyship timely notice.* And he was as good as his word, giving her advice of his Nomination to the Bishopric of *Exeter.* She also was not worse than hers, presenting him with the first Lawn Sleeves he ever wore."

When the Headship of Jesus College, Oxford, became vacant in 1659, Ward was elected and admitted Principal. But he and the Fellows who chose him were cited to appear at Whitehall. The Fellows were severely reprimanded, and the election was annulled; but "Dr. Ward was treated with great civility and complimented and dismiss'd not without promise of particular favour." Shortly afterwards he was elected President of Trinity owing to the influence of his friend Ralph Bathurst, the ablest of the Fellows and afterwards President.* But the Restoration put an end to Ward's presidency in less than a year. His biographer states that

"'tis true he left *Trinity College* and Oxford ἐκὼν ἀέκοντί γε θυμῷ, with an unwilling willingness, for he was contented with his Condition and so pleased with a Collegial Life and the Charms of that sweet place that he would willingly have remain'd there the rest of his days; and in order to that, propos'd Dᵣ *Potter* an Equivalent, which was refus'd."

This is Hannibal Potter, ejected President, who was reinstated in 1660. Pope goes on to remark that, if Ward

"had kept that Headship, I mean been buried alive in *Trinity College,* hiding his glorious Light under that Bushel,

* Blakiston, *History of Trinity College,* p. 149.

Exeter and *Salisbury* could not have boasted of so good a Bishop and Benefactor. . . . He might have publish'd more Treatises in Divinity and Mathematics, but he could not possibly have done so much good."

In 1661 he was made Dean of Exeter ; some years before he had been nominated Precentor of that Cathedral, but was never admitted.   In the West Seth Ward was much beloved ; and when the See of Exeter became vacant in the following year, the country gentlemen pressed his claims on Charles II., " at that criticall time when the House of Commons were the King's darlings."   Aubrey says that

"the old bishops were exceedingly disgruntled at it, to see a brisk young bishop, but forty years old, not come in at the right door, but leap over the pale."

In 1667 he was translated to Salisbury, and afterwards procured for that See the honour of the Chancellorship of the Garter, which had formerly belonged to it.   In both his dioceses he was reputed to be an excellent organiser and disciplinarian, " keeping a watchful eye over the dissenters."   He died in 1689 and was buried in Salisbury Cathedral.   Besides a text-book on Trigonometry and several treatises on Astronomy he wrote *Exercitatio in Hobbii Philosophiam* and *Vindiciae Academiarum* ; in the latter he defended the Universities against those who styled them "nurseries of wickedness, nests of mutton tuggers, and dens of formal drones."   In addition to considerable benefactions at Salisbury and elsewhere, the Bishop endowed four scholarships at Christ's College.   Pope says that "he had designed to place this his benefaction at

Sidney College, but upon some disgust altered his intention."

Having sketched the career of one of Sidney's most illustrious sons, we now return to the "stricken field" of Cambridge. In other Colleges we meet

" with many moans in this kind: how soldiers were now quartered in their Colleges; chapels abused; materials for building colleges taken away; Jesus College Grove (no idolatrous one) cut down to the ground; and the ancient coins of St. John's taken away."

Sidney had less to complain of than most Colleges. In its post-Reformation Chapel the iconoclast William Dowsing found no cherubims or saints to demolish. He visited the Chapel on December 30, 1643, and reported thus: "We saw nothing there to be amended." There was, however, one greater grievance which pressed hard on all the Colleges.

" Chiefly it vexed them that their lands, hitherto exempted from payments, and, like *his* father's house who should conquer Goliath, free in Israel, were now subject to taxes, wherein the raters were heavier than the rates, being taxed by the townsmen. And how 'odious is a handmaid that is heir to her mistress'; but much more when mistress of her mistress, as here the Town, in some sort, was over the University, where such who set the lowest price on learning put the highest valuation on the Professors thereof." (Fuller.)

Before filling up the vacant Fellowships, Manchester desired the Master and Fellows to send the names of such Scholars as were judged most capable of Fellowships, that they might be examined and made Fellows,

if upon examination they should be approved. The
College decided that one of the five vacant Fellowships
should not be filled at present for the reason explained
in these two Orders :

(1) "There was like order made for paying Mr Lukyn
all that was due to him in Mr Lawsons yeare for beere."

(2) "The M^r and ffellowes unanimously ordered that
the profits of the fellowship which was Mr John Pawson's
should bee reserved to the Treasury use till such time as
the detriment which the Coll. hath sustained by Mr John
Lawson bee repaid."

Four of the five vacant Fellowships were filled up in
December 1644 by the admission of Francis Quarles,
John Rowlet, William Wells, and George Thorne.
Before their admission they made solemn declarations
to the effect that they

"being appointed and constituted by the Right Honourable the Earl of Manchester who is authorised thereunto
by an ordinance of Parliament "

to be Fellows of the College,

"with the approbation of the Assembly of Divines now
sittinge at Westminster, doe solemnely and seriously
promise in the presence of Almighty God the searcher of
all heartes "

to promote piety and learning in themselves and the
students of the College,

"agreeable to the late solemn national League and
Covenant, by them sworne and subscribed, with respect to
all the good and wholesome statutes of the said Colledge
and of the University correspondent to the said Covenant."

A high compliment was at this time paid to a former Fellow of Sidney. It appears from the short autobiography of Thomas Gataker, prefixed to his *Adversaria*, that in 1645 he was pressed by the Earl of Manchester to take the Mastership of Trinity. His brethren of the Assembly of Divines, especially those who had been placed by the same authority over other Colleges, strongly urged him to accept. But with characteristic modesty he declined the high office, for which he was admirably fitted. In his autobiography he pleads that he has not strength for the task, having already " one foot in the grave." The interesting fact remains that one Sidney man offered to another Sidney man the Mastership of Trinity. Gataker died in 1654. He had been four times married.

In 1646 the plague broke out again in Cambridge. William Sancroft of Emmanuel, afterwards Archbishop of Canterbury, writing to his father, says : " No College stirs but Christ's in whose vicinage the infection is. We are the next to them, but yet our lads budge not." Apparently the lads of Sidney were no less courageous. There was another visitation in the following year, when booths were set up on Jesus Green and Coldham Common for the reception of the plague-stricken.

In the next year we find our old friend Fuller seeking shelter at Boughton House, the residence of Edward Lord Montagu, where a Sidney man might be sure of a welcome. He went there with his six-year old son, a broken-hearted exile, grieving over the loss of his library and his country's calamities. His friend's hospitality soon restored him to his former self ; so he tells us. During the last four years Fuller had led an adventurous life. In 1643 he joined the King at Oxford, where he lived for seventeen weeks in Lincoln College. He alleges that these seventeen weeks at Oxford cost him more than his seventeen years at Cambridge, even all that he had, *i.e.*, his property and preferments. On account of the calm and moderate tone of his sermons at Oxford the high royalists accused him of lukewarmness. To justify himself, he took the post of chaplain in Lord Hopton's regiment. After Hopton's defeat at Cheriton Down, Fuller took part in the defence of Basing House ; where on one occasion he headed a sally upon the enemy's trenches. He was afterwards regarded as one of the "great cavalier parsons." During the time of the war, he tells us, when apologising for the non-appearance of his *Church History*,

"I had little list or leisure to write, fearing to be made a history, and shifting daily for my safety. All that time I could not live to study, who did only study to live."

In 1655 he published his *History of the University of Cambridge*.

In 1649 a Sidney man gained the highest office in the University. After the triumph of his forces at Marston Moor, Manchester had been quite indifferent about the progress of the war. Hence came his quarrel with Cromwell and retirement from his military command. It has been remarked that the misunderstanding between Manchester and Cromwell was due to

"the difference of point of view from which the two men regarded the ultimate purpose of the War. Manchester, like many others, never got beyond the idea that the War was an armed protestation. . . . Cromwell's idea that the Earl's apathy sprang from a fear lest they should beat the King too well went to the root of the matter." (Kingston, *The Civil War in East Anglia*, p. 176.)

In January 1649, in the House of Lords, Manchester had strongly opposed the ordinance for the King's trial; and, when the inauguration of a Commonwealth appeared to be inevitable, he retired from political life. In March he was appointed Chancellor of the University.

In October Parliament passed a momentous ordinance, viz., (1) that the Committee for regulating the Universities should cause all Heads, Fellows, College Officers, and Graduates to subscribe the "Engagement," which ran thus:

"I do declare and promise that I will be true and faithful to the Commonwealth of England, as the same is now established, without a King or House of Lords";

also (2) that thenceforth no person should be admitted to any degree or bear any office in the Universities without subscribing to this Engagement. In 1650 several Heads of Houses and many Fellows were ejected because of their refusal to subscribe. The Committee sat at the Bear Inn; they did their best to coax objectors into subscribing.

"It was declared twice or thrice," says Samuel Dillingham, "that we were to stand engaged; 'for,' said they, 'it is no reason you should partake of the benefit and fruit of the government, unless you engage to do your best to maintain it'."

I

The Master and Fellows of Sidney did not cut a very noble figure.

"D' Minshull, though he joined first with the rest, crept at night to their lodgings and put his hand to the parchment, his whole College ambling next day in the same step. . . . To sixty-six subscribers there were nearer six hundred refusers, if they may be so called who make account they have not given their final answer, and, if the second woe come, . . . will, in all suspicion, say a new lesson for fear of whipping." (S. Dillingham, *Letter to Mr. Sancroft*.)

The Earl of Manchester showed greater independence than the authorities of his own College. In the Commons' Journals for November 4, 1651, we find this statement :

"Sir Henry Mildmay reports, from the Committee for Reformation of the Universities, that the present Chancellor of the University of Cambridge does not comply with the Act of Parliament in subscribing the Engagement; whereby the University doth suffer."

On November 27 the Committee for regulating the Universities removed the Earl from the office of Chancellor. The ejector was himself ejected. The Committee appointed in his stead Oliver St. John, Lord Chief Justice of the Common Pleas.

In the following year Cromwell showed some consideration for the University, addressing the following order to officers and soldiers under his command :·

"These are to charge & require you upon sight hereof not to Quarter any Officers or Souldiers in any of the

Colledges, Halls, or other Houses belonging to the Universitie of Cambridge, nor to offer any Injurie or Violence to any of the Students."

In the *Cambridge Portfolio* it is stated on the authority of Noble that Sidney was never "rifled" by soldiers; and Carter in his *History of the University* says that " Oliver Cromwell, a Student of the House, left them a large Quantity of Old Plate, *i.e.*, he did not take it from them as he did from others."

On November 4, 1652, " Dr. Minshull was elected in the Regent house Vice-Chancellor and entered upon the office." Baker relates that at the Commencement in the following summer the Vice-Chancellor "being seized with a strange sort of deafness," Dr. Tuckney of St. John's moderated for him ; "after which the Vice-Chancellor was happily restored to the use of his ears." In 1658 Dr. Minshull contributed verses to the *Musarum Cantabrigiensium Luctus et Gratulatio,* on the death of the Protector and the accession of his son Richard.

On May 11, 1660, Charles II. was proclaimed King by the Mayor of Cambridge. The Earl of Manchester had taken a leading part in bringing about the Restoration, and, as Speaker of the House of Lords, welcomed the King on his arrival. He was loaded with honours. On May 26 the House of Lords made an order that the Earl of Manchester be restored to " the exercise of his Chancellorship of the University "; and on June 4 it was ordered that " such persons who have been unjustly put out of their Headships, Fellowships, or other Offices . . . be restored." On the following day Dr. Minshull, who was not, as might have been expected,

disturbed in his Mastership at the Restoration, waited
on the King at Whitehall with the other Heads and
the University officers. After the ceremony "some
went to dyne at Ordinarys, & some went and dyned
with their Friends & Acquaintance." During the
summer Manchester issued many warrants for the
restoration of ejected Masters and Fellows. At Sidney
no such restoration was necessary. In the following
year the Senate passed this Grace:

*Placeat vobis ut omnia rescripta jussiones et mandata Oliveri
nuper dicti Protectoris reliquaque istius tyrannidis monumenta
quae in Registro hujus Academiac vel alibi prostant visenda
deleantur et de medio penitus tollantur.*

On August 3 the King issued a mandate empowering
Magdalene, Emmanuel, and Sidney Colleges to nominate
Proctors, Taxors, and Scrutators, according to a " proportion and order " to be decided by the Vice-Chancellor
and the major part of the Heads. This privilege had
been already granted by the University in 1650; and
Sidney nominated its first Proctor in 1651 (see p. 135).
But apparently the concession was thought to be *ultra
vires.* The new cycle for the nomination of Proctors,
&c., came into force in 1666.

In 1660 Fuller paid his last visit to Sidney. On
August 2 he took his D.D. degree by royal mandate,
"as a scholar of integrity and good learning who had
been hindered in the due way of proceeding." He died
on August 16 in the following year. He was buried in
the chancel of Cranford Church, of which he had been
appointed Rector in 1658. His epitaph says truly
that " while he was endeavouring to give immortality

to others, he himself attained it." In the words of Echard, "by his particular temper and management he weathered the late great storm with more success than many other great men."

By the Act of Uniformity in 1662 Heads, Fellows, and College officers were compelled to subscribe (before St. Bartholomew's day) to a declaration of assent to the Liturgy of the Church of England. The declaration also contained clauses (1) against taking arms against the King, and (2) against the Solemn League and Covenant. Deprivation was the penalty for failure to subscribe. No member of the Sidney Society was deprived at "Bartletide."

In 1665 on account of the prevalence of the plague a Grace was passed by the Senate for discontinuing Sermons at St. Mary's and Exercises in the Schools. The pestilence raged with great violence for some months. In March of the following year it was announced that Cambridge had a clean bill of health. But in the summer the plague broke out again, and all public meetings in town and University were suspended. This was the year of the great fire of London ; shortly after that event some riotous individuals threatened to "make Cambridge a second London." The Vice-Chancellor gave orders that five or six Scholars of each College should act as watchmen in their respective Houses.

On May 5, 1671, the Earl of Manchester was gathered to his fathers. In 1667 he had become a Fellow of the Royal Society, and married his fifth wife. His character is well indicated in these statements : " The Earl was a gentleman of debonair nature, but very facile and changeable" (Sir Philip Warwick); "of a soft and obliging temper, of no great depth, but universally beloved" (Burnet). His successor in the Chancellorship was George Villiers, Duke of Buckingham, who received Charles II. on the occasion of his first visit to Cambridge on October 4, when, as the King passed the Market place, "the conduit ran with Claret wine."

A statement of the numbers at the different Colleges, published in 1672, gives Sidney the eighth place, with 122 residents. The total number was 2522. In the next year Benjamin Johnson, Fellow of Sidney and Junior Proctor, was compelled by the Heads to recant for an abusive speech made at the Commencement.

When Sancroft was made Archbishop in 1677, the hope that a Sidney man—"Seth Sarum"—might reign at Canterbury was finally dissipated. The following entertaining story bears on this subject, though its truth may very fairly be doubted.

"When K. C. intended to shut up the Exchequer he asked this Bishop (Ward) if he had no monys there, intending to give him a friendly warning. He said he had none, fearing the King would borrow it. 'But are you sure?' said the K. 'Have you not £3000?' 'No,' said he (*verba sacerdotis*), 'I've not a groat.' The K., knowing it, said, 'Let him goe like a knave and his money with him.' By this he lost his hopes of the A.B^p of Canterbury and £3000. Being Chancellor for the Knights of Windsor—the K. usually allowed to the Chancellor the surplusage of what he gave for the Installments. At 7 years end the K. called for the Accompts. He told him he had £3000 and he would put 2000 more to it and build houses for the p^oo^r Knights. The K. said, 'I am a poor

Knight ; I'll have the mony myself' ; and so he lost £3000 more." (*Some hystoricall passages out of Mr. Woodcock's papers* printed in the *Cambridge Review,* vol. vii. p. 274.)

In 1681 many graduates of the University combined to pay a compliment to an old Sidney man. Roger L'Estrange (see p. 98) was still writing vigorously in defence of the Church ; and a Cambridge subscription of £200 was raised as an acknowledgment of his services. Recently he had been accused of being a papist ; whereupon he published his tract, *L'Estrange no Papist,* in which he wrote : " The whole kennel of Libellers is now let loose upon me as if I were to be beaten to death by Pole-cats." He had already written innumerable tracts and broadsides against the Dissenters. He now started the *Observator,* in which he carried on his warfare for some years ; the journal had a very powerful influence. Nahum Tate said of this effort :

" He with watchful eye
Observes and shoots their treasons as they fly ;
Their weekly frauds his keen replies detect,
He undeceives more fast than they infect."

At the Revolution L'Estrange lost his office of Press Licenser. He died in 1704 within a few days of his eighty-eighth birthday.

From 1645 to 1660 the Society was subject to very frequent changes. One Fellow was elected in 1646, one in 1648, two in 1649, three in 1650, two in 1651, two in 1654, three in 1655, three in 1656, three in 1658, two in 1659. Only three of these were men of any eminence, Gilbert Clerke, Malachi Thruston, and John Luke. Clerke was the first man ever nominated by the College

for the Proctorship. This was in October 1651. The
signatures affixed to his nomination tell us the constitution of the Society at that date. They are : "Ri. Minshull, Carolus Pendreth, Theoph. Dillingham, Edm.
Matthews, Elias Pauson, Fra. Quarles, Will. Welles,
Gilb. Clerke, Tho. Buckingham, Tho. Rolt." Clerke
was a really celebrated mathematician. Mr. Ball gives
this account of him in his *History of Mathematics at
Cambridge* (p. 39) :

"He lectured for a few years at Cambridge, but in 1655
was forced to quit the University by the Cromwellian
party. He had a small property in Norfolk, and lived
there till his death. His chief mathematical works were
the *De plenitudine mundi*, published in 1660, in which he
defended Descartes from the criticisms of Bacon and Seth
Ward ; an account of some experiments analagous to those
of Torricelli, published in 1662 ; a commentary on Oughtred's *Clavis*, published in 1682 ; and a description of the
'spot-dial,' published in 1687. He was a friend of
Cumberland and of Whiston. He died towards the end of
the seventeenth century."

Clerke was also an advocate of Unitarian principles,
and wrote an attack on Bishop Bull's *Defensio Fidei
Nicaenae*. Thruston, who was educated at Blundell's
School, entered the College in 1645, and was elected
Fellow in 1651 ; he afterwards became Fellow of Caius.
He was a physician of some celebrity, and took his
M.D. by royal Mandate in 1668. He wrote *Diatribe de
Respirationis usu primario*, a book much criticised by
another Sidney man, Sir George Ent. John Luke,
who became Fellow in 1654, was the second Proctor

nominated by the College. He was afterwards Fellow of Christ's and Professor of Arabic.

For about the first half of Minshull's Mastership— *i.e.*, the twenty-three years ending with 1666, the number of admissions were generally small. In eighteen of these years the number was under twenty ; in one year, 1649–50, it reached thirty-three ; in 1658–59 it was only seven. During the eight years 1666–74 there was a great improvement, the numbers being 38, 41, 31, 22, 31, 26, 29, 34. Then followed twelve lean years, 1674–86. In seven of these the number was below twenty ; in one year it was only six ; in another nine ; the highest entry being twenty-seven. These lists of Fellows in two different years during Minshull's reign are worth recording :

(1) October 1664. Edmund Matthews, B.D., John Luke, B.D., Richard Kitson, B.D., William Freer, M.A., Walter Brace, M.A., Joseph Moore, M.A., Anthony Nethercott, M.A., James Johnson, M.A., David Jenner, M.A., John Fuller, M.A.

(2) October 1679. Edmund Matthews, B.D., Joseph Moore, B.D., James Johnson, B.D., Thomas Goodlad, B.D., Thomas Fowler, B.D., William Scott, M.A., Joseph Craven, M.A., John Saunders, M.A., Samuel Richardson, M.A., Jeremy Priestley, M.A., Samuel Coyne, M.A., Walter Strange, M.A., John Abell, M.A.

During the Restoration time appointment by King's Mandate was very frequent. In 1660 James Johnson was admitted Fellow *ex Mandato Regio* in the room of Mr. Quarles. In 1661 " Mr. George Downing was admitted into a Coxwould fellowship by the K's

Mandate," and Thomas Freeman was made Clerke Fellow and afterwards Freestone Fellow " by vertue of the same authority." In the same year

" April 17. Ralph Barker was admitted into the place of George Downing *ex Mandato Regio*. May 3. George Downing was readmitted and Mr. Barker's letters revoked by the K's command."

In 1663 David Jenner and James Johnson, junior (afterwards Master) were admitted after the usual examination and election ; but in the same year John Fuller, son of the celebrated Thomas Fuller, was appointed by Royal Mandate. However, a memorandum in the *Acta Collegii* shows that some members of the Society were not prepared to submit tamely to the pleasure of the Merry Monarch. In fact John Fuller was only admitted thanks to the Master's casting vote.

" Jan. 21, 1663. Mr John Fuller was admitted Fellow by vertue of the King's mandate. Mr Luke protested against his admission in behalfe of Sr Green and Sr Sacket. The M^r, Mr Matthews, Mr Frere, Mr Brace, Mr Moore were for his present admission. Mr Luke, Mr Kitson, Mr Nethercot, Mr Johnson, Mr Jenner were for petitioning to the King for a free election."

With regard to another of the King's nominations some doubts or difficulties had arisen, as may be seen from this Order :

" Aprill 30th, 1663. Whereas it was the King's will and pleasure signified by his letters to the Maister and Fellowes of Sid. Suss. Coll. bearing date July 23, 1661, that Edward Condy, B.A., and student of the s^d Coll.

should forthwith be admitted into such Fellowship as was then vacant . . . the M^r and Fell. did admit him the s^d Edward Condy Aug. 3rd, 1661, and doe hereby declare that he was admitted into the s^d Fellowship."

From 1664 to 1670 seven Fellows were duly elected and admitted by the statutory process. In 1666 Edward Alston was put into John Fuller's place *virtute Mandati Regii*. In 1668 Thomas Fowler, and in 1672 Richard Reynolds were appointed Fellows by Royal Mandate; so also were John Grant and William Scott in 1673. With regard to Scott's admission the College was inclined to be rebellious. After prolonged dis- cussion, he was in 1674 induced by the College to acquiesce in this form of admission :

" By virtue of the King's Letters I admit you into a Fellowship of Sir John Hart's Foundation of this College to receive ten pounds per Annum, being the Allowance by his will, and four pounds and fourteen shillings or whatso- ever is due from Sir John Brereton's Gift annexed to that place ; but no dividend whatsoever mentioned in his Majestie's Letter aforesaid unlesse it doe appear by Law or Determination of the Visitors to be your Right."

We have more instances of appointment by Royal Mandate in 1675, 1679 and 1684. In 1676 and 1678 Abraham Channon and Jeremy Priestley were statutably elected ; but both of them died in College not long after election. There were eight other normal elections in the years 1676–86.

Several distinguished men, besides those already mentioned, were at Sidney under Minshull. John

Sterne, who was admitted in 1642, was a man of extraordinary ability. He is described in his epitaph as
Philosophus, Medicus, summusque Theologus. He was a
nephew of Archbishop Usher and a scholar of Trinity
College, Dublin. At the time of the Irish Rebellion he
fled from Ireland to Cambridge with his little brother
James, who joined the Perse School and entered Sidney
in 1645. John Sterne stayed at Cambridge for seven
years; during this time he collected materials for his
first book, *Animi Medela*, which he dedicated to Henry
Cromwell. Subsequently he went to Oxford, where he
received a warm welcome from Seth Ward. In 1656
we find him again in Ireland, as Fellow and Hebrew
Lecturer in Trinity College. In 1660 he became
Professor of Law, and in 1662 Professor of Medicine.
All this time he was practising as a leading physician in
Dublin. He is best known as the founder and first
president of the Irish College of Physicians, which
obtained its charter in 1667. It is said that he cared
much more for theological study than for his profession.
He died in 1669 at the age of 43.

Peter Pett, who entered in 1645, was the son of Peter
Pett, chief shipwright to Charles I. After taking his
B.A. he migrated to Pembroke, Oxford, and was afterwards elected Fellow of All Souls. In 1663 he was one
of the first batch of members of the Royal Society; but
he was expelled in 1675 for " not performing his obligation to the Society." It was thought, apparently, that
he gave too much attention to literary work of a
polemical character. He published books on *Trade,
Liberty of Conscience,* and other subjects. He also
practised as a barrister, sat in the Irish Parliament, and

was Advocate-General for Ireland, where he was knighted. He died in 1699.

Edmund Calamy, who entered in 1652, was the son of Edmund Calamy, the famous Nonconformist divine, and the father of another Edmund Calamy, well known as the biographical historian of Nonconformity. After taking his B.A. he migrated to Pembroke. He received Presbyterian ordination and spent most of his life in London, ministering to small congregations.

In 1658 Thomas Rymer was admitted. He was noted as a dramatic critic and still more as a historian. One of his first works was a play called *Edgar, or the English Monarch*, which was highly royalist in tone. Afterwards he devoted himself to the criticism of the drama. Pope describes him as "on the whole one of the best critics we have ever had." Later on he became interested in historical studies. In 1692 he was appointed Historiographer to the King. In this capacity he compiled his *Foedera* in sixteen volumes, a monument of patient industry, which has been invaluable to subsequent historians. He died in 1713.

John Thompson, afterwards first Baron Haversham, entered the College in 1664. He was made a baronet in 1673, and sat in the House of Commons from 1685 till 1696. He was an enthusiastic Whig, and took a leading part in inviting the Prince of Orange to come to England. In 1696 he was raised to the peerage, and was Lord of the Admiralty from 1699 to 1701. Taking offence at some action of the Government, he joined the Tories. In 1709 he vehemently opposed the impeachment of Sacheverel, and supported the cry of "the Church in danger." He died in 1710.

William Wollaston, who was admitted in 1674, and gained a scholarship, was the author of a very famous book, *The Religion of Nature delineated*. Mr. Leslie Stephen (*English Thought in the Eighteenth Century*, vol. i. p. 131) says that

"in his youth Wollaston suffered from the impecuniosity of himself and his nearest relatives, and turned the Book of Ecclesiastes into Pindarics in order to give vent to his feelings."

Curiously enough, Voltaire confused him with another Sidney man, Thomas Woolston, who was admitted in 1685. To the record of his entry a later hand has added these words: *Hic ille fuit Haereticus qui an. 1728-9 Salvatoris sui miracula palam oppugnare, immo et ludibrio habere non erubuit.* He was a Fellow, a great student of Origen, and an able, but very eccentric, writer. The names of Wollaston and Woolston are important in the literary history of the eighteenth century; we shall return to them hereafter.

Thomas Comber was admitted in 1658 at the age of fourteen; he afterwards became Dean of Durham. John Lamb, Dean of Ely, was admitted in 1664. In the following year Thomas Walker, who had been seven years at Charterhouse, entered as a Sizar; he afterwards gained a Fellowship and became Headmaster of his old school. John Billers, who was admitted in 1666, was afterwards Fellow of St. John's and Public Orator.

A few benefactions were received during Minshull's Mastership. In 1644 Richard Dugard, B.D., formerly Fellow, bequeathed to the College £120 to be employed for "some good permanent use," according to the dis-

cretion of the then Master and Fellows. He also left
£10 to buy books for the Library. In 1657 Charles
Pendreth, B.D., formerly Fellow, bequeathed effects to the
value of £83 8s. 5½d. for the use and benefit of the whole
Society. This legacy, together with that of Mr. Dugard,
which was not paid into the College Treasury till 1653,
was ordered by the College to be part of the sum paid
for the purchase of Evanis Hall at Polstead in Suffolk,
"and for charges since." In 1680 Downham Yeomans,
of the town of Cambridge, Dyer, bequeathed to the
College all his lands at Denston in Suffolk, and his
houses and lands at Stradishall in the same county, of
the annual value of £24, for the benefit of three Bedfordshire men, being Scholars of the College. Two
livings were also bequeathed to the College, the Vicarage
of Peasmarsh in Sussex, by John Gyles in 1654, and the
Vicarage of Wilshamstead in Bedfordshire by James
Riseley, of High Holborn, in 1649. The latter benefice
was afterwards exchanged for that of Week St. Mary in
Cornwall. Philip Stanhope, Earl of Chesterfield, gave
£100 to the Library.

The low state of the College finances at this time is
well illustrated by several Orders dealing with repairs
and the payments for them:

(1) "Febr: the 11th, 1670. It was agreed that the
Mason should provide tile and other necessaries for the
Library roofe aforehand and that the slate thereof should
be taken off and imployed to mend the roofe of the
Colledge hall and the north side and middle row of
building."

(2) "July 29th, 1671. The Mr and all the ffellowes at
home agreed that Mr Urlin should have these peices of

Plate, viz., M' Thomas Power's [and eight other Fellow-commoners'] Pots,* M' Calmady's broaken Boll, a broken Salt and two broken Spoones . . . weighing in all 191 ounces . . . for the summe of fourty-five pounds seventeen shillings and six pence, which have been laid out for tiling and other repaires of the Chappell roofe and thereabouts."

(3) "May 8, 1679. It was ordered by the Master and Fellowes of the Colledge that their old broken and bruised plates should be sold towards the new slating of the Colledge."

Then follows a list of the different pieces of plate with the names of the Fellow-Commoners who gave them concluding with "one spoon of Mr. Armstead's and six other broken spoons." After noting these indications of the poverty of the College Treasury, it is pleasant to record the following Order:

"Aug. 7, 1680. It was agreed and ordered by the Master and Fellows that ten pounds should be given to the Vice-chancellor towards the repairs and building of St. Paul's Church in London."

Minshull's financial management is severely criticised by a later Master, Dr. Parris:

"The purchase money (of the Evanis Hall estate) was in great part taken out of the Treasury and was what Dr. Ward by duly attending to the rights of it had been collecting all his life. But the rent of the estate instead of going to the Treasury was suffered, and is still suffered, tacitly to pass into the dividend of the Master and Fellows. This, considering their narrow circumstances at that time,

* All Fellow-Commoners were obliged to give £5 worth of plate to the College.

had been reasonable enough perhaps, if the other rights of the Treasury had been preserved ; but these too, one after another, went silently the same way, till scarce anything was left to the Treasury. I have no excuse for Dr. Minshull, the Master, who suffered all this, unless that by thrusting himself, as he had done, illegally into his office he was all his life long obnoxious and never his own master."

It would seem that Minshull had great difficulties in the management of his students. The wholesome discipline of the rod enjoined by the Statutes had fallen into disuse, wisely, perhaps, at a time when some of the students were armed with more effective weapons in the shape of swords and pistols. The College Order Book contains many instances of dissolute and violent conduct in his time. Here is a striking example:

"Aprill 15th, 1669. Memorandum. That William Butler Bach : Arts of the Second Year and Schollar of Mr. Peter Blundell's foundation having been divers times statutably admonished and not reforming his ill manners and having on the day of the date hereof for high mis-demeanours then committed been summon'd to appear before the Master and Fellowes and refusing to come, and with his sword and pistoll threatning some and assaulting others, was by the unanimous consent of the Master and Fellowes deprived of his Schollarshipp and expelled the Colledge."

Another B.A. espoused the cause of William Butler, " distempered himself with drinks and committed out-ragious insolences against the Dean in breaking his Windowes with Brick-batts," and " publickly defied all

K

the censures of the Society by throwing off his Gown."
He too was expelled.   In another case B.A.s are sufferers
from the violence of undergraduates, three of whom are
admonished by the Master "for being chiefe sticklers
in an assault made upon the Bachelers of Arts in the
buttries." Memoranda like the following are common
at this time:

"Richard Payton was Publickly admonished before the
M^r, Senr Fellow and Dean of the Coll. for Drunkenness,
intollerable Impudence, making a disturbance in the Town,
coming in after twelve o'clock and then making a disturbance in the Colledge, and very seldom in his chamber when
the Dean visited."

"Mathew Munday was out of the Coll. at the Dolphin
where he distempered himself by excessive drinking and
came not into the Coll. till 12 of the clock at night to the
disturbance of the same : as also the next night he was at
the same place till nine of the clock and came into the
Coll. distempered and did swear divers oaths that were
publickly heard ; for which fault he was solemnly admonished by the Master in the presence of the sen: fellow
and Dean : and ordered at the same time to read a publick
Recantation in the Hall."

The College appears to have been very long-suffering
in matters of discipline ; for shortly afterwards the same
Mathew Munday is again admonished for being "distempered with drinks and assaulting Wilson, sen^r
Sophister of this Coll., and other misdemeanours."
Three months afterwards being accused of throwing the
stone "which came in at Mr. Alston's study window and
was likely to have done him a mischief" and of keeping

unstatutable hours, he is assured that for the next
offence he "should be convented before the Society."

Another note refers to an impudent attempt by
undergraduates to commit a burglary at the Master's
Lodge. Minshull gives this account of the College
meeting on the subject:

"When we were met I declar'd unto them (*i.e.*, the
Fellows) the cause of my calling them, which was this. A
discovery was made to me of a robbery that was committed
in S^r [=Sophister] Charles Pym's chamber by Thornton
and Huggins; Woodall also (as he confessed to his Tutor)
knew of the same. Thornton also by the confession of
Huggins told Berry that Thornton had been with him
severall times to attempt the like upon the M^r; but he
would never consent to him nor for the world endeavour
it. Likewise Berry and Taylor senior were told by Avis
the Joyner last week that Thornton and Woodall had been
with him now and then above a quarter of a yeare to assist
them in the same, but he denied them; whereupon (as
Woodall confest to his Tutor) Thornton and Woodall
endeavoured the breaking open of my doore and cut the
holes which were found there, and Woodall told them since
that Thornton gave him money to buy the instrument with
which they did it. Upon this information the Society
procceded to the Expulsion of Huggins, Thornton and
Woodall, and expell'd they were the day above written by
unanimous consent."

Misconduct was not confined to the students. Witness this College Order of October 30, 1663:

"That Mr. Daniel Nailer having been diverse times
statutably admonished and not reforming his ill manners
being convented before the Master and Fellows hee was

deprived of his Fellowship by the unanimous consent of the said Master and Fellows whose names are here under-written."

Nor were the College servants without reproach. The Master writes this pathetic memorandum:

"William Beale our Cooke had an admonition given by me in the Hall after dinner before the Society for going away without leave and staying eleven dayes wandring whither we know not."

But this admonition did not suffice.

" Febr : 2, 1681.   William Beale had a publicke and his last admonition before the whole Society for his intoler-able extravagancies. 1683. He had another ultimate admonition."

The following Order goes to prove that the Fellows as a body were not given to excess :

" It was ordered by the M^r and Fellowes that whosoever shall hereafter be elected and admitted into a Fellowship in this Colledge shall (instead of the Supper which the new-elected Fellowes heretofore usually gave to the Society) pay forty shillings into the Maister's or the Steward's hands . . . to be layd out in bookes for the Colledge Library."

On December 30, 1686, Dr. Minshull died after a reign of forty-three years. The retention of his Mas-tership for so long in those dangerous days is a testimony more to his moderation than to his strength of character.

CHAPTER IX

AN INTERLOPER

AFTER the death of Dr. Minshull the College was the unfortunate victim of the University policy of James II., which is well explained by Burnet:

"The Jesuits fancied that, if they could get footing in the University, they would gain such a reputation by their methods of teaching youths, that they would carry them away from the University Tutors, who were certainly too remiss. Some of the more moderate among them proposed that the King should endow a new College in both Universities. . . . But either the King stuck at the charge which this would put him to, or his priests thought it too mean and below his dignity not to lay his hand upon these great bodies. So rougher methods were resolved on. It was reckoned that by frightening them they might be driven to compound the matter, and deliver up one or two Colleges to them ; and then, as the King said sometimes in the circle, they who taught best would be most followed. They began with Cambridge upon a softer point.* The King sent his letter, dated February 7th, 1687, to order Father Francis, an ignorant Benedictine Monk, to be received a Master of Arts ; once to open the way for letting them into the degrees of the University."

The cruel treatment of the Vice-Chancellor, which

followed this attempt at Cambridge, and also the King's tyrannical dealings with Magdalen College, Oxford, are well known through Macaulay's interesting narrative. Sidney was the Cambridge College singled out by James for a special exemplification of his policy. He took advantage of the opportune vacancy in the Mastership caused by Minshull's death. The Fellows were compelled, quite illegally by Royal Mandate, to admit to the Mastership Joshua Basset, B.D., of Caius. He was born in or about 1641, was admitted at Caius as a Sizar in 1657, and was elected a Fellow there in 1664. He had declared himself a Papist in January 1687, and the King dispensed him from taking the statutory oaths before his admission, which took place on March 7, 1687. The Fellows complained that he was thus "let loose upon them to do what he liked." Basset had made a name for himself by a successful attack on Mr. Spence of Jesus College, who had satirised the Roman Church in a speech before the University on November 5, and was compelled to make a public recantation in the Senate House. Afterwards Basset was looked upon as very crotchety in his religious views even by his Romanist friends. Dr. Craven, a later Master of Sidney, writing to Bishop Reynolds, also a Sidney man, says that he was "such a mongrell Papist, who had so many nostrums in his religion that no part of the Roman Church could own him." In the first year of his Mastership was published a book entitled *Reason and Authority, or the Motives of a late Protestant's Reconciliation to the Catholick Church.* This book is attributed to Basset in the Catalogue of the Bodleian Library; and there seems to be little doubt that it is his work.

At the new Master's instigation, the "Commissioners for Ecclesiastical Causes and the Visitation of the Universities" revised the Sidney Statutes, annulling all provisions against "Popery, Heresy, and Superstition"; also the promise to be made by the Master and Fellows to prefer the authority of the Scriptures before the opinions of men; and the clauses which forbad any election to be influenced by "mandates," "letters," &c. They also gave power to the Master to admit any students he wished without the consent of the Fellows. In one copy of the Statutes we find these alterations duly noted; they are stated to have been made *tempore Jacobi 2ᵈⁱ a Commissionariis Ecclesiasticis, Basset et aliorum Papistarum introducendorum causa.* The King addressed to the Master and Fellows this letter confirming the order of the Commissioners:

JAMES R.

James the Second, by the Grace of God, King of England, Scotland, France and Ireland, Defender of the Faith, &c. To our trusty and well-beloved the Mʳ and Fellows of Sydney-Sussex College in our University of Cambridge, & to their Successors, Greeting.

Whereas our Commissioners for Ecclesiastical Causes, & for the Visitation of the Universities, & of all & every Cathedral & Collegiate Churches, Grammar Schools, Hospitals & other the like Incorporations or Foundations & Societies, have thought it requisite to abrogate and abolish several Clauses in the Statutes of that our College, as by their Order, hereunto annexed, more fully appears: We having seen and considered the said Order, do, by these Presents, approve, ratifye & confirm the same, willing and requiring you to cause these Presents, & the

said Order to be entered in, and added to your Book of
Statutes; & for the time to come, to observe the same;
any order, constitution, statute or usage of the said College
to the contrary, in anywise notwithstanding : & for your so
doing, this shall be your Warrant.   Given at our Court of
Windsor the 2d Day of July 1687, in the 3d year of our
Reign.

By His Majesty's Command,

SUNDERLAND P.

The Fellows attempted, by petition and the interest of
friends, to obtain a reversal of these orders ; but in vain.
One of the Commissioners, Bishop Sprat, writing in
1688, says that he himself " absolutely resisted all the
alterations in the Statutes of Sidney College . . . for
the advantage of popish priests and students."

On November 5, 1687, the Master requested the Fellows
to omit the special service ordered for that day.   But
they stoutly refused.   Basset then locked up the Chapel
and " hindered Divine Service for that time."   He also
threatened that Popish services should be introduced
into the Chapel.   It has been stated that he actually
" set up the Mass " there; but this is untrue.   He fitted
up a private chapel of his own in the Master's Lodge.
Cole, writing in the next century, states that he had
met several Cambridge people who had heard Mass
there ; he adds that the altar-piece of Basset's Chapel
was left in the Lodge at his departure.   Cole saw it
many years afterwards hanging over one of the doors of
the " Audit-room " (now the Master's dining-room).

On November 7 William Thompson, Scholar of Caius,
was admitted a Fellow *secundum tenorem regiarum
literarum*.   On November 19 Valentine Husband, who

had been three years at Caius, was admitted *a Collegii magistro Joshua Basset, S.T.B. et sub illius tutela.* We may conjecture that these two were Basset's pupils at Caius, and Romanists. Only four other students were admitted during his Mastership. One of these, Samuel Taylor, who entered in July 1688, was afterwards a munificent benefactor to the College (see p. 174). Apparently no College Orders were made during Basset's time; but the Annual Officers were appointed as usual. Theophilus Pickering, who was elected a Fellow in 1686, was Steward and Ecclesiastical History Lecturer (October 1687) and Dean (October 1688). He was afterwards Canon of Durham and a liberal benefactor to the Church and the poor. Dr. Craven, who, as a Fellow, had had experience of Basset's rule, writes thus in 1726:

"As to his government, we found him a passionate, proud, and insolent man wherever he was opposed, which made us very cautious in conversing with him, who saw he waited for and catched at all occasions to do us mischief in what concerned our religion. I do not deny that he had learning and other abilities to have done us good; but his interest lay the contrary way."

In October 1688 Archbishop Sancroft and other bishops then in London petitioned the King that he would

"restore the Universities to their legal state and to their statutes and customs, . . . and that he would not permit any persons to enjoy any of the preferments in either University but such as are qualified by the statutes . . . of their several foundations."

Alarmed by the news of the coming of the Prince of Orange, whose fleet anchored in Torbay on November 5, James proceeded to a complete reversal of his University policy. He dissolved his Ecclesiastical Commission. The orders of the Commissioners with regard to the Sidney Statutes were rescinded in the following letter, which was sent to the Senior Fellow :

JAMES R.

Trusty and well-beloved, we greet you well. Whereas our late Commissioners for Ecclesiastical Causes & for the Visitation of the Universities, Colleges, &c., did make several Alterations in the Statutes of that our College, which said Alterations we did by an Instrument under our sign manual ratifye, approve of, & confirm; & whereas we are pleased to restore the Statutes of our said College, as they were before the said Alterations were made ; we do accordingly by these Presents rescind, revoke and annul, as well the said Decree, made by our said late Commissioners, as our said Instrument of Confirmation thereof: willing and requiring, that the Statutes of that our College be observed & pursued in all things, & to all intents & purposes as if the said Alteration had not been made : and we do also hereby authorise & empower you to proceed to the Election of a Master, Fellows, or other Officers of our said College, in the room of those who are not qualified by your Statutes ; any form, letter, order or directions to the contrary notwithstanding. And so we bid you farewell.

Given at our Court at Whitehall the first Day of December 1688, in the fourth year of our reign.

By his Majesty's command,

MIDDLETON.

On December 9 James Johnson, B.D., one of the Fellows, was unanimously elected Master. Basset had terminated his inglorious reign by absconding. He took his departure none too soon; immediately afterwards there was a No Popery riot in Cambridge. In Alderman Newton's diary we read under December 13, 1688:

"This night & several nights before there were upp in armes a great many in this Towne, some nights 2 or 300 (many scholars among them) of the rabble called the Mobile, who at first under a pretence to seek for papists & such who had favoured them & to ransack their houses for armes, at last came to be very insulting & wherever they pleased to enter men's houses & doe them much mischief."

Owing to his hurried departure Basset left most of his effects in the Master's Lodge. Later on he was in necessitous circumstances. One day, meeting his successor in London, he asked that his goods might be sent him from the College; Johnson answered the poor man roughly, threatening to inform against him as a popish priest if he did not abandon his claim. In 1713 Basset published *Ecclesiae Theoria Nova Dodwelliana Exposita*. An anonymous work of considerable importance, published in 1704, has been ascribed to him by competent authorities. It is entitled *An Essay towards a Proposal for Catholick Communion, by a Minister of the Church of England*. This book was thought worthy of republication a few years ago. Basset's financial circumstances never improved. He died in London in 1720. He was possessed of great gifts and excellent intentions; but his appointment to the Mastership of Sidney was a serious misfortune both for himself and for the College.

From a photograph by]

THE NEW COURT

[J. Palmer Clarke, Cambridge

CHAPTER X

DULL DAYS

" Happy the people whose annals are vacant ! " During the fifteen years of Dr. James Johnson's Mastership (December 1688 to December 1703), Sidney nearly attained to this blissful state. The new Master entered on the Vice-Chancellorship on November 4, 1699, and being a thoroughly jovial person (as his portrait testifies) gave orders for a grand University celebration of the new King's birthday.

In 1689-90 the College was saddened by two deaths from small-pox. Burke Brereton, who belonged to the family of our benefactor, Sir John Brereton, and had recently joined the College at the age of seventeen— *florentissima gemma*, as the Register says—*variolis correptus magno cum omnium maerore succubuit*. Out of respect for Sir John's memory, his young relative was buried in the College Chapel. A few months afterwards John Downe, Fellow and Praelector, fell a victim to the same disease. The ordinary number of admissions at this time was from fifteen to twenty. But in the year 1698-9 there is only one entry recorded in the Register; probably this was due to a serious epidemic of small-pox. The most distinguished man who joined the College in Johnson's time was

Richard Reynolds, afterwards Bishop of Lincoln. He was the son of Richard Reynolds, Rector of Leverington, and was admitted in 1689 at the age of fifteen, gaining a scholarship in the next year. Apparently he studied law for a time, for he migrated to Trinity Hall in 1694, and took his LL.B. in the following year. In 1701 he proceeded to the LL.D. from Sidney. Afterwards he took Orders and married a daughter of Bishop Cumberland of Peterborough. He became in succession Chancellor, Prebendary, and Dean of Peterborough. In 1721 he was made Bishop of Bangor, and in 1723 he was translated to Lincoln, which See he held till his death in 1744.

Johnson must have been a precise disciplinarian, if we may judge from the following entry concerning one of the few offences recorded by him :

"Sʳ Swan was admonished for frequent neglect of being at Chappel, particularly for absenting himself on the Lady's day, Palme Sunday, and other times, not being at Church that day."

The Master's will bears testimony to his kindness of heart. He bequeathed £1200 to the College for the purchase of livings, and his estates at Cherry-Hinton, near Cambridge, and Swine in Yorkshire for the maintenance of three or four " poor widdows of Clergymen who have been of the College "; "for want of such widdows" the rent of the estates is to go to Exhibitions for four orphans of clergymen. He left his estate at Higham for the augmentation of four specified livings as an encouragement to the incumbents to preach afternoon sermons on Sundays and catechise children ; for the furnishing of whom with Catechisms, Bibles, and books of devotion, he bequeathed to the College

"£100 to buy lands, and also £100 for lands for cloaths or coals for poor prisoners or widdows, at the discretion of the Master and Fellows."

In a codicil to his will he left to the College the advowson of the Rectory of Rempstone, near Lough-borough, on condition that within a year after his death the Society should "settle a catechist" to discharge that office in the College according to the Statutes. Unfortunately Dr. Johnson signed his will without witnesses, and the freehold estates at Cherry-Hinton, Swine, and Higham went to the heir-at-law. The College, however, purchased the Cherry-Hinton estate. In 1706 the College spent £350 of the legacy in the purchase of the living of South Kilvington in Yorkshire. In 1710 another sum of £350 was spent from the same source on the living of Swanscombe in Kent.

Bardsey Fisher, D.D., Rector of Newmarket and a former Fellow of the College, was elected Master on January 22, 1704. The portraits of this comfortable-looking divine and his handsome wife, painted by Kneller "in his best manner," still adorn the Master's Lodge. Fisher's reign was very uneventful. The only fact of any interest recorded in the Order Book during his time is the public expulsion of a student by order of the Vice-Chancellor and Heads.

"These are to require you to order the name of Remington to be cutt out of your college buttery tables forthwith, he being expell'd the University by us the Vice-Chancelour and Majority of the Heads of the Colleges.

" Witnesse our Hand, JOHN BALDERSTON, pro-can."

" The said order was executed in the Hall publickly in the presence of the Master, Fellows, and all the Scholars, May the 6th, 1707."

Fisher was Vice-Chancellor in 1705–6. As regards numbers, the College was fairly prosperous under his rule. In fact, the entries were now larger than at any other time during the eighteenth century. In 1709–10 there were twenty-two admissions; in 1714–15 the number fell to six. The usual entry during Fisher's Mastership was about ten.

The names of four sons of the celebrated William Wollaston (see p. 142) appear in the Admission Register at this time,—Charlton, the eldest son (admitted 1708), William, the second (1710), Francis, the third (1712), and John, the fifth (1715). Wollaston's loyalty to the College is very remarkable after the unjust treatment which he suffered there. His story casts a lurid light on the state of the College in his day. In his autobiography, which is printed in Nichols' *Literary Illustrations*, he acknowledges that he was treated well for four or five years, and that he had a reputation as a scholar which was in later years a " matter of amazement " to himself. After that he had " unjust usage and many more melancholy hours " than he ever had before. The trouble arose thus. One day, after he had taken his B.A. degree, he had to " answer in the Schools." A question was given him which seemed to require a " speech " in answer. This he tried

to shirk ; but some others, who said that they meant to
make speeches, prevailed on Wollaston to do the same
"contrary to the modesty of his nature."

"Speeches upon this occasion," he continues, "are jest-
ing and of the same nature with those of the *Tripos's* and
Prevaricators, as they are styled. Mine was something
merry, but I thought perfectly innocent. The misfortune
was that it pointed principally at a man that would bear
nothing, and at a story that, though it implied no wickedness, yet implied great folly and rendered him very
ridiculous ; and, more than that, he was the Dean of the
College and had some power to revenge himself. The
man immediately took fire, and his passion was not to be
extinguished. Not content to punish me in the usual
methods of the College, he suborned a parcel of illiterate,
scandalous fellows, that were already enemies on that
account to the best of my year, to blacken us all and especially me with lies and many stories that had not the least
foundation in truth. Some time after this when my
contemporaries began to look after preferments, there was
one who fixed his eye upon a Fellowship ; and he having,
by a certain transaction that I could tell, luckily got an
interest in one of the junior Fellows, a bawling driving
man, that man engaged for him most of the other junior
Fellows. This club of them determined, if possible, by
right or wrong, to remove all obstacles to the advancement
of their friend, of which, it seems, I was yet looked upon as
one of the greatest."

This " persecution " and " the perversion of all he said
and did " was successful. Wollaston never gained a
Fellowship. He took his M.A. and was ordained in
1681, and left Sidney in September of that year.

L

"The place I loved notwithstanding all unkindness. The way of living was regular and fixed, which suits with my temper; there was some freedom allowed among friends and contemporaries not to be found elsewhere. . . . I was going into the wide world quite in the dark as to my future circumstances. In short, no man ever carried a heavier heart from Cambridge than I did."

He gave vent to his sorrow in a " Pindaric " beginning thus :

When driven by the tyranny of Fate,
I left the banks of Cam and Muses' antient seat,
Loaded with grief I slowly went.

After leaving Cambridge, Wollaston was for some time an Assistant Master at King Edward's School, Birmingham. In 1684 he went to London "thirsting after repose and settlement," and " paid his addresses to a very amiable young lady who caught the small-pox and died just before their nuptials." Her lover wrote a graceful epitaph for her tomb, containing these words :

attraxit ad se amantem
W. W.
qui veniendo videndo victus
eam solam speravit uxorem.

In 1690, having come into a large property, he married a lady of fortune, and settled in Charterhouse Square. There, in the heart of the busiest city in the world, he lived a life of contemplation, never absent from home for a single night during thirty years. " His life," says Mr. Leslie Stephen, " approached that of a monastic student as nearly as is possible to a man who begets eleven children." In 1703 he printed a little Latin Grammar for the use of his family. Four of his boys, as has been mentioned, were sent to Sidney; they were all born and educated in Charterhouse Square. They were entered as Fellow-Commoners. Francis Wollaston followed his father's example and sent four sons to Sidney. Wollastons came to the College even to the fifth generation.

Joseph Craven, B.D., Senior Fellow, was elected to the Mastership on February 25, 1723. After a brief tenure of the office he died in December 1728. He was Vice-Chancellor at the time of George II.'s accession and took up the loyal address of the University, with the Chancellor, six bishops, and others. Craven's short reign was a very remarkable one in the literary history of Sidney.

In 1723 the eccentric Thomas Woolston (see p. 142) was Senior Fellow. For some time he had absented himself from College beyond the limit allowed by the Statutes. The Society " compassionating his case and judging it to be in some degree the effect of a bodily distemper," allowed him to go on receiving his dividends. Woolston, greatly put out at the view taken by the College, went up to Cambridge with the intention of convincing his colleagues that he laboured under no disorder. He now definitely refused to reside, and thus lost his Fellowship. It was at this time that he began to publish his *Free Gifts to the Clergy*; these volumes contain signs of incipient insanity. He gives out that Origen has said of him that he is " best skilled of any man in the spirit of prophecy." In 1727–30 he published his six *Discourses on the Miracles*, dedicated

to six bishops. He had now, it appears, become quite
mad with the love of allegorising, which he had imbibed
from much study of Origen. These discourses on the
Miracles, though not of any intrinsic value, were very
important in the literary history of the eighteenth
century on account of the "Woolstonian Controversy"
to which they gave rise; several pages in the library
catalogue of the British Museum bear witness to its
extent. The sale of Woolston's books was very large.
To Mr. Leslie Stephen he appears to be

"a mere buffoon jingling his cap and bells in a sacred
shrine, and his strange ribaldry is painful even to those
for whom the preternatural glory of the temple has long
utterly faded away."

Woolston was prosecuted for blasphemy. At his trial
in the Guildhall the poor man told the Lord Chief
Justice that it was very hard to be tried by a set of men
who were "no more judges of the subjects on which he
wrote than he himself was a judge of the most crabbed
points of law." He was fined £100 and imprisoned in
the King's Bench. Dr. Samuel Clarke made great
efforts to effect his release. But Woolston died in
prison, soon after his committal, in January 1733.

In 1724 was published the most famous work ever
written by a Sidney man,—William Wollaston's *Religion
of Nature Delineated*. The book had been privately
printed in 1722; it was addressed to " A. F. Esq.," in
answer to certain questions of his about Natural
Religion.

" I have printed a few copies of this *Sketch*," writes the
author, "not with any design to make it public, but merely

to save the trouble of *transcribing ;* being minded since I have made it, to leave it not only with you, but perhaps also with two or three other *friends ;* or, however, with my *Family* as a *private monument* of one that meant well. Tho as to the disposal and fate of it much will depend on your judgment and manner of acceptance."

In the preface to the 1724 edition * Wollaston thus explains his reasons for publishing the book :

" A few copies of this book, tho not originally intended to be published, were printed off in the year 1722. But, it being transcribed for the press hastily and corrected under great disadvantages, many *errata* and mistakes got into it, which could not all be presently observed. With a great part of them therefore still remaining four or five of the copies were given away ; and some more, taken from the printing-house, passed through hands unknown to the author, and he supposes were sold privately. There has, beside, been some talk of a piratical design upon it ; and if that should take effect, both it and he might suffer extremely. For these reasons he has thought fit to reprint it himself."

It is interesting to note that Benjamin Franklin, who was at this time working as a compositor in London, " set up " part of this edition. " I was employed at Palmer's," he says in his autobiography, " on the second edition of Wollaston's *Religion of Nature.*" Ten thousand copies of the book were sold in a few years,— an enormous sale for the eighteenth century. Pope in one of his letters says sarcastically that it was a

* Mr. Alfred Worthy, of Cambridge, has recently presented to the Sidney Library a copy of this edition, which once belonged to Dr. Isaac Watts and, before that, to our own Thomas Twining.

great favourite with the ladies. As a matter of fact, it was a really important philosophical work.* Very soon after the publication of the *Religion of Nature* Wollaston broke his arm. He was at the time in very poor health, and this accident hastened his end, which came in October 1724. Before his death he burnt several treatises as being " short of that perfection to which he desired and had intended to bring them." Some of his manuscripts which escaped the flames bore testimony to the extent of his learning, especially in Semitic languages and antiquities.

Another Sidney philosopher of this time was John Gay, who was elected Fellow in 1724. His short career as a College officer is an extraordinary one, and it illustrates the remarkable way in which the annual College offices changed hands at Sidney. Gay must have been a most versatile person. In five years he held all offices except the Mastership. In 1725 he was Steward, Keeper of the Common Chest, Hebrew Lecturer, and Catechist; in 1726, Praelector, Hebrew Lecturer, Ecclesiastical History Lecturer, and Catechist; in 1727, Dean, Hebrew Lecturer, and Greek Lecturer; in 1728, Hebrew Lecturer and Mathematical Lecturer; in 1729, Praelector and Hebrew Lecturer.

---

* " Wollaston's theory of moral evil, as consisting in the practical contradiction of a true proposition, closely resembles the paradoxical part of Clarke's doctrine, and was not likely to approve itself to the strong common sense of Butler; but his statement of happiness or pleasure as a 'justly desirable' end at which every rational being 'ought' to aim, corresponds exactly to Butler's conception of self-love as a naturally governing impulse; while the ' moral arithmetic,' with which he compares pleasures and pains, and endeavours to make the notion of happiness quantitatively precise, is an anticipation of Benthamism."—H. Sidgwick, *History of Ethics*, p. 195.

During these years he was also the leading Tutor in the College. In 1731 he published a *Dissertation concerning the fundamental principle and immediate criterion of virtue*, which attracted considerable attention.

In July 1724 William Pattison, the "Sidney poet," entered the College. He was the son of William Pattison of Peasmarsh in Sussex, and was educated at Appleby School. After the register of his admission these words were subsequently added:

Idem in lucem edidit versus quosdam lingua vernacula conscriptos, qui felicem satis ingenii venam indicarunt, bonum que olim augurati sunt poetam. At juvenem carmina famamque meditantem (sic Deo visum est) "abstulit atra dies et funere mersit acerbo."

Academic life seemed to Pattison most irksome. For a time he consoled himself by his devotion to poetry and fishing. He loathed the Disputations of the Schools; these lines express his resentment at being carried off thither by some of his studious friends:

As the brute world to father Adam came,
Requesting with inquiring looks a name,
To every beast a title he assign'd
And nominated all the sylvan kind.
So savage multitudes about me throng;
Did Adam's talent but to me belong!
Yet though they cheat the world by their disguise,
They are but *asses* to poetic eyes.

The friend to whom he addressed his *Epistle from Cambridge* says that "even at school an early fondness for Ovid's *Epistles* began to dawn in his breast," and "that as to a new translation he knew none more equal to the undertaking." His poems, which are printed in the eighth volume of the *Poets of Great Britain* along with those of Pope, Gay, Savage, and others, are, many of them, thoroughly Ovidian in character. His description of *College Life*, written in the artificial style of the time, is interesting. Here are some extracts from it:

> Wak'd by the promise of a day we rise,
> And with our souls salute the dawning skies;
> All summon'd to devotion's fane repair,
> And piously begin the day with prayer;
> Thence, led by reason's glimmering light, descry
> The dark recesses of philosophy;
> Through classic groves the wily wanton trace,
> And logically urge the puzzling chase.
>
> But when the sounds of the presaging bell
> Noon's pleasurable invitation tell,*
> Moods, methods, figures swim before my sight,
> And syllogisms wing their airy flight.
> Confus'd the fairy vision flits away,
> And no ideas but of dinner stay. . . .
>
> Now those whom recreating toils invite,
> Pour'd on the plain, indulge their lov'd delight:
> Now flies aloft in air the whirling ball,
> Anxious the learned rabble waits its fall;
> Pursu'd by wafting caps the fury flies,
> Rises in height and lessens in the skies.

---

* We have seen that in the early days of the College the dinner-hour was 10; it was now 12; by the end of the eighteenth century it was 3.

Thus healthfully refresh'd we leave the plain,
For pleasure oft repeated is but pain.
Now we survey the vast capacious ball,
And take long journeys o'er the learned wall;
Or from her tender birth Britannia trace,
And all her glories center'd in great Brunswick's
race.

.   .   .

Now to the Muse's soft retirement fly,
Or soar with Milton or with Waller sigh;
Each fav'rite bard o'erpays my curious view;
For who can fail to please who charms like you?

To find us thus, Apollo takes his way
To sooth the sultry labours of the day;
The tuneful Muses charm his list'ning ears,
And in soft sounds he bears away his cares.
Thus, dearest Florio, thus, my faithful friend,
In learned luxury my time I spend.

Pattison soon grew utterly tired of the restraints of
College life. He foolishly quarrelled with his Tutor,
John Bell, whose rigour, he tells us, "was not easy to
brook." Owing to "threats of expulsion," Pattison cut
his name out of the Butteries. In thoughtless gaiety
he left Cambridge for London, having pinned to his
gown this apology for his unceremonious departure:

Whoever gives himself the pains to stoop
And take my venerable tatters up,
To his presuming inquisition I
In loco Pattisoni thus reply :
Tir'd with the senseless jargon of the gown,
My master left the college for the town;

Where from pedantic drudgery secur'd,
He laughs at follies which he once endur'd ;
And scorns his precious minutes to regale
With wretched college wit and college ale.
Far nobler pleasures open to his view,
Pleasures for ever sweet, for ever new.
Bright wit, soft beauty, and ambition's fire
Inflame his bosom and his muse inspire ;
While to his few, but much endearing friends
His love and humble service he commends.

Pattison's Sidney friends were much concerned at his departure. They urged him to return, or, at least, to send an apology to the Master and Fellows. He consented to apologise, but did not return to College. Benjamin Wase, a Shrewsbury boy, who was in Pattison's year at Sidney, wrote thus:

"I advise you to send a decent epistle to the Master with an impartial account of ill treatment which you have met with under Bell ; display therein his *severe usage* in moving terms, and urge that he was the chief cause of your *abrupt departing hence*. Bell is not as yet returned ; the Fellows begin in an open manner to complain of his *misbehaviour* to them and *dishonesty* to his creditors ; they have met together twice to consult some means of redressing the *grievance* of college *servants* and *others*."

In another letter Wase says :

"Bell threatens to give you trouble ; but on what score is unknown to me. He seems exceedingly incensed at your leaving college counter to his permission, . . . and takes no small pains to enumerate in emphatical words what mighty services he has done, and what vast kindnesses he always showed you whilst in College. He opened his books to my view yesterday morning, wherein I perceive you stand indebted to him, all matters justly calculated, but for a mere trifle; for he has your *caution-money* in his custody, being ten pounds, and exhibition money, &c., to receive on your account; all which will near amount to a complete disbursement of himself, &c."

Another friend, however, asserted that he " knew of no severities from his Tutor but what were necessary to make him sensible of his doings." His biographer adds that

" the apology which he made to avert the reproach of expulsion met with a reception very favourable. . . . So unwilling was the Society to lose him that his exhibition was kept in suspense for some time in expectation of his return to College."

His friends pressed him to come back. Pattison replied to Wase, " I will be at Cambridge by next *Division*, for I am afraid I cannot dispatch affairs before." Evidently he never meant to return. His voluptuous nature was already too fascinated with the delights of London life. " I meet every day," he says, " with very great encouragement among persons of distinction, and, in short, live so happily, that I begin to be in love with the town." He made the acquaintance of Pope, to whom he addressed an *Epistle*, and who promoted the subscription to Pattison's *Miscellany* of poems, which was projected to save him from starvation. At last he was in the direst straits, as may be seen from this miserable letter:

"If you was ever touched with a sense of humanity, consider my condition; what I am, my proposals will inform you ; what *I have been*, Sidney College in Cambridge can witness; what *I shall be* some few hours hence, I tremble to think—spare my blushes—I have not enjoyed the common necessaries of life these two days."

He found a friend in Mr. Curll, the famous bookseller, who took him into his house early in June 1727. Pattison died in the following month.

"Though the small-pox," says his biographer, "contributed to deprive us of so great a genius, yet it was his dying declaration ; *His heart was broke, through the misfortunes he had fallen under ;* which I wish I could not say were wholly owing to himself."

On January 17, 1728, Walter Chambre, B.D., was elected Master. He was a former Fellow and now held the College living of South Kilvington. Our Register states that, in a letter sent from Kilvington on February 1, Mr. Chambre *magistratu se abdicavit.* He was probably very comfortable in his Yorkshire Rectory, and had no ambition to preside over a College, which, as we shall see, was now by no means in a prosperous state.

A fresh election to the Mastership was necessary ; on February 12 the choice of the Society fell on John Frankland, D.D., Dean of Gloucester, a former Fellow. He was not admitted till April 18. On November 4 he entered on the Vice-Chancellorship. While Master he was appointed to the Deanery of Ely, which was, of course, much more convenient than Gloucester for a Cambridge Head. He died in the summer of 1730.

The admissions during Frankland's three years numbered 8, 9, and 14; but among these 14 were no less than six Oxford Graduates, who joined the College merely to take an *ad eundem* degree,—a frequent practice at this time; of the remaining eight, three were Eton boys.

Two College Orders of Frankland's time present a dismal picture of tottering buildings and financial depression:

(1) "Nov. 7, 1729. Whereas the College of the Lady Frances Sidney Sussex in the University of Cambridge is at present in a ruinous condition as to its buildings, which cannot be put into tolerable repair without very great charge & expence, & whereas there are great arrears of Rent due to the same, part of which will in all probability never be recover'd, & whereas it is at present engaged in a tedious and expensive Lawsuit concerning Sr Francis Clarks foundation, whereby £140 per Annum are not only detain'd from it, but is likewise oblig'd to be at great charges in carrying on the said Lawsuit, we the Master & Fellows of the same by a power committed to us by the 19th statute of the said College, do agree, order & determine that the fellowship of the foundation now vacant by the resignation of Mr. Harrison shall not be fill'd up or chose into (untill the affairs of the College shall so alter as to make it reasonable to take off this suspension), and that in the mean time twenty pounds each Audit [*i.e.*, half-yearly] shall be paid out of the profits of the said fellowship into the treasury in order to defray the necessary expences of the said College, & the payment of the first £20 to be made at this Audit being Mich. Audit 1729. J. Frankland, Ric. Allin, J. Adams, J. Taylor, J. Gay, R. Read, W. Murdin, Fran. Sawyer Parris."

(2) " May 7, 1730. In consideration of the ruinous and miserable condition our College is in as to its buildings, which cannot be put into sufficient repair by the ordinary method of College expences, we the Master and Fellows of the same do agree to borrow the sum of two hundred pounds . . . and to repay the same by twenty pounds each Audit for the space of six years . . . and we do further agree that the College Seal be fix'd to a Bond given by the College to Frederick Frankland, Esqr, of Westminster. . . ."

On September 15, 1730, John Adams, B.D., one of the Fellows, was elected Master; he held the office for sixteen years. He was Vice-Chancellor in 1735–36. The chief event of his Mastership was the receipt of the Taylor bequest, which in after years proved a most valuable accession to the College endowments. Samuel Taylor, of Dudley, a former student (see p. 153) died in 1732, bequeathing to the College houses and land at Dudley and some other property, of the clear annual value of £60, on condition that the Master and Fellows should from time to time apply the profits thereof for the establishing of a Fellowship in the College and for the maintenance of a person learned in the Mathematics; the person so elected to pursue his studies in all kinds of Mathematical Learning. This learning the Testator "apprehended to be of publick benefit and observed in his time to be much neglected in the College." The person appointed is once every week at least to read a Mathematical Lecture to the students of the College and of any College of the University who shall please to come. It is further directed that

" if any money should hereafter be raised out of the estate from any coal or other mine upon it, the produce be applyed, first, in making good any deficiency in the rent of the said estate by working the said mines, and then to the maintenance and education of one or more such students of the College as shall principally apply themselves to the study of the Mathematics."

Doubts having arisen whether the establishment of the Fellowship desired by Mr. Taylor was consistent with the Statutes which required all the Fellows to apply themselves to the study of Divinity, application was made to Chancery for leave to institute a Lectureship instead of a Fellowship. This was granted. Subsequently the College passed this Order:

"March 28, 1740. Whereas it is appointed by Mr. Taylor's will as explained and confirmed by Decree in Chancery that his Lecturer shall read one Lecture at least in every week throughout the year; it is agreed by the Master and Fellows that, provided the said Lecturer do read three Lectures in every week during the three several Terms of the University, he may be at liberty to discontinue his said Lectures in non-Term."

The first Taylor Lecturer was the well-known Mathematician, John Colson of Emmanuel, Lucasian Professor. He was appointed in 1739 and held the lectureship till his death in 1760.

The payment for repairs in the Master's Lodge was frequently a bone of contention between the Master and Fellows. Complaint was made against Adams, because he had incurred considerable charges in this way without the consent of the College, notwithstanding the wretched state of its finances. Accordingly this Order was passed:

" Oct. 21, 1734. It is agreed by the Master and Fellows that for the future the College shall not be liable above fifteen shillings each half year for work done within the Lodge without the consent of the Society first obtained for the doing of the said work."

Financial depression did not prevent the College from giving a striking proof of its loyalty at the time of the rising of the Young Pretender. On September 21, 1745, Charles Edward won the battle of Preston Pans, and then pursued his victorious career as far as Derby, which he reached on December 4. It was at this exciting time that the Society passed the following Order:

" Nov. 29, 1745. Agreed by the Master & major part of the Fellows of Sidney College that one hundred pounds be advanced out of the College Treasury for the service of his Majesty on occasion of the present unnatural rebellion."

This is signed by the Master and nine Fellows.

The most distinguished Fellow of Adams' time was John Garnett, who migrated from St. John's in 1728 and gained a scholarship in the same year. He took his degree in 1729 and was elected Fellow in 1730. He was appointed Praelector and Greek Lecturer in 1733, Hebrew Lecturer in 1735, and Dean in 1734 and 1737. In 1749 he published a *Dissertation on the Book of Job*, of which Dr. Richard Garnett writes:

" The author's theory, by which the book of Job is referred to the period of the Captivity, and the patriarch regarded as the type of the oppressed nation of Israel, is remarkably bold and original for a divine of the eighteenth century. The execution is unfortunately in striking contrast, being prolix to a degree which would have taxed all Job's patience and surpasses ours."

In 1751 Garnett went to Ireland as Chaplain to the Lord-Lieutenant, and in the following year he was made Bishop of Ferns; in 1758 he was translated to Clogher. He died in 1782. He is described as

"a prelate of great humility and a friend to literature and religion. Though he had but one eye, he could discern men of merit."

Francis Sawyer Parris, B.D., one of the Fellows, was elected Master on August 20, 1746. He became Vice-Chancellor on November 4 in the following year. He was a man of very great industry, and must have been very useful as Principal Librarian * of the University, to which office he was appointed in 1750. We still possess his MS. account of our College Endowments, a very thorough piece of work. He was also the author of a valuable compilation dealing with University history, of which Dyer writes thus in the Introduction to his *History of Cambridge*:

"The principal of my sources are two MS. volumes, in quarto, entitled 'An Index to Hare's Collections of the Charters and Privileges of the University, from the earliest time, together with a Collection of Statutes, Graces, Decrees of Heads, Interpretations of Statutes, and King's Letters, from the year 1570, when Elizabeth's Statutes were first given, to the middle of the last Century, made from the Vice-Chancellors' and Proctors' Books, and from

---

* In 1845 the two offices of *Bibliothecarius Publicus* and *Protobiblio-thecarius* were united.

M

the Grace Books and other Records of the University, and since revised and corrected with some care; signed and written by F. S. Parris, 1735.' "

We have an entertaining record of the receipt by the Master of a "Valentine," which he did not at all appreciate; the sender was a junior Fellow:

"Mem. Ap: 22, 1747. At a meeting of the Society in the College Parlor, viz: The Master, Mr. Allin, Mr. Barnes, Mr. Walter, Mr. Wood, Mr. Bell, the Master made complaint against Mr. Wood for writing & sending to him on or about the 14th of Feb: last a false, scandalous, & abusive Letter, directed *To the Master of Sidney College;* which Letter was produced & read before Mr. Wood, who did not deny his writing and sending the same."

Mr. Wood had to eat humble pie. He consented to make public acknowledgment of his offence and to beg pardon for the same,

"promising for the future to carry myself towards the Master and all others with more decency & respect; and I do consent that this my recantation & submission be publickly read in Chapple after evening service in my name & in my presence."

To show the Master's magnanimity, it is added that

"the Master has consented at the particular request of Mr. Wood not to publish the above recantation in Chapple, Mr. Wood giving no provocation of the same kind for the future."

The curious ceremony of a recantation in Chapel was performed many years afterwards by an undergraduate, who, for misbehaviour in Chapel, "is ordered not to miss Chapel, Gates, Hall, or Lectures till Trinity Sunday next inclusive, and also ordered to speak an English Composition after Evening Prayers on Thursday the 5th of May on the Nature of his offence."

In 1749 two students were very unruly;

"having a second time made great disturbances in the College, and, contrary to the order of Mr. Barnes, Locum tenens in the absence of the Master, to keep their chambers, appeared abroad, taken their names off the Buttery board, put off their gowns, and shewn themselves so about the town, they were publickly sent away by the Master with the approbation of the Fellows."

During Parris's Mastership the College was still deep in the slough of financial depression. It was necessary to suspend several Fellowships in order to carry out some indispensable repairs.

"Oct. 1, 1746. Agreed by the Master & the major part of the Fellows to continue the vacancy of the Foundation Fellowship, late Mr. Parris's, beyond the time ordinarily allowed by our Statutes, for the necessary reparation and decent refitting of the College Hall."

In 1748 it was agreed to suspend two more vacant Fellowships "both for repairing and refitting the College Hall, and for other repairs, particularly of the drain." The Fellowships already kept vacant for the former purpose had not proved sufficient, and there was no money in the Treasury for the latter. This the Society "consents to the rather, as there are none of our College of six years standing & fit to fill the said vacancys." It appears that in this year and for several years afterwards there were never more than three or four Fellows in residence. In the same year, 1748, it was ordered that " in consideration of the great decrease in the value of money " the students' payments *in usus Collegii necessarios* be increased ; and that the Chamber rents be applied to the Treasury. It was also agreed " for the speedier fitting up of the College Hall and other necessary repairs " to borrow the sum of £400, " interest and principal to be repaid again out of money arising from the Fellowships kept vacant." In 1749 yet another Fellowship was suspended ; the state of the College Gateway being mentioned as the reason in addition to the repairs of the Hall and drain ; and again " there is no one of our College fit to fill the said vacancy." In 1752 there were only five Fellows in all.

The restoration of the Hall was completed before 1753 ; for Carter writing in that year says that " the Hall was wholly repaired and beautified within these two years, and is a grand apartment." The flat ceiling and the music gallery were introduced at this time, and the Hall assumed the Italian character which has not been altered since. The position of the Gateway, as shown in Loggan's print, was not changed ; but it was replaced by one of classical design, which in its turn was removed and now forms the entrance to the Fellows' Garden near All Saints' Church.

In April 1756 another Fellowship was suppressed ; but at the same time it was agreed " to fill one of the Fellowships kept vacant for extraordinary repairs at Christmas next." The College now begins to be surprisingly generous.

From a photograph by]

THE HALL

[J. Palmer Clarke, Cambridge

"Mar. 24, 1757. Mem. At a meeting of the Society it was agreed unanimously to allow the Cook out of the Treasury or Coll : Stock one shilling a week towards the wages of a Skull in the Kitching."

This is the last College Order recorded by Dr. Parris. The next, in Dr. Elliston's handwriting, is dated December 11, 1760.

In Parris's time the number of students was very small, as indeed it was during most of the eighteenth century. The number of residents, including Fellows, was now generally about forty ; but then it must be remembered that throughout the University the numbers were small, the total on the Boards being only 1500 at this time.

In 1755 the College received £1000, a legacy from Sir John Frederick, which was appropriated to the College Fund for purchasing livings. Dr. Parris bequeathed £400 for the same purpose. Out of this fund in 1765 the College bought for £1400 the advowson of the Rectory of Gayton in Northamptonshire. In 1753 William Barcroft, Rector of Kelvedon, a former Scholar of the College, gave £50 "for glazing and beautifying the College Chappell." In the following year he gave £400 for founding an Exhibition in the College for a clergyman's son or orphan ; in 1755 he gave another £400 for the same purpose. In 1776 Thomas Lovett, a former Scholar, left £2000 for founding two Exhibitions for sons of clergymen in Priest's Orders " duly qualified for such Orders by having taken a regular degree either at Oxford or Cambridge." Successful candidates must engage to enter into Deacon's

Orders at the age of twenty-three years. Preference is
to be given to scholars from Grantham and Oakham
schools. Mr. Lovett's legacy was laid out in the
purchase of land at Melton Mowbray, producing about
£80 per annum. Curiously enough, this is the present
rent of the Lovett estate.

During Parris's reign Sidney did remarkably well in
the Tripos. In 1748 John Cranwell was Second
Wrangler; in 1751 William Byrch was Eighth; in
1752 Robert Ravald was Third; in 1754 William
Nesfield was Second; in 1758 George Wollaston was
Second. George Wollaston was the fourth son of
Francis Wollaston (see p. 160) and grandson of the
famous William. He was admitted in 1753 along with
his brother, William Henry. They were both educated
at Charterhouse. The two elder brothers, Francis and
Charlton, entered in 1748. Francis was afterwards
Rector of Chislehurst and Precentor of St. David's.
Nichols says that Charlton Wollaston was " one of the
most admired physicians of his day and sure of dis-
tinguished eminence," if he had not been cut off by a
fever before he was forty. George Wollaston became a
Fellow in 1758, and succeeded John Colson as Taylor
Lecturer in 1760; he lived till 1826.

In December 1755 that excellent scholar, Thomas
Twining, entered the College. He is described in the
Register as *filius natu maximus Daniclis Twining Theae
Mercatoris* (= Tea-dealer). Having been sent into his
father's business, Thomas was very unhappy; for " his
passion for books, provided they were not books of
business," had manifested itself. Accordingly he was
allowed to leave that celebrated Tea house. In 1756 he

was elected to a Scholarship. He graduated in 1760 as a Senior Optime; he was a candidate for the Classical Medals, and, though not successful, he gained, according to his brother Richard, "upon his examination a high degree of credit." Certainly this was as much as could be expected of him; for, being intended for business, he had been sent to a small school near his home at Twickenham. His contemporaries placed him in the first rank of classical scholars. Writing many years afterwards to his nephew Daniel, Thomas Twining gave these reminiscences of his Sidney life:

" If any young person is disposed to abuse the liberty of a college life, there is hardly any kind of vice or folly that he has not in his power to practise, if he chooses it. It is a wide and common field; the gates all wide open and the fences (now I fear) almost all thrown down, and even while some of them remained standing, they were easily climbed over. A man must have the *murus aëneus* in his own breast; and so as much brass in your inside, and as little in your face, my dear, as you please. I think in college it used to be the fashion in my time to wear it chiefly upon the face. . . . If in the course of your studies you should meet with difficulties, . . . I shall have a particular pleasure in giving you any assistance in my power. It is an opportunity that I often wanted and wished for when I was a young student, but never had. I was obliged to fight my way through thick and thin *proprio Marte*, the only sort of Mars a Twining is constructed to have anything to do with."

Thomas Twining was elected Fellow in December 1760, the year of his degree. He must have been a singularly

charming accession to that small society. To his other
accomplishments he added great musical gifts.

"My brother's ˙musical talent," says Richard, "discovered itself at a very early age, and it met with
encouragement from his father, who was himself a performer, though by no means a distinguished performer,
on the violoncello and the organ. . . . My brother performed extremely well upon the organ before he went to
Cambridge, and during his residence there bore a con-
spicuous part in the oratorios and at other musical
meetings."

On the Apple-roaster in the Sidney Combination Room
Twining wrote this *jeu d'esprit* after the manner of
Linnæus, whose mongrel terminology he abhorred :

"MELOPTEUM stanneum, monopum, versatile ; *seu* Ap-
plé-ro-aster. *Corpore* versatili, circumactili ; fossulis stan-
neis, melo-decis, parallelis, intus distincto : *Cacumine*
fastigiato, suggrundiato ; *Latere* uno pendulo, circumjectili,
ambidextro, tinnitu crebro gaudenti ; alteris fixis, bullatis.
Habitat in Conclavi Combinatorio seu Combibatorio Collegii Sidney-Sussex in Academia Cantabrigiensi."

His colleague, Thomas Martyn, tells us that the *wycked
wyghte*, who was the author, and who had afforded him
" many hours of rational pleasure and innocent cheer-
fulness," used " to lounge in my College rooms and read
Linnæus's works and question me much about them."

But Fellows' Parlour and Apple-roaster were soon to
know T. T. no more. Before going to Cambridge he
read with Mr. Palmer Smythies of Colchester, whose
daughter Elizabeth used to study Latin and Greek

along with Twining, special attention being devoted to the conjugation of *amo*. And now he was able to write in the first page of an account book : "ELIZABETH TWINING, January 21, 1764. *illi sint omnia curae et juvet in tota me nihil esse domo.*" The happy pair settled at Fordham, near Colchester, of which parish Twining had the sole charge; they lived in Fordham parsonage for nearly thirty years. Twining's great literary work was his *Translation of Aristotle's Treatise on Poetry, with notes and two dissertations on Poetical and Musical Imitation* (1789). Dr. Samuel Parr, who, when at Colchester, saw a great deal of Twining, wrote these words in his presentation copy of the Aristotle :

" The gift of the author whom I am proud and happy to call my friend, because he is one of the best scholars now living, and one of the best men that ever lived."

To Richard Twining Dr. Parr wrote after the death of Thomas :

" M' Twining, no critic of his day excelled your brother Thomas; he understood Greek and Latin, and he wrote perfect English. I have many letters of his, and they are most precious in my sight."

Many of Twining's delightful letters may be seen in *Recreations and Studies of a Country Clergyman*, and in *Selections from Papers of the Twining Family*. He died in 1804 at Colchester, where he held the Rectory of St. Mary's during the last years of his life.

The year 1758 was a very remarkable one in the

annals of the College. The buildings had now been completely restored, and the suspension of Fellowships might well cease. There were now only four Fellows. On April 27 the six vacant places were filled up. Only two members of the College were regarded as fit for Fellowships, Samuel Harness and George Wollaston. So four distinguished aliens were elected,—William Elliston, of St. John's, Fourth Wrangler in 1754; John Hey, of St. Catharine's, Eighth Wrangler in 1755; Owen Hughes, of Jesus, who just escaped the " Wooden Spoon " in the same year; and Thomas Martyn, of Emmanuel, who was a Senior Optime in 1756. We shall see that of these four one (Elliston) became Master of the College, and two (Hey and Martyn) Professors in the University. Martyn had been disappointed in his hopes of winning a Fellowship at Emmanuel, where two persons from the same county could not be Fellows at the same time. A son of the Master, a native of Middlesex, Martyn's county, had been recently elected, so there was no room for Martyn at his own College. In January 1758 Martyn received this letter from his Tutor at Emmanuel :

" An affair for your advantage has been under consideration these two months, and seems now to be drawing towards a conclusion. . . . I can now venture to ask whether you would accept of a Fellowship at *Sidney*. The Fellowships require a good deal of residence, which possibly may not be disagreeable to you, who, if I am not mistaken, do not dislike an University life. Some knowledge of Hebrew is necessary ; the rest of the examination is usually in Philosophy, Aristotle's Rhetoric, some part of the first six books in Homer, and Virgil's Georgics. . . .

I have nothing further to say than to desire your answer to this proposal, as soon as you have well considered it; and to assure you that, had your county been open here, you would have been the last person that should have been recommended to another College by your affectionate tutor and friend, H. HUBBARD."

In October 1758 the annual College offices were entirely filled by the new Fellows. Elliston was elected Steward and Keeper of the Chest; Hey, Praelector and Greek Lecturer; Hughes, Dean and Ecclesiastical History Lecturer; Harness and Wollaston, *Sublectores*. Early in 1760 Elliston and Hey were appointed joint Tutors. The old tutorial system had now become obsolete; and for many years to come we shall find the tutorship held jointly by two of the Fellows. On May 1, 1760, Dr. Parris died at the age of fifty-six. He had been a good Head of the House during a very difficult time.

CHAPTER XI

ELLISTON'S MASTERSHIP

William Elliston was elected Master on May 8, 1760. Strange to say, the government of the College had now fallen entirely into the hands of novices; for the four Fellows of the old stock went out of residence in 1760, two of them to take College livings. In 1761 four new Fellows were elected; of these the best known is John Lettice (see p. 219). The Master and John Hey held the tutorship together till 1763. From that year till 1774 Hey and Thomas Martyn served as joint Tutors. The bond was dissolved by Martyn's marriage. Hey continued as Tutor till 1779, with another distinguished man, Christopher Hunter, as his colleague. Richard Hey,* in a notice of his brother John in the *Gentleman's Magazine* for April 1815, states that when Tutor he gave lectures on Moral Philosophy which were attended "by several persons voluntarily, amongst whom were the late Mr. Pitt and other persons of rank," besides those students whose presence was required. In 1780 he was elected the first Norrisian

---

* Richard Hey, who was Third Wrangler and Senior Classical Medallist in 1768, migrated from Magdalene to Sidney after taking his degree, and was elected Fellow in 1775. His dissertations on the *Pernicious Effects of Gaming*, on *Duelling*, and on *Suicide* were highly thought of.

Professor of Divinity. In 1785, and again in 1790, the professorship became vacant by the will of the Founder; and Hey was re-elected on both occasions. In 1795 he ceased to be Professor, being too old to be re-elected according to the terms of the will. While Professor, he had held the Rectory of Passenham near Stony Stratford, together with the adjoining Rectory of Calverton. Passenham was his ordinary residence at this time, except when the duties of his Professorship called him to Cambridge. He held his two livings till 1814, when he resigned and moved to London, where he died in the following year. In 1796–98 he published in four volumes *Lectures in Divinity delivered in the University of Cambridge from 1780 to 1795.* These Lectures continued to be a standard work for divinity students for half a century. Hey's beautiful portrait hangs in the Hall, where as Tutor and Professor he lectured for twenty-seven years. Thomas Twining, in a letter describing a visit to Cambridge after a long absence, gives this charming account of his old friend's manner of lecturing :

" Not the worst part of my entertainment was my attendance upon two of Dr. Hey's Norrisian lectures in Sidney College Hall. Nothing could be more opposite to everything that is dull, heavy, tiresome, trite, &c. He has no papers, no notes at all. He looks over his written lectures before he goes into the Hall ; but all is perfectly easy, clear, unembarrassed. His manner exactly the thing, with just enough of authority, without anything pompous or dogmatical. His audience were very attentive, and most of them took notes. The Professor stands at a small desk, and has a bench near him, on which are placed such books,

Latin, English, or Greek, as he has occasion to quote ; and
in the course of his lecture he takes them up and reads
the passages.   This relieves, and makes a very pleasant
variety.   The lectures were extremely entertaining to me.
He mixes extempore talk with his memoriter, and alters
sur le champ the language of his written lectures ; but all
seemed very well of a piece ; there was no jolt in passing
from written to unwritten.   I assure you I was very much
pleased, and could not help expressing my surprise that he
had not a larger audience.   They were mostly young men,
and many came scattering in the midst of the lecture, for
which I told him I should *job* them."

As a divine, Hey belonged to the somewhat colourless
school of Paley.   On such subjects as subscription
to the Articles his views are thoroughly easy-going.*
An episcopal critic takes him to task for leading his
readers into "all the labyrinths of a loose and a per-
fidious casuistry."   However that may be, in his
modesty and fairness Hey is a model to all teachers.
For instance, having discussed with extreme delicacy
the views of his erratic fellow collegian, Thomas Woolston, he writes thus in one of his lectures :

" I am not ashamed to conclude with owning that I feel
more compassion, when I think of Woolston, than indig-
nation. . . . He was a man of learning and probity ; nay,

* His treatment of obsolete statutory promises is a good illustration of his point of view : "(1) *I will say so many masses for the soul of
Henry VI.* may come to mean *I will perform the religious duties required
of me by those who have authority.*   (2) *I will commonly wear a gown with a
standing collar ; in my journeys a priest's cloak*, etc. ; this may come to
mean *I will observe a decency in dress suitable to my profession.*   (3) *I will
preach at Paul's Cross* may mean *I will endeavour to propagate true
religion.*"

of wit and humour, however misapplied. It would have reflected more honour upon our religion and upon our civil government to have committed him to the care of his relations and friends (for friends he had to the last of the greatest eminence in the Church) than to let him support himself in prison by the sale of his writings and end his days in confinement."

Hey's lectures are often "extremely entertaining," as Twining truly says. There is no "donnishness" about this Professor. Commenting on 1 Tim. iii. 2, he writes :

"Dr. Thomas, Bishop of Lincoln in 1757, was said to be married to his fourth wife and to have, as a motto of a ring, *If I survive I'll make it five.* The same story has been told of others ; it is only mentioned here as proving that a succession of marriages was not disreputable even to a prelate."

When discussing the difficulty of understanding the things of common life as expressed in dead languages, he supposes the following "familiar letter" (which presumably relates his own experience) to be explained to a Chinese eighteen hundred years hence :

"Cambridge, April 5, 1780. Sir, on Thursday I was at the Assizes for this County ; as only one felon was to be tried, and he likely to be only transported, I sate in the *Nisi-prius* end of the Shire-Hall. The Jury were ignorant, but followed the direction of the Chief Baron, who sate as Judge ; I dined at two o'clock with the Sheriff, as his Chaplain, at Trinity Lodge ; the Judge dined in his coat and waistcoat, without his gown or full-bottomed wig. A small party adjourned to the Rose ; we had a round of toasts, and drank all the leading members of both Houses,

Whigs and Tories. The Punch and Tobacco being too much for me, I went into the Bar, but some people being there engaged with Whist and Backgammon, I went into the Balcony and got a little Porter; and below in the Market-place I saw a Mob, in which a Brazier's Apprentice got so hurt, that some shillings were gathered for him, and he was sent to the Hospital. What enraged them was fancying they had found part of a Press-gang; so they pulled off their hats, huzza'd, and cried out 'Wilkes and Liberty!' A Quaker passed by, but he would as soon have put on a sword as taken off his hat; tho' he was offered plenty of roast beef and plum-pudding. But the post is just going out; so I must in haste subscribe myself your obedient servant, J. H."

Hey calculated that fifty-four dissertations might be written on this letter, "such as those of Graevius or Gronovius."

The story of Thomas Martyn's long career as Professor is very interesting. From his early years he had imbibed a taste for botany from his father, John Martyn, Professor of Botany at Cambridge; and he had become acquainted with the writings of the "illustrious Swede." Some of his own statements on the matter are worth quoting:

(1) "About the year 1750 I was a pupil in the school of our great countryman, Ray. But the rich vein of knowledge, the profoundness and precision which I remarked everywhere in the *Philosophia Botanica* withdrew me from my first master." (2) "I had long before been acquainted with the *Systema Naturae, Genera Plantarum,* and *Critica Botanica,* which Linnæus himself had presented to my father, But that inestimable work, the *Philosophia*

Botanica, in 1751, and, above all, the *Species Plantarum,* in 1753, which first introduced specific names, made me a Linnæan completely." (3) "Being then (1753–6) engaged in academical studies, and afterwards (1756–9) in those of the profession (clerical) I had determined to adopt, Botany was rather the amusement of my leisure hours than my serious pursuit."

At the end of 1761 Professor John Martyn signified his wish to resign the Botanical Professorship. In the following February Thomas Martyn was elected to succeed his father, who had occupied the Chair for twenty-nine years. Thomas filled it for sixty-three years. The elder Martyn had been very anxious to establish a Botanic Garden. It was not till 1761 that his hopes were realised by the generosity of Dr. Walker, Vice-Master of Trinity, who purchased the site of the Monastery of the Austin Friars for that purpose, and appointed Thomas Martyn the first "Walkerian Reader." In 1763 he writes:

"You will be glad to hear that the Botanic Lectures have been well attended. I have had 50 pupils; and though probably but a small proportion of this number will attend to much purpose, yet upon the whole, if we can keep up our Garden, the science will certainly flourish among us. You may be sure that I teach the system of Linnæus."

In 1766 he writes rather sadly:

"My pupils are but few in number; and there are fewer still who give any attention to the science. . . . The Garden gets on very well in point of plants; but our income is still very scanty. Indeed, we are obliged to use a degree of

N

frugality not very consistent with the dignity of an university or the usefulness of the design; but we keep it on foot for better times!"

His biographer, George Gorham, tells us that

"when he had read Lectures in the science, which was his favourite study, for a few years, he found it necessary to add the other branches of Natural History, Animals, and Fossils; *Botany* not being then sufficiently popular to keep together a class on that single subject!"

In 1770, on the departure of Charles Miller, the Curator of the Botanic Garden, Martyn undertook to perform that office gratuitously in addition to his duties as Tutor of Sidney, Professor of Botany, and Walkerian Reader. To the Professorship and Readership no emolument was attached except the amount of fees received from students, which was trifling. In 1771 the Duke of Grafton, Chancellor of the University, who was then Prime Minister, was about to procure from the Crown an endowment for the Professorship. Unfortunately a change of Ministry put off the completion of the scheme for twenty-two years. In December, 1773, Martyn married Martha Elliston, sister of the Master of Sidney. Having thus vacated his Fellowship, he undertook the sole charge of the parish of Triplow, near Cambridge. In 1776 Sir J. B. Warren, a Sidney man, gave him the living of Little Marlow, Bucks. From 1778 to 1781 he travelled abroad, and returned "like a giant refreshed" with abundance of new materials for his lectures. In 1786 he was elected a Fellow of the Royal Society.

"In the midsummer term of 1796," writes his biographer, "the Professor read his last course of lectures
at Cambridge; having continued them for a period of
34 years, without interruption, except in the years 1779,
1780, when he was abroad, and the year 1785, when his
lecture-room was rebuilding His state of health now
unfitted him, in a great measure, for this annual labour;
and in truth there was so little zeal for the study in the
University that it was scarcely possible to form a class.
Very few persons would have persevered so long in the
effort to excite a taste for the elegant science to which his
life had been devoted."

Another Sidney Professor of Elliston's time was
Francis John Hyde Wollaston, who entered the College
in 1779. He was the eldest son of Francis Wollaston,
Rector of Chislehurst (see p. 182), and was educated at
Charterhouse.* He was Senior Wrangler in 1783, and
Taylor Lecturer from 1783 till 1785, when he migrated
to Trinity Hall and gained a Fellowship there. In
1788 and 1789 he was Moderator. While holding this
office, he was reprimanded for admitting Francis
Wrangham's *Carmen Comitiale* (now called "Tripos
Verses") on a prize-fight between Humphrey and
Mendoza. In 1792 he was elected second Jacksonian
Professor of Natural Experimental Philosophy. He
carried out the wishes of the Founder, who had directed

* His brother, Charles Hyde, was admitted in 1789. Their cousin,
Henry John, son of Frederick Wollaston, LL.D. (who was a grandson of the celebrated William Wollaston), was admitted in 1788; he
was afterwards Rector of Scotter and Chaplain to the King. His
son, Henry John, joined the College in 1824; he was the thirteenth
member of the Wollaston family who came to Sidney; he also was
Rector of Scotter.

that "the natural bodies which are the subject of
inquiry be exhibited at the lectures" and a course of
experiments made upon them "in the way of chemical
analysis." It is said that the optical experiments of his
predecessor, Isaac Milner, had been little more than
"exhibitions of the Magic Lanthorn on a gigantic
scale." Wollaston gave alternate courses on Physics
and Chemistry till 1795. When Samuel Vince in 1796
"broke through the bad example of preceding Plumian
Professors" by lecturing on Experimental Philosophy,
Wollaston issued this notice :

"In consequence of the election of Mr. Vince to the
Plumian Professorship, Mr. Wollaston will discontinue his
lectures in Experimental Philosophy, and intends to read
Chemistry annually."

His physical apparatus he handed over to Vince. In
1807 Wollaston was, as we shall see, elected Master
of Sidney; but his tenure of the office was very short.
He held his Professorship till 1813. His only publications were *A Plan of a Chemical Course of Lectures,
1794*, and *A Charge delivered to the Clergy of Essex in
1815;* for he ended by becoming an Archdeacon. He
died in 1823. Professor Vince, who was Senior Wrangler
in 1775 and occupied the Plumian chair till 1822, was a
Caius man; in 1777 he was admitted a member of
Sidney, and held the Taylor Lectureship for a few
years. He took his M.A. from Sidney in 1778.*

* Dr. Samuel Parr writes thus of the Cambridge Professoriate at
this time: "In regard to Cambridge, the persons there appointed to
Professorships, have in few instances disgraced them by notorious
incapacity or criminal negligence. A late work of Dr. Hey furnishes
us with a decisive proof of his abilities and his activity. Dr. Waring

In 1784 there was established in Cambridge the "Society for the promotion of Philosophy and of General Literature." There were twenty members, of whom four belonged to Sidney, — H. W. Coulthurst (Tutor, 1788–91), Martyn, Vince, and F. J. H. Wollaston. Owing to inadequate support this little Society was dissolved at the end of 1786. They had determined to occasionally publish papers under the title of *Tracts Philosophical and Literary by a Society of Gentlemen in the University of Cambridge*. Amongst the dissertations actually printed were two by Vince and one by Martyn.

During twelve years of Elliston's reign (1783–1794), Sidney did wonders in the Tripos. F. J. H. Wollaston was Senior Wrangler in 1783, as has been said already; in the same year Robert Heslop was Fourth Wrangler and Senior Classical Medallist, and Nelson Ryecroft was Eighth Wrangler. John Holden was Second Wrangler in 1784, and Joseph Watson was Third in the following year. In 1786 Rowland Ingram was Seventh Wrangler, and Robert Harris Tenth in 1787. In 1791 John Haggitt was Eleventh; in 1792 Thomas Woodcock Fifteenth and John Bromby Seventeenth. In 1793 Godfrey Sykes was Tenth and Charles Hyde Wollaston Fourteenth. In 1794 George Butler was Senior Wrangler and John Browne Seventh.

George Butler was the second son of the Rev. Weedon Butler; he was born in 1774, educated at his

and Mr. Vince in their writings have done honour to the science, not only of their University, but of their age. . . . Mr. Vince has by private instructions been very useful, both to those who were novitiates, and to those who were proficients, in Mathematics."

father's school at Chelsea, and admitted at Sidney on January 12, 1790. His elder brother Weedon was admitted on the same day. Both were elected Scholars in November, 1791; in the following October George was elected to the Taylor Mathematical Exhibition, which was founded by College Order, on the day of his election, out of part of the balance of "Mr. Taylor's Mathematical Estate." In the Long Vacations of 1792 and 1793 he read with the famous "Coach," John Dawson, surgeon, of Sedbergh. The son of a poor "statesman," Dawson had taught himself mathematics while looking after his father's sheep on the mountains. From 1781 to 1794 he numbered eight Senior Wranglers among his pupils, and he taught four more Senior Wranglers of later years. This extract from a letter of George Butler's, written on his first arrival at Sedbergh in June 1792, is interesting:

"I waited upon Mr. Dawson and settled the Terms, &c., in about 5 Minutes, being 5 Shillings per week for Instruction. I then returned to the King's Arms Inn, the best in the Town, and hired an excellent Room in the Inn for 1s. 6d. per week . . . where I shall continue during my whole time, as I think it much more convenient and full as cheap as living in a private house—Dinner 10d., Breakfast 2d. per Day."

On January 16, 1794,* Weedon sent this note to Chelsea:

* On the hundredth anniversary of this auspicious day a portrait of Dr. George Butler was most kindly presented to the College by his son Dr. Montagu Butler, Master of Trinity.

" HAPPY FATHER,

Thank God ! George is *Senior Wrangler.*   He beat them *all, hollow !*

" Yours in haste,

" W. BUTLER."

Weedon, according to the amusing statement of the grandiloquent Nichols (in his *Literary Anecdotes*), "declined all attempts at Mathematical Honours from an undisguised conviction of a beloved brother's more splendid talents."

On January 24 George wrote to his father:

"Your fears for my health were groundless. . . . Suffice it to say that I both am and look better than at any former period of my life, and it was remarked in the Senate House that I had more the appearance of an idle lounger than of a candidate for Academical Honours. Indeed I could scarcely avoid being of the same opinion when I beheld the ghastly looks of my competitors.   One of them fainted away on the first morning of Examination ; several declined the contest from mere debility ; and most of those who did endure to the end looked more like worn out rakes than men under three and twenty in the bloom of youth and in the prime of manhood."*

The College authorities now wished their Senior Wrangler to sit for the Chancellor's Medals.   On February 1 Weedon writes :

* The Second Wrangler of the year was John Copley of Trinity, afterwards famous as Lord Lyndhurst ; he wrote home thus on January 17 : " My health was my only enemy. I am more pleased at my place, as this study has only been adopted by me within these nine months, whereas several of my opponents have been labouring for years.".

"George is as sorry as myself at this provoking, unexpected delay on his side [in visiting his parents at Chelsea]. The cause is this: As George has so greatly distinguished himself in the Mathematical way, and has gained in his own College the prize for Classics, our Master expects that he will sit for the Medal. . . . He wished much not to be a candidate; but the Master and Fellows united in persuading him, and say that, if he only passes a good examination, without obtaining a Medal, they will be amply satisfied."

To this letter George appends the following note:

"Sir,

As you value my happiness do not mention the above to any Cantabs, or indeed to any body else. I would not have it told in Cambridge that I was a candidate upon any account until the very time of contest, for reasons too obvious to mention. Ambition, how absurd a frailty! But how totally ridiculous is that College Ambition which actuates Master and Fellows to the destruction of the comfort and joy of

"Your disappointed Son,

"G. Butler."

In the end ill health prevented George from being a candidate for the Medals and from having the chance of realising the sanguine expectations of his friends. The following extract from a letter, one of many written to his Sidney friend, John Browne, tells of his election to the Taylor Lectureship and also gives a delightful picture of the Master:

"Old *Sidney* for ever. 20 June 1794. . . . Imprimis, you are to congratulate me upon my final Election to the vacant Mathematical Lectureship, an honour which Dr. Elliston notified to me a few days ago. He began his information as usual by desiring me to sit down in the Jobation Chair; then, putting aside a Book which he affected to hold in his Hand for the Purpose of Reading, he seemed, during a silent Interval, which I had not Courage or Inclination to break, to envelope himself with his most impenetrable Gloom of Dignity, and at last he *oped his Mouth* and said: 'I suppose, Sir, you know the Reason of my sending for you.' 'No Sir,' said I very innocently, imagining he alluded to my scaling the College Walls, a practice which I had of late very frequently adopted, and which I feared he might have discovered. At length, however, I found myself happily disappointed, and left him in Exultation to relate to my Friends the joyful Occurrence."

We have more about the Master in another letter to Browne:

"Cambridge. 24 July, 1794. Dear Jack . . . would you think it, you rustic swain? I had the honour of drinking Tea with the Master this Evening at the Lodge, after having played at Bowls with him and Mr. Ingram for an Hour this Afternoon. When I say he was what he can be when he chuses, but what he seldom chuses to be to Undergraduates, you will not be at a Loss to supply my Meaning and to conjecture that the time was spent agreeably. . . . Nay even he laid aside his bands. Tate is coming into College and talks of residing the Long Vacation; we are going to fagg Classics together, or rather I with him."

The "Tate" mentioned in this letter is James Tate, who entered the College in 1790. He was a Senior

Optime in Butler's year, and was elected Fellow in 1795. He is best known as the excellent Headmaster of his old school, Richmond in Yorkshire, over which he presided from 1796 to 1833. As a classical scholar he was very famous. Sydney Smith, after being his travelling-companion on a coach, told a friend that he had met a man "dripping with Greek." Besides several classical school-books, Tate published in 1832 *Horatius Restitutus*, which went through three editions. In 1833 he was appointed to a Canonry at St. Paul's, which he held till his death in 1843.

In 1797 Butler announces to Browne the taking of his M.A. and his appointment as Classical Lecturer :

"Sid. Coll. 12 April, 97. . . . 'Master of Arts' . . . Last Friday I was qualified at the trifling expense of £12 to mount the magisterial Hat and Gown, take out Books in my own name from the University Library, cut Gates with total Impunity, &c., &c., and to be elected Member of the Drum Coffee House, which election has actually taken place. Pemberton of Emman., Richmond, Trin., Bourdillon, Queens', &c., were magistrified at the same Time—a jolly Set of us ! . . . Old Sidney is just now remarkably gay ; our *back Piece* is in full Employ. 'Tis the Military Parade of our loyal Townsmen, who have united into a Body to learn their Soldier Duties under the Direction of some Professional Men. Every afternoon they are Exercised from 5 to 6, and very well indeed do they perform. Their uniform is a blue Coat lined and faced with White, red Cape and Cuffs, white Waistcoat and nankin Breeches."*

* Butler was himself an officer of the University Volunteers who were enrolled in 1803.

" 19 Oct., 1797. . . . I have just been appointed Classical Lecturer,* and had previously engaged myself with 3 Private Pupils,—all which + Mathematical Lectureship will amount to 5 Lectures per Diem."

He does not forget his old Mathematical Coach, John Dawson. Several Sidney men are sent to Sedbergh. He writes thus to his father in July 1797 :

" I have received a letter from Jackson, dated Sedbergh, to my no small joy. If he makes good use of his time, he will thank me for sending him thither to the last day of his life ; for he will succeed and success will insure a habit of application. I have dispatched thither also my friend Mr. Cruttenden of at least equal abilities. Sidney shall shine among the Colleges."

Butler was elected Fellow in December 1797 (at the same time vacating the Taylor Lectureship) and Praelector in October 1798. He shared the Tutorship with John Holden from 1797 till 1804. In 1800 he is Senate-house Examiner and finds it tremendous work ; so he tells Browne. " Sid. Camb., 10 Dec. 99. . . . I am appointed one of the four Senate-house Examiners. Do you not envy me ? "

"S. S. C. C. 22 Feb. 1880. Your long letter found me just returned from a trip into Hampshire, where I had been spending a month in the very centre of everything sportsmanlike : in fact I wanted some such relaxation after the confinement of the Senate house, in which I had the honor to officiate as Examiner. From Monday morning till Thursday night I had but nine hours' rest in bed."

* His official title was *Lector Graecus.* In the *Cambridge Calendar* for 1802 it is amusing to read that "the *Belles Lettres* or *Classics* in most Colleges are studied with diligence and success."

The following extract is interesting:

"S. Suss. Coll. 22 Oct. 99. The University, thanks probably to the war, is very, very thin; in our small College we have only *one* freshman coming up. . . . Govett is still at Dawson's delighted with the man and with his instructions . . . Porson has just edited the *Phoenissae*."

With the first sentence in the above it is instructive to compare these words, written sixteen years later:

"Harrow, 25 Feb. 1816. . . . How do you account for the surprising fulness of our Universities? At Cambridge even the little Colleges overflow into the Town; and at Oxford—at least in all the principal Colleges—you must bespeak your admission two years or more from the destined time. Can it be that our population increases with our bloodshed? Or that Commerce stagnates, and therefore Learning finds votaries?"

In September 1800 Butler was ordained deacon by Bishop Pretyman of Lincoln. In October 1802 we find him Dean of his College and Ecclesiastical History Lecturer. Unfortunately for Sidney, his residence in College was brought to a close by his appointment in April 1805 to the Headmastership of Harrow in succession to Joseph Drury,

"after exhibiting to the Governors of the School and to his Grace the Archbishop of Canterbury such honourable testimonials of character from the chief Dignitaries and Schoolmen of Cambridge as perhaps were never before bestowed on any member of that body."

So writes Nichols *more suo*. The Cambridge testimonials were indeed remarkable. One of them was signed by twenty-four graduates, including seven Heads of Colleges and seven Professors, among whom was the great Richard Porson. Butler held his Headmastership till 1829, when he retired to the College living of Gayton in Northamptonshire.* He had vacated his Fellowship in 1815. In 1836 he was made Chancellor of Peterborough ; and in 1842 Dean of Peterborough, on the recommendation of Sir Robert Peel. He died at his Deanery in 1853, and was buried at Gayton.

The coming of our great treasure—the Cromwell Portrait—is an interesting episode in Elliston's Mastership. As an incorrect version of the story has been often repeated, our documentary evidence on the subject may be given here. In January 1766 there arrived at the College the following mysterious communications and also a case containing the Portrait :

" An Englishman, an Assertor of Liberty, Citizen of the World, is desirous of having the honor to present an original Portrait in Crayons of the Head of O. Cromwell, Protector, drawn by Cooper†, to Sydney Sussex College in Cambridge. London, Jan. 15, 1766.

* He had been presented to the living in 1814. Nichols, after stating that in 1814 Weedon succeeded to the management of the school at Chelsea where he had assisted his father for nineteen years, adds that "the venerable Principal calmly and contentedly retired to the village of Gayton to be Curate to the Master of Harrow."

† Samuel Cooper (1609-1672) is best known as a miniature painter. Two of his miniatures of Cromwell are in the Duke of Devonshire's collection. Aubrey calls Cooper "the Prince of Limners." Pepys says in his Diary (1669), "My wife sate to Cooper ; he is a most admirable workman and good company. . . . He hath £30 for his work, and the crystal and gold case come to £8 3s. 4d. more." Pope's mother and Cooper's wife were sisters.

' I freely declare it, I am for old Noll ;
Though his Government did a Tyrant resemble,
He made England great, and her Enemies tremble.

'A. Marvell.'

" It is requested that the Portrait may be placed so as
to receive the Light from Left to Right ; and to be free
from Sunshine. Also, that the favour of a line may be
written on the arrival of it, directed ' To Pierce Delver,
at Mr. Shove's, Bookbinder, in Maiden Lane, Covent
Garden, London.'

" To the Master and Fellows of Sydney Sussex College,
    Cambridge."

"A small case was sent yesterday by the Cambridge
Waggon, from the Green Dragon in Bishop's gate street,
directed 'To Dr. Elliston, Master of Sydney Sussex College,
Cambridge. Free of Carriage.' It contains a Portrait,
which the Master and Fellows of that College are *requested*
to accept. London, Jan. 18, 1766."

Dr. Elliston did not acknowledge the safe arrival of the
Portrait till March 26 ; he pleads as an excuse "an
absence of some months," adding that he has great
reason to think himself further indebted to " Pierce
Delver " for a set of Prints, and begs that his " particular obligation may be expressed to him for that
mark of his regard." The mystery as to the donor was
solved by the publication of the *Memoirs of Thomas
Hollis*, who died on January 1, 1774. This passage
from his *Memoirs*, which appeared six years after his
death, identifies him with " Pierce Delver ":

" Jan. 15, 1766.   He sent to Sidney College in Cambridge, where Cromwell had his academical education, an
original portrait of that hero, painted by Cooper. . . . It
has indeed a terrific aspect and gives some credit to a
report which circulated in Cambridge at the time that the
King of Denmark * visited that University. . . . Contem-
plating the picture with attention he expressed his feelings
in these or like words, *il me fait peur.*" †

The College buildings were considerably improved in
Elliston's time.   In October 1774 the College decided
to suspend a Fellowship to provide funds for the rebuilding of the Chapel and Library, which were in a
ruinous condition.   Dyer draws a fancy picture of the
Master " reviving the ancient character of the ecclesiastic,
superintending and directing the building according to
his own taste."   As a matter of fact, an architect was
employed—the well-known James Essex, who suggested
several alternative plans.   In October 1775 Elliston
produced at a College meeting a new plan drawn by
Essex " according to the Master's idea of a new Chapel
and Library."   This was " in general preferred to the
other plans."   Cole says that the old Chapel was pulled

* This was Christian VII., who visited Cambridge on August 30,
1768.

† In Hollis's papers underneath his memorandum of his present to
the College are the three lines from Marvell given above. On May 22,
1765, he records the giving to Christ's College of four copies of *Para-
dise Lost*, two of them first editions.   Milton was Hollis's great hero
and model.   In 1761 he sent to Trinity his portrait of Newton.   He
was also very liberal in presenting books to the libraries of Harvard,
Berne, and Zurich.   He was a great collector of republican literature of the seventeenth century, and was himself accounted a
"republican "; but, according to his own account, he was a " true
whig."

down in July 1776, and adds the utterly untrue statement that the late Master, Dr. Parris, had " well-nigh
ruined the College by suppressing Fellowships for the
ornamenting of the Hall and his Lodge." Essex laid
the foundation-stone of the new Chapel on October 1
"at half an hour after eleven." The Master and
Fellows being busily engaged over the College Audit,
no one was present at the ceremony but the Master-
bricklayer and a labourer who assisted the Architect in
laying the stone. The situation of the new building is
almost identical with that of the old, but not on the
original foundation. The work proceeded very slowly.
As late as May 1779 we find the College empowering
" Mr. Essex to employ Mr. Clarke the plasterer to begin
the ceiling and walls "; and in November it was agreed
to use deal for the panelling instead of oak. It was not
till March 1782 that Essex received his fee of £100
" for superintendence of the New Building." The slow
progress of the work was due to lack of means ; in 1777
it was decided to continue the suspension of three
Fellowships " for the expense of rebuilding the Chapel,
Library, and Offices of the Lodge "; in 1781 another
Fellowship was suspended ; and in 1779 £40 per annum
was set apart for the purpose. Dyer, writing in 1814
(*i.e.*, before the buildings were stuccoed), gives this
account of the appearance of the College after the
alterations made under Parris and Elliston :

"The entrance to Sidney is by a good Doric portico ;
the first court is a neat little brick building, but with
nothing in it remarkable.; in the second court is the
Chapel with an agreeable interior : a few years since it

was rebuilt ; and a new direction given to it, to make the court more uniform."

Of the old Fellows' Garden, which in 1890 was sacrificed to make way for the New Court, Dyer writes with enthusiasm :

" Here is a good garden, an admirable bowling-green, a beautiful summer-house, at the back of which is a walk agreeably winding, with variety of trees and shrubs inter-twining, and forming, the whole length, a fine canopy over head ; with nothing but singing and fragrance and seclusion; a delightful summer retreat; the sweetest lover's or poet's walk, perhaps, in the University. So our traveller is left to his meditation."

Elliston died on February 11, 1807, aged seventy-six, after a not inglorious reign of nearly forty-seven years. In his time the College, though small in numbers, had played an important part in the intellectual life of the University.

CHAPTER XII

MODERN TIMES

THE story of the next Mastership is short, but interesting. On February 18, 1807, the choice of the Society fell on Francis J. H. Wollaston, B.D., Jacksonian Professor (see p. 195). It is said that a strong wish was expressed that Dr. George Butler might become a candidate; but it could hardly be expected that he would so soon abandon his great work at Harrow. The election of Wollaston was most extraordinary; for he had never been a Fellow of Sidney, and, unless his supporters could show that no suitable candidate could be found amongst (1) present Fellows of the College, (2) former Fellows, (3) members of Trinity College, his election was clearly a violation of the Statutes (see pp. 26, 27). A discontented minority appealed to the hereditary Visitor, John Shelley Sidney. A long delay ensued before he gave his decision to the effect that the election was void; for we find Wollaston still acting as Master on January 15, 1808. The Visitor's decision must have been announced within a few days of that date, as the next Master was elected on January 31. Gunning gives us this piece of gossip in his *Reminiscences* :

THE NEW COURT: GARDEN FRONT

" Notwithstanding his disqualification, Wollaston took possession of the Lodge, and believed himself so firmly fixed in the Mastership that he directed the gardener, when he pruned the trees, to leave as much bearing wood as possible, as he should want a great quantity of fruit during his Vice-Chancellorship ; which, as no one expected he could remain Master, afforded a considerable deal of amusement."

The new Master was Edward Pearson, B.D., one of the Fellows, who was admitted as a Sizar in 1778, and graduated as a Senior Optime in 1782. For a time he acted as Curate to our old friend, Dr. Hey, at Passenham. From 1791 to 1798 he was joint Tutor, his successive colleagues being Christopher Hunter, Joseph Watson, and John Holden. In 1796 Elliston presented him to the Vicarage of Rempstone, this living being in the gift of the Master. Pearson published in 1798 *Thirteen Discourses to Academic Youth*, 'sermons preached at St. Mary's. He was highly esteemed as a preacher. At Rempstone he was a model parish priest, attending each week-day at his church "for the purpose of reading portions of the Liturgy and expounding passages of Scripture," and "rigorously presiding over the moral and religious education of the children" (Nichols). In 1806 Pearson proposed that a Professorship of Ritual should be established at Cambridge. In this he was strongly supported by Spencer Perceval, then Chancellor of the Exchequer. But the proposal did not meet with a favourable response in the University. Perceval thought very highly of Pearson's writings; he was induced " by their perusal alone to find out the author in his privacy," and " to cultivate a confidential inter-

course with him, which terminated only with his life."
In 1807 he secured for Pearson the Warburtonian
Lectureship at Lincoln's Inn. Pearson was elected Vice-
Chancellor in the first year of his Mastership, and in
1810 Christian Advocate on Hulse's foundation. He
revelled in controversy, vehemently attacking both
the Utilitarianism of Paley and the gloomy Calvinism
(as he thought it) of Charles Simeon. He still kept his
country living. In 1811 he had an apoplectic seizure
while walking in the garden of his parsonage, and died
a few days afterwards on August 17. It appears from
our account books that in his Bursarial business Pearson was a sad muddler.

A distinguished scholar joined the College in Pearson's time—Thomas Mitchell, who, after ten years at
Christ's Hospital, was admitted at Pembroke in 1802:
He was Senior Chancellor's Medallist in 1806. In 1809
he was elected to a Fellowship at Sidney, but vacated
it in three years, being unwilling to take Orders.
His translation of Aristophanes is well known;
Byron pronounced it to be "excellent." In the years
1834–9 he published editions of several plays of Aristo-
phanes with English notes ; and afterwards he edited
Sophocles (1839–43). He died in 1845. Josiah Rowles
Buckland, who graduated from St. John's as Fifth
Wrangler in 1807, became Fellow and Tutor of
Sidney, and afterwards Headmaster of Uppingham.
Another distinguished Fellow of this time was George
Cecil Renouard, who migrated to Sidney in 1800
from Trinity, where he had resided for two years.
He was Lord Almoner's Professor of Arabic from
1815 to 1820.

Dr. Pearson's successor was John Davie, one of the
Fellows. He was born in 1774, entered the College in
1794, and graduated as Senior Optime in 1799. He
was elected Master on August 30, 1811, and Vice-Chancellor on November 4 in the next year. In one of Miss
Edgeworth's letters, dated May 1, 1813 (vol. i. p. 198),
there is an amusing account of a visit to Dr. Davie's
Lodge, where she went to see the Cromwell Portrait.*

"After having recruited our strength, we set out again
to the Vice-Chancellor Davie's to see a famous picture of
Cromwell. As we knocked at his Vice-Chancellorship's
door, Mr Smedley said to me, ' Now, Miss Edgeworth, if you
would but settle in Cambridge, here is our Vice-Chancellor
a bachelor . . . *do* consider about it.' We went upstairs ;
found the Vice-Chancellor's room empty ; had leisure
before he appeared to examine the fine picture of
Cromwell, in which there is more the expression of great-
ness of mind and determination than his usual character
of hypocrisy. This portrait seems to say, ' Take away that
bauble,' not ' We are looking for the corkscrew.' The
Vice-Chancellor entered, and such a wretched, pale,
unhealthy object I have seldom beheld ! He seemed
crippled and writhing with rheumatic pains, hardly able to
walk. After a few minutes had passed, Mr Smedley came
round to me and whispered, ' Have you made up your
mind ?' ' Yes, quite, thank you.' "

In the same letter Miss Edgeworth writes :

"I suppose you know that Mr Smedley has published
minutes of the trial of that Mr Kendall who was accused
of having set fire to Sidney College, and who, thoug

* The Portrait is now in the Hall,

brought off by the talents of Garrow, was so generally thought to be guilty, and to have only escaped by a quirk of the law, that he has been expelled the University."

The "Mr. Smedley" mentioned in Miss Edgeworth's letter is Edward Smedley, who was elected Fellow of Sidney in 1812. He was at Westminster and entered at Trinity in 1805. He graduated as "Wooden Spoon" in 1809, and gained the Member's Prize for a Latin Essay in 1810 and again in 1811, also the Seatonian Prize in 1813 and in three subsequent years. He vacated his Fellowship by marriage in 1816 and died after much ill-health in 1836. He was one of the editors of the *Encyclopaedia Metropolitana*, and published *Sketches from Venetian History* in two volumes (1831-2). His *Poems and Memoirs*, edited by his widow, were published in 1837. His minutes of Kendall's trial for arson cannot be traced.

There were several attempts to set the College on fire in Davie's time; but in all cases the flames were extinguished before any serious damage was done. In 1812 the Senate passed this Grace, offering £300 reward for the discovery of the supposed incendiary:

"Cum gravis suspicio orta sit, incendium quod Collegii Sidneii aedibus nuper erupit a quibusdam sceleratis consulto excitatum esse: Placeat vobis ut iis, qui criminis indicium facient et quorum testimonio incendiarii praedicti sub judice damnari possint, summa trecentarum librarum concedatur et quod haec summa eo nomine persolvenda e communi cista erogetur."

Gunning states in his *Reminiscences* that

"in the early part of 1813 Sidney College was again on fire in two places, but no material damage was sustained. Suspicion fell on Frederick Kendall, B.A., of that College, who was committed for trial. He was tried at the Lent Assizes before Mr Serjeant Marshall. Sir William Garrow Solicitor-General, who was specially retained, defended the prisoner, and he was acquitted."

In the *London Packet* for March 22, 1813, this paragraph appears:

"SIDNEY COLLEGE, CAMBRIDGE.—Friday last the trial of Mr Kendal, charged with setting fire to the College, commenced at the Cambridge Assizes. Before the Solicitor-General had finished the cross-examination of Paterson the watchman, such a scene of perjury was displayed that Mr Kendal was immediately acquitted."

The College in its *forum domesticum* dealt with the matter in its own way. On March 20 it was ordered by the Master and Fellows that "in consequence of the events which have lately taken place" Mr. Kendall's name should be erased from the Boards of the College.

Dr. Davie died in October 1813, a martyr to duty.

"The delicate state of his health," says Gunning, "made him ill fitted for the office (of Vice-Chancellor); but so anxious was he not to neglect his duties that his life was sacrificed before the expiration of his Vice Chancellorship. He persisted in going to the Senate-house at the Bachelors' Commencement, although he had but just risen from a sick bed. I begged he would allow me to represent his state, and assured him that I could easily procure a deputy. He said he had been unsuccessful in the first application he had made, and that he would sooner die than subject himself to another refusal. It snowed very hard all the day ; the weather was remarkably severe, and he was in the Senate-house for five hours. As soon as he reached home, he went to bed, where he was confined for some weeks. .When able to undertake the journey, he proceeded into Suffolk. He lived some months, but died in his Vice-Chancellor's year."

William Chafy was elected Master on October 17, 1813. He was born in 1779 and entered Corpus as a Sizar in January 1796 ; in October of the same year he migrated to Sidney, where he was also admitted as a Sizar. In 1800 he graduated as a Senior Optime, and was elected Fellow in the following year. After his ordination he held for a time the curacy of Gillingham in Kent. In 1807 he succeeded John Holden as sole Tutor of the College. Very soon after his election to the Mastership he became Vice-Chancellor (November 4, 1813). He took an early opportunity of showing the University what manner of man he was. In the summer of 1814, William, Duke of Gloucester, Chancellor of the University, visited Cambridge, in order to preside at the Commencement ceremonies. It had been arranged that an Address to both Houses of Parliament in favour of the abolition of the African Slave Trade should be laid before the Senate on the Monday in Commencement week "under the express sanction of his Royal Highness." The proposed Address regretted that Ministers had not sufficiently insisted on the abolition in their negotiations with Foreign Powers. The story may be continued in Gunning's words :

"As usual, the Address was laid before the Heads in

the vestry of St. Mary's Church after the evening sermon. Chafy objected to the Address *in toto* in the most violent terms. He said it was a censure of the Ministry that he supported, and that he was determined to negative it in the Caput. He spoke so loudly and so vehemently, that the parishioners (who had in leaving the church to pass the vestry door) crowded together in order to learn the cause of this uproar. His Royal Highness at length broke up the meeting without replying otherwise than by merely observing that the language and the tone of the Vice-Chancellor were very unsuitable to the place and the occasion."

On Monday in the Senate House, Chafy, who was well aware that the Address had the hearty support of the Senate, was determined to *non-placet* it. On a division it appeared that only the Vice-Chancellor and a subservient Fellow of Sidney, Francis Henson, voted against the Grace. A distinguished visitor witnessed this strange exhibition.

"Blucher came that morning to Trinity Lodge, to which place he was drawn by the multitude, who met him at Trumpington and took the horses from his carriage. . . . A few minutes at the Lodge sufficed for toilet and refreshment, and he then accompanied the Chancellor to the Senate-house, where the first business was to make him LL.D. He had scarcely taken his place amongst the Doctors, when, by the opposition of Chafy, he unexpectedly found himself amongst the voters. If he voted at all, it was with the majority, as, by the return of the Proctors, there were only two dissentients."

The sequel is still more extraordinary :

" On the Commencement Tuesday, before the business of the day was quite concluded, the Vice-Chancellor was about to leave the Senate-house, without even the courtesy of bowing to the Chancellor, who, seeing his intention, told him that he proposed leaving the University at 4 o'clock, previously to which he should be glad to see him. He fixed 3 o'clock as the hour at which the Vice-Chancellor should call upon him at Trinity Lodge, that he might deliver up to him the keys, the Statutes, and the insignia of office. The Vice-Chancellor did not appear at the time appointed. After waiting three-quarters of an hour, Beverley was sent to Sidney Lodge, to announce that his Royal Highness was waiting for the Vice-Chancellor. He shortly returned with the information that the Vice-Chancellor was gone for a ride, and it was very uncertain when he would return."

If Chafy could deal thus with a royal Chancellor, we may well shrink from inquiring how he conducted himself towards members of his own College.

In 1818 the old Sidney Professor, Thomas Martyn, made an unwilling appearance in the arena of Cambridge politics. With the sanction of the Vice-Chancellor, he had made the apparently innocent arrangement that Sir J. E. Smith, President of the Linnæan Society, should lecture as his deputy. At once the Tutors of Colleges were up in arms. Eighteen of them protested to the Vice-Chancellor that they disapproved of their pupils attending the lectures of " any person who is neither a member of the University nor of the Church of England." Martyn wisely determined to give up his plan. But Sir J. E. Smith in high dudgeon provoked a savage paper war on the subject. The aged

Professor was not much disturbed by the controversy ; he wrote thus to a friend :

" If not much of a philosopher, I am too much of a Christian to be affected by any thing that is passing at Cambridge or any where else ; for, standing as I do on the very verge of both worlds, I am looking forward to *Yellow Meads of Asphodel and Amaranthine Bowers*."

Martyn died at Pertenhall in Bedfordshire (of which parish he was Rector for the last twenty-seven years of his life) on June 3, 1825, in his ninetieth year.*

In Chafy's time the College enjoyed remarkable financial prosperity. During the great war the rental of the estates had, of course, considerably increased, and now the proposal to grant a mining lease on the Taylor property at Dudley opened up new visions of wealth. In 1818 and 1823 private Acts of Parliament dealing with the Taylor Estates were passed. " Taylor Trustees " were appointed, and authorised, out of the proceeds of the mining lease, to augment the stipend

---

* Martyn's literary labours had been enormous. His biographer enumerates nearly 40 publications, mostly on botanical subjects, some of them in several volumes. But the Professor's interests were by no means limited to his special subject. In 1766 he published in two volumes *The English Connoisseur, containing an account of Paintings, ' Sculpture, &c. in England*, and in 1773 (in conjunction with another Fellow of Sidney, John Lettice) *The Antiquities of Herculaneum, translated from the Italian*. The first part, containing 50 excellent plates, was all that was published of the latter work ; for "the Court of Naples made a formal remonstrance, by their Ambassador, to the English Court, against the publication of a work 'designed exclusively for *presentation* to Sovereigns, Princes, Noblemen, and Ambassadors '! Notwithstanding these lofty pretensions, and the fear expressed of a debasement of a Royal Italian Work, by its vulgar exposure in the literary market of England, the translators had themselves *purchased* the original for fifty pounds."

of the Taylor Lecturer, to found additional Taylor
Exhibitions, to provide funds for the erection of a
Mathematical Library, and for the purchase of books
and instruments, and to provide room's for the residence
of the Exhibitioners. Between 1821 and 1833 the
sum of £13,000, of which a large portion came from the
Taylor funds, was spent on the College buildings. In
October 1821 the Master and Fellows agreed to seal
contracts for building the Mathematical Library and
making other improvements in the east and west fronts
of the College, "according to the plan and specification
of Jeffry Wyatt." In April 1831 it was agreed to
repair and alter the central range of buildings, and to
make a new entrance and gateway tower, "agreeably
to the plans of Jeffry Wyatville." Another Order was
passed in June 1832, directing that the north wing of
the Hall court and the south wing of the Chapel court
be altered and repaired, and that a new Combination-
room be built in the Fellows' garden.

Wyatt (or Wyatville, as he afterwards called himself)
was the architect employed at Windsor Castle, and
would on that account commend himself to the taste of
Dr. Chafy, Chaplain to the King. Cooper says that
Wyatt then enjoyed "great, but undeserved repute
as an architect." The style which Wyatt selected for
the "improvement" of Sidney was the "pseudo-
Elizabethan Gothic." Its characteristics need no
description; they are only too well known to all
Cambridge men. The chief structural alterations made
by Wyatt were these:—Ten buttresses were built on
the garden front of the Hall and Lodge, the wall being
found to be in a ruinous condition. A projecting

structure was added to the west front of the Hall court, containing the Taylor Library and additions to the Lodge; and this side of the court was crowned with a new lantern turret. The attic storey of the Hall court was rebuilt, and the rooms in it considerably enlarged. The old ' portico opposite to the Hall entrance was removed to the corner of the garden near Jesus College, and a new gateway tower was built. This tower is of stone; the rest of the building was now cased with Roman cement. The new Combination-room, pro-jecting into the garden, adjoined the old Fellows' Parlour (now the Taylor Reading-room). In 1890–1 Wyatt's room was demolished and replaced by the present Combination-room; at the same time the gable end of the Hall, cleared of Wyatt's cement and em-battled parapet, was restored to its pristine simplicity. In 1833 Dr. Chafy "repaired and beautified" the Chapel at his own expense.

On November 4, 1829, Dr. Chafy was again elected Vice-Chancellor. In speaking of his second term of office, Gunning dwells on his love of lavish hospitality:

" After his election he invited, according to ancient custom, the members of the Senate to drink wine with him. The numbers had for some years been decreasing; but the Vice-Chancellor's wine bore so high a character that there was a strong muster on this occasion. . . . Chafy's entertainments were always on a costly scale; and I believe nothing pleased him better than to provide the most choice wines that could be procured, and to see them freely taken. I can well remember that at the Installation of the Marquis Camden, in 1835, he gave a sumptuous breakfast in Sidney Gardens. Many amongst his guests

were obliged to leave to dine with the Vice-Chancellor at
Jesus College. On returning from this dinner between
eleven and twelve o'clock, we heard the sound of music and
revelry at Sidney Gardens. Several of us (and, if my
memory does not fail me, Mr. Baron Parke and Sir James
Scarlett were amongst the number) agreed to go in by way
of finish. We found in a large marquee Dr. Chafy and
many distinguished guests who had been enjoying his good
fare. There were even at that late hour the remains of a
splendid dessert upon the table, and about two hundred
persons were dancing or walking about the gardens. I used
frequently to hear Chafy boast, with much apparent satisfaction, of the quantity of champagne and other expensive
wines that were consumed on that occasion."

A Sizar in his own undergraduate days, Chafy is said
to have discouraged poor men from entering Sidney.
At first he tried to specialise in Fellow-Commoners; but
this policy was not a success. He failed to enhance
either the reputation or the popularity of the College.
Very few men of distinction were there in his time.
Alldersey Dickin (Twelfth Wrangler in 1814) was
afterwards Fellow of Peterhouse and Headmaster of
Tiverton. John Hind, who graduated from St. John's
as Second Wrangler in 1818, became Fellow and Tutor
of Sidney. Robert Bentley Buckle, Fourth Wrangler
in 1824, was a Fellow. In 1826, the third year of the
Classical Tripos, John Gibson was Fourth Classic; he
was afterwards Fellow and Tutor, and four times
examiner for the Classical Tripos. He enjoys the
distinction of being the only Classical First-classman
from Sidney, as long as the order of merit was retained in that Tripos. In 1830 James William Lucas

Heaviside was Second Wrangler and Second Smith's
Prizeman; he became Fellow and Tutor, and was
afterwards Professor of Mathematics at Haileybury
and Canon of Norwich. Edward Bickersteth, who was
a Senior Optime in 1836, was Dean of Lichfield for
many years. Samuel Phillips, who entered the College
in 1836, but left after a short stay owing to the
death of his father, attained some celebrity in literary
circles. He was best known as a writer in the *Times*.
Two volumes of his *Essays from the Times* were published in 1851 and 1854. His *Memoir of the Duke of
Wellington* was also reprinted. In 1844 he published
a three-volume novel, *Caleb Stukely*.

Dr. Chafy died in May 1843, bequeathing £1000 for
the augmentation of College livings. He was succeeded
by Robert Phelps, who was elected Master on May 23.
A good account of Dr. Phelps's life was contributed to
the *Cambridge Review* (vol. xi., pp. 152-3) by one who
knew him very well, after his death on January 11,
1890. From this biography some interesting passages
may be quoted here.

"The family is a well-known one in Somersetshire; but
the branch of it to which Dr. Phelps belonged had for
some generations been settled in Devonport, where, it has
been remarked, his father must have been a man of consequence, because, when during the war with Napoleon a
Volunteer Corps was raised for the defence of Devonport,
he was chosen as its commander. He was twice married,
and rests, with his two wives, in the picturesque churchyard of St. Stephen's by Saltash, just across the estuary in
the county of Cornwall. His youngest son by the second
marriage, who was named Robert Turner, was sent to the

well-known Grammar School of Richmond, and when there showed such exceptional mathematical abilities as determined his friends to send him to the University."

Robert Phelps entered Trinity College in 1829 and graduated in 1833 as Fifth Wrangler. In April 1836 he was appointed Taylor Lecturer at Sidney, and in October 1838 he was elected to a Fellowship; he became Tutor in January 1840. He also took many private pupils for the Mathematical Tripos, and published a treatise on Optics, which long remained the text-book on the subject at Cambridge.

"We believe that as a private teacher he was not so successful as might have been expected from his acknowledged powers. He was in the habit of saying that he himself had never needed the services of a Coach, and possibly his self-reliant nature found some difficulty in understanding what the sort of help was of which weaker students stood in need. From this drudgery he was set free in 1843, when, on the death of Dr. Chafy, he was elected to the Mastership of the College, an appointment which then included the Bursarship, both of which offices he held until his death. It may surprise those who have only known him by reputation in later times to find him acting on the Committee to secure the re-election of Mr. Goulburn, M.P., for the University of Cambridge, when that politician's conversion to the doctrines of Free Trade had offended the 'stern and unbending Tories' of the University. The most important incidents in his biography which remain to be mentioned are, his marriage, which took place shortly after his election to the Mastership, and his appointment to the Rectory of Willingham in 1848. He had been Vice-Chancellor for the second time in the previous year. . . ."

"Immersed in happy domesticity, his life for many years seemed free from any cares beyond those of his family of five children; however, the public side of the Master's character came out when in the years 1868-9 the fate of the Irish Church was decided. At the meetings which were held in its defence the Master of Sidney was always present, and he laboured unceasingly, both by speech and writing, in a cause which seemed to him to be also that of the Church of England. . . . It was, however, his determined resistance to the Universities Commission of 1876 which at once placed him in the list of historic Masters of Colleges. The Commissioners in that year commenced their operations by demanding from every College at Oxford and Cambridge a detailed account of the revenue at their disposal. This the Master of Sidney refused to furnish. We are inclined to regard the story of his having declared that *nothing short of the rack* would make him yield as apocryphal. . . . His action was sharply criticised at the time by the advocates of the new system. . . . At the same time he felt that his refusal to furnish information might be misconstrued, and he consequently published a pamphlet, in which all the sources of the income of the College were stated. . . . He carried his point so far that it was from this pamphlet, and not from any official return, that the income of Sidney is estimated in the Blue-book. . . .

"After the completion of the work of the Commission, Dr. Phelps took but little further share in the political life of the University, and after the death of his life-long friend, Mr. Beresford Hope, M.P. for the University of Cambridge, with whose views on Church matters he entirely agreed, he may be said to have retired from public life. However, it is not as a politician that his friends will remember him, but rather as the eager fisherman, who

P

when long past three score and ten, would still recount with glee how he caught his first salmon in the River Blackwater below Lismore; as the artist whose works filled all the walls of his charming old house and over-flowed into many portfolios; or as the musician whose clarionet might be heard in the court below for many a happy year."

At one epoch in Dr. Phelps's Mastership his eldest son, Edmund Louis, seemed to his youthful contem-poraries a more important member of the College than the venerable Master himself.   He rowed number six in the two victorious Cambridge Boats of 1870 and 1871, when the famous Goldie was stroke.   It was in the first of those years that Cambridge won after a series of nine defeats.   In 1868 and 1869 Sidney won the University Fours with a crew of which Phelps was a member.*   In 1870 the College Boat left off fifth on the River.   The *Record of the University Boat Race* (by Treherne and Goldie) gives the names of two other Sidney Rowing Blues, William Simson Longmore, who rowed in 1851 and 1852, and Edward Hawley (after-wards Vicar of Worksop), who rowed in 1852 and 1853. Hawley was President of the C.U.B.C. and Longmore Secretary.   The early history of Sidney rowing is interesting.   In 1845 the Boat rose from the Second to the First Division, and in the Lent Term of 1848 it finished fifth on the River, and in the May Term gained the high place of third.   Curiously enough, our Boat Club record goes on to state that in Lent 1849 the Boat was taken off the River " owing to most of the

---

* He also rowed a dead heat for the Colquhouns and won the Magdalene Pairs.

men taking their degree." In 1857 Sidney again reached a high place, seventh on the River, and this,. " despite the fact that there were only ten men in the College :

> "There were eight to row and one to steer
> And one to run on the bank and cheer."

The Tutors under Dr. Phelps were William Towler Kingsley, B.D., John Clough Williams Ellis (Third Wrangler, 1856), and the present Master, Charles. Smith (Third Wrangler, 1868). The success of the College in the Mathematical Tripos during the years 1877–1891 was remarkable. A list of our high. Wranglers of that time may be recorded here :

1877, S. R. Wilson, 5th ; 1878, J. Edwards, 4th, and. J. A. Martin, 10th; 1879, S. H. Haslam, 11th; 1881, F. W. Stokes, 8th ; 1882 (January), S. L. Loney, 3rd, and H. C. Robson, 6th; 1882 (June), R. H. Piggott, 5th; 1883, G. W. Küchler, 9th ; 1884, A. Anderson, 6th ; 1888,. A. G. Cracknell, 6th ; 1891, R. H. D. Mayall, 2nd.

These successes were followed by a spell of many First Classes in Natural Science, which has not yet been broken.

Though, since the Statutes of 1860, Sidney has ceased to be a " Divinity College " strictly so called, it still continues to play its part as a *Seminarium Ecclesiae*.. Among living Church leaders, educated at the College, may be mentioned John Lloyd, D.D., Bishop of Swansea ; Charles William Stubbs, D.D., Dean of Ely ; and John Rundle Cornish (formerly Fellow and Dean), Archdeacon of Cornwall. The names of Robert.

Machray, D.D., Archbishop of Rupertsland and Primate of Canada, and John Wale Hicks, M.D., D.D., Bishop of Bloemfontein, are on the present list of Fellows; among whom are also three Fellows of the Royal Society,—Harry Marshall Ward, Sc.D., Professor of Botany, Francis Henry Neville, and Ernest Howard Griffiths. The present Master was elected on February 5, 1890. The first important event of his reign was the erection of the new buildings, which were begun in July 1890, and opened in October 1891; the Architect was Mr. J. L. Pearson, R.A., who, before his death, provided plans for the completion of the New Court and the erection of a new Chapel. The enthusiasm displayed at the Tercentenary festivities in February and June 1896 showed that the College may still depend on the loyal support of its members, old and young.

APPENDIX

SUMMARY OF HALF-YEARLY ACCOUNT, MICHAELMAS AUDIT 1648.

RECEIPTS.

Rents.	£	s.	d.
Saleby (p. 23)	76	1	10
Clee (p. 51)	41	7	11
Cridling (p. 92)	70	0	0
Wootton (p. 90)	70	0	0
Stamford (p. 53)	12	10	0
Burwash (p. 49)	7	10	0
Evanis Hall (p. 143)	4	10	0
Abbots Langley *	15	0	0
Sir J. Hart's estate (p. 52)	21	0	0
"Robson's tenements" (*i.e.,* houses over against the College)	12	3	4
Grantchester	0	10	0

* In 1641 Francis Combe, of Hemel Hempstead in the County of Hertford, bequeathed part of his library to the College and "all that he hath at Abbots Langley and the Lordship there and the Meadow in St. Stephen's with the appurtenances" to this College and Trinity College in Oxford, to be divided equally between them for the education of four of the descendants of his brothers and sisters,—"the Lease of Langley aforesaid to be let at one third part under the true value to his wife's kindred, viz., brothers and sisters there and at Harrow." Francis Combe was grand-nephew of Sir Thomas Pope, Founder of Trinity College, Oxford. His estate had once belonged to St. Alban's Abbey. This bequest was from the first a subject of controversy ; it is now regulated by a new Statute of 1861, interpreted in a judgment of the Lord Chancellor, March 24, 1869.

	£	s.	d
Rent-charges.			
Bagington (p. 23)	15	0	0
Copingford (p. 57) . . .	10	0	0
Other Sources of Income.			
Chamber rents	6	7	2
Payments by Fellow-Commoners and Pensioners	4	4	0
	366	4	3
Deduct for Cridling . .	70	0	0*
„ „ Bagington . .	1	0	0
	£295	4	3

EXPENDITURE.

The Master : from the College . .	10	0	0
„ Mr. Freestone . .	1	0	0
„ Sir J. Hart . .	1	0	0
„ Mr. Blundell . . .	2	0	0
his allowance on the quarter's bills	5	8	0
8 Fellows of the Foundation	33	5	0
16 Scholars of the Foundation . . .	21	4	6
2 Freestone Scholars	5	0	0
Sir J. Hart's 2 Fellows	10	0	0
„ 4 Scholars	5	14	6
Sir F. Clerke's 1 Fellow	6	8	4
„ 3 Scholars	7	16	0
4 Blundell Scholars	15	8	0
3 Montagu Scholars	4	6	6
2 Combe Exhibitioners	6	18	0
Other expenses	82	19	10
	£218	8	8

The balance, amounting to £76 15s. 7d., is stated to have been "divided at several times" amongst the Master and Fellows. Compare p. 66.

* Distributed as stated on p. 93.

INDEX

Printed by Ballantyne, Hanson & Co.
London & Edinburgh

www.ingramcontent.com/pod-product-compliance
Lightning Source LLC
Chambersburg PA
CBHW020556030726
47497CB00007B/1969